Copyright © 2023 by Mike Nevin

All rights reserved.

No part of this publication may be reproduced, distributed, or transmitted in any form or by any means, including photocopying, recording, or other electronic or mechanical methods, without the prior written permission of the publisher, except as permitted by U.K. copyright law. For permission requests, contact howcaring.com

The story, all names, characters, and incidents portrayed in this production are fictitious. No identification with actual persons (living or deceased), places, buildings, and products is intended or should be inferred.

Book Cover Design by Keroles Raaft

Fourth edition 2024

Published by howcaring.com

We love staying in Dirleton

DIAMONDS OF DEATH

BOOK 1

MIKE NEVIN

From the Author
M. Nev.

HOWCARING.COM

Contents

Dedication	VII
Acknowledgements	VIII
1. Chapter 1	1
2. Chapter 2	13
3. Chapter 3	28
4. Chapter 4	40
5. Chapter 5	60
6. Chapter 6	77
7. Chapter 7	94
8. Chapter 8	110
9. Chapter 9	127
10. Chapter 10	143
11. Chapter 11	161
12. Chapter 12	173

13.	Chapter 13	185
14.	Chapter 14	202
15.	Chapter 15	218
16.	Chapter 16	233
17.	Chapter 17	246
18.	Chapter 18	259
19.	Chapter 19	279
20.	Chapter 20	293
21.	Chapter 21	309
Also By Mike Nevin		326

Dedication

Dedication

To my amazing wife Mary, without whom this book would never have been written. Her patience, encouragement and sense of fun keep me going. She is my rock, my love, and my life.

Acknowledgements

Acknowledgements

I am so grateful to everyone who helped me with this book. Most of my best ideas came from my wife, Mary. My imagination has merely transformed her stories and ideas into print.

A fantastic writing group in Wellington, Somerset, headed by Peter Blaker, encouraged me along the way. They so loved Hilda; it inspired me to keep writing about her.

My daughter Sandy read early drafts, and my daughter-in-law Rachel lent a helpful hand. Their input has been invaluable.

An American writer friend, Ashley, has been a sounding board and source of encouragement along the way. She patiently read my drafts and pointed out my glaring errors to do with America. Any that snuck into the final book are entirely down to me.

The Cleve Hotel Wellington, Somerset, holds a special place in my memory. It was a delightful location where I spent many hours writing in peace and quiet - in the early years.

Without all my family and friends, I couldn't have finished this book.

Chapter One

Autumn 1937

Big D's Farm, Mill Lane, Marlan, Ohio, USA

Ruby stood in the doorway and stared. Her parents lay dead on the kitchen floor. Her best friend screamed first, arriving just after Ruby. One lad also screamed, though he denied it later. Ruby would never forget the sight of her parents' bodies. She'd seen one other dead body before, Old Ma Jenkins. Ruby was delivering a food parcel to her and found Ma Jenkins unmoving in her bed. Ruby thought her asleep at first. Her cold staring eyes gave a lie to that. This was different. Someone had heartlessly dumped Ed and Ginny's lifeless corpses onto the floor. No thought about how they lay. Fortunately, Ruby didn't study their bodies closely. The savagery of the stabbings would have been an enduring memory. The fact of their death enough to destroy her innocence and security.

Sixty years later

July 1997

Big D's Farm, Mill Lane, Marlan, Ohio, USA

The old building was fast returning to a pile of lumber. If it hadn't been for the sign at the entrance to the driveway, they would never have known this was once a working farm. Pearl stared at it in dismay. All hopes of finding any clues about her sisters' whereabouts seemed as forlorn as the place before her. Pearl turned around to speak to her best friend and travel companion, Hilda. The sight that met her caused her to stare for a moment. She knew Hilda well, but this was a new one. After watching in amazement for a while, she asked, 'what *are* you doing?'

Hilda was tapping her toes rhythmically on what may once been part of an old tractor. Now it lay flattened and abandoned in the yard. Hilda smiled at her friend. 'This metal makes a wonderful sound when tap dancing.'

'But, Hilda,' said Pearl. 'Why are you tap dancing at all? Have you forgotten why we're here?'

'You know dancing always cheers me up and you were looking rather sad, dear,' said Hilda. She sped up her tap routine and then did a spectacular finish and jazz hands.

Pearl would have contradicted Hilda, but she owed her so much. They would never have made it this far without Hilda's off the wall plan to travel across America. Typical of her to decide on a whim to travel over from England and hire a giant camper van, the man at the hire centre called it an RV. Then travel from coast to coast. Also typical of Hilda to drop all her plans when Pearl had told her about her long-lost sister. As the two septuagenarians stood in the midday heat in the dusty yard, Pearl felt gratitude for that. She had been wondering how to set off on this search until Hilda phoned had invited her on this road trip.

Pearl glanced back at their large camper van, parked on the road at the end of the driveway. She longed for a sit down and a cup of tea. Then she looked back at Hilda acting like a twenty-year-old, tap dancing and now singing. Pearl smiled. Hilda's plan to cheer her up had worked.

A sharp voice broke in on the moment of joy. 'You ladies lose something?' It came from a man in a dark T-shirt and tatty jeans at the end of the drive. Judging by the lines on his face and few remaining grey hairs, he seemed to be a similar age to the two ladies. He made an imposing figure, tall and wiry. The newly arrived stranger yanked at an unkempt dog by his side. The poor creature made no response, perhaps used to such treatment.

Pearl approached the stranger hesitantly. 'Sorry, is it your farm… now, I mean? Are we trespassing?'

'Neighbour.' The man gave the word a less friendly feel than is usual. He pulled his shoulder back.

'We're looking for someone who lived her, a long time ago,' said Pearl. 'Maybe you knew them, Ruby Davies or her parents Ed and Ginny?'

Hilda strode forward, hand outstretched. 'I'm Hilda Shilton and my friend is Pearl Parker.' The man stared at her hand, but left it unshaken. 'Ah, well, I guess you don't know us yet, dear. We're very nice, you know. It's lovely to meet you anyway, whoever you are.' Hilda looked back at Pearl and shrugged.

'Orville.' The sharp announcement caused Hilda to jump a little. Orville grinned, displaying his few remaining yellowed teeth.

Pearl stepped closer to him and asked, 'did you know the Davies family?' Hilda stood behind her friend.

'Family was ere you mean?' Orville stared hard at the ladies. There was something in his eyes, like a lion studying its prey. He glanced up and down the road. It was deserted.

Pearl was too focussed on her search to notice any danger, and said, 'yes, my sister, Ruby and her parents.'

Orville stared at her with empty grey eyes. Then said, 'Ruby's sister, eh?' He licked his lips as if hungry. 'Never knew she had one. You look like her, though.' His eyes narrowed.

'I only found out about Ruby recently. Umm, we were adopted.' Pearl hesitated, unsure why she had said so much.

'Adopted? That figures.' Orville scratched the few grey stubbles on his chin with a gnarled fist. As he did so, the muscles in his arms rippled. For an older man, he looked strong.

'What happened to Ruby?' Pearl, focussed on her quest.

Orville bared his teeth. Or was it a smile?

Hilda shuddered. She said to Pearl, 'I think we should be going.'

Pearl span around, put her hand up to Hilda and said, 'wait!' Then turned back to Orville, 'do you know?'

Orville yanked his dog's lead extra hard. This time it yelped pathetically. 'The murder you mean?'

'My sister was murdered?' Pearl stumbled back.

Orville howled. Maybe he laughed that way. '*Her parents*, not Ruby. She was out.' He breathed deeply, as if drawing in a scent. 'At a *dance*.' He spat out the last word and scowled. 'Never invited *me* though.' He stood silently for so long; that

Pearl opened her mouth to speak. Then Orville continued, 'shouldn't have seen what she did.... T'aint right.'

'Who?' asked Pearl.

'Ginny, that's Ruby's ma.'

'Passing madman, sheriff reckoned.' Orville made a sound that may have been laughter. 'Ginny was out fetching wood.' He stared at the remains of the farm building as if seeing events unfold. 'Her apron was dirty, a smudge of soot on her face.'

Pearl stood frozen to the spot, white faced. Hilda gripped her hand.

Orville continued. 'She screamed so loud.' He nodded as if in satisfaction. Then continued. 'Her wailing brung out Ed.' He looked across at Pearl; his tongue ran around the inside of his mouth. 'He should ave stayed inside.'

'I really think we should go,' said Hilda.

'What about Ruby?' asked Pearl desperately. Orville took a step closer to her and shouted. 'Ruby never got over it, her parent's dying like that. Ran off to New York.' Then he looked drained, empty, and whispered. 'She just left.' His face distorted. Were they tears? Pearl recoiled from him.

Hilda grabbed Pearl's hand and pulled her towards their RV. Orville turned from the ladies and strode off, dragging his dog behind. From the safety of their vehicle, Hilda and Pearl watched him depart - both shaking.

Back to 1937

Big D's Farm, Mill Lane, Marlan, Ohio, USA

Ed and Ginny Davies were having a terrible year. Flooding in January had damaged buildings and equipment. A late cold snap slowed down the planting. Now, as they prepared for harvest, a storm front was moving in.

America had been a bold new start for the Davies family back in 1920, a new life and a new start. In England, everything just seemed to go wrong for them. Ed lost the job he had since school, a farmhand. Farming in England was struggling. He was a casualty. They were not blessed with children.

***

One night, sitting by the fire, Ginny said, 'I was reading about farms you can buy over in America.'

'Buy with what?' Ed stared at his wife.

'Don't get cross with me. I looked into selling my mother's jewellery.'

Ed opened his mouth, but Ginny held up her hand. 'I know what you'll say. But my parents are gone now. They would rather we found a better life.'

'Somewhere we don't know, with no friends or family?'

'We can have family, at least. I read in the paper that The Kilburn Maternity Home has babies for good homes. We're a good home aren't we?'

***

Seventeen years later and settled in Ohio, that dream may have become tarnished. Everything seemed to niggle Ed. He'd been up for hours planning the harvest - an impossible task. By breakfast he was smouldering with frustration. Ruby twirled into the room, thinking of the dance that evening. The day seemed heavenly. What was not to enjoy?

'Why are you so happy?' asked Ed. He stared up at her from the kitchen table. Ginny stood by the stove, stirring a pan of steaming porridge.

'I don't know, I just am, pa,' said Ruby. Her face a picture of youthful joy.

Ed growled and pointlessly studied some papers. He cast them aside. Ginny brought over the pan of porridge, 'get a move on young lady, you haven't even washed up ready for breakfast.'

'Just a minute.' Ruby bounded outside to use the old hand pump.

Once back inside, Ruby's pa was talking, '... short straw again. Last to get the co-op harvester. That storm'll be here any time.' He stared darkly at the table.

Ruby skipped up to the table. 'It's another lovely day.'

'You never got the hang of farming,' Ed sighed. 'Weather changes quickly round here.'

'We could do with a bit more help from you.' Ginny's voice was harsher than her face. 'If not on the farm, then around the house.'

'I have a life, ma... a job, friends,' said Ruby.

Ed stared at his daughter - His eyes hard. 'Fine, you get on with your life.'

Ruby walked sluggishly to work. When she returned that afternoon, her parents were even more negative than at breakfast. When Ruby said, 'looks like rains coming in.' Her pa just grunted.

The farm with the harvester was going slower than planned. All the farmers helped on each farm and Ed had been there all day. The evening meal was a muted affair. Afterwards, Ruby offered to wash the dishes - she did it fast.

As Ruby left for her dance, she called, 'don't wait up,' and received two curt responses. They were the last words she ever heard them speak. When she tried to recall them later, she couldn't even remember the words. Life is strange. We see so far behind us and no distance at all in front. It's as if we are always walking into a solid wall. No idea what lies beyond. As Ruby left that evening, it's certain that had she known the future, she would have acted differently.

***

After the dance, the young people all headed home. Ruby's farm was on its own, down a long road. Her friends always accompanied Ruby home, then headed back as a group into town. They started doing that when eleven-year-old Jill died six years earlier, not that anyone liked to talk about her death.

Laughing and joking, they all processed up the lane. The group of four girls and two lads. As they approached the silent farmhouse, they shushed each other. Unaware that no amount of noise would ever disturb Ed and Ginny again. A shadowy figure of a man standing near the house moved deeper into the darkness. He was watching the house keenly. One lad noticed the movement and said, 'a ghost,' he used his best spooky voice. He received a slap from Ruby. 'I have to sleep here tonight.' Not knowing she would never sleep there again.

Her friends stood nearby as Ruby advanced slowly towards her front door. On arriving, she shivered. But not from the cold on such a sultry night. Her best friend giggled. The lad who had suggested a ghost made a quiet wailing sound. Ruby turned and stared at him. The man studying them had retreated to a distant group of trees. He stood and waited, unseen by the group.

Ruby opened the outer door to a buzzing sound. She paused and glanced behind at her troop of friends. They were walking off. 'Hey!' she waved them over. They turned and joined her on the porch. 'Hear that?' she asked.

The lad who had joked about ghosts now sounded hesitant and said, 'just flies?'

'Why so noisy?' Ruby looked at him wide eyed.

'Your ma prob'ly left some meat out,' said the lad. With more hope than certainty.

Ruby stared at him for a moment and then back towards the closed kitchen door. The loud buzzing was coming from the other side.

'Come with me?' Ruby appealed to her friends, and they agreed. In the dark hallway, all laughing stopped. The lad who had suggested spooky visitors opened his mouth, then closed it. The group of five young people inched their way along the corridor. Ruby put her hand on the kitchen door, took a deep breath, then swung it wide. It was at that point she saw her parents bodies lifeless on the hard, cold, kitchen floor and her life changed forever.

***

The sheriff's investigation concluded that a crazed madman had attacked Ed and Ginny outside; then dragged the bodies into the kitchen. Blood trails led from outside. He concluded the attacker wanted to draw Ruby inside and murder her, too. Taking her friends inside may well have saved her life.

***

Ruby stayed at a friend's house for the next couple of weeks while investigations were underway. Groups of armed locals scoured the area. They found no madman hiding in the vicinity. It is just as well no stranger was passing through. The locals were not making good judgements while their blood was up.

Ruby was so shaken by it all, she slept fitfully. The image of her parents' dead bodies replayed in her mind. It made no sense. When the sheriff visited her at her friend's house to give his final verdict. She was too stressed and exhausted to treat the sheriff with respect. Instead, she said, 'a madman, but why? You suggested they were lying in wait for me, too. Footprints outside, you said. Why me as well? Wouldn't a madman just have run off? Do madmen plan like that?'

'Don't you worry your pretty little head,' said the sheriff as he sat back in a rocker on the porch. 'Mind if I smoke?' He took out a Lucky Strike.

'Yes,' shouted Ruby.

'Oh, sorry, Miss,' the sheriff stood. 'Well, I guess there's nothing more I can say. I'll be going.' With that, he left, and Ruby sat looking at the wooden floor.

Her friend had been listening in. She came out and asked, 'everything alright?'

'Incompetent fool,' Ruby got up and walked to the railing around the porch. 'I can't stay in Marlan. If someone wants me dead too and it can't have been a madman. I need to get away. I'm going to New York.'

'On your own?' Her friend stared, wide eyed.

Ruby didn't seek approval from anyone. She decided that a change of scene was what she needed. Her boldness may have shocked her friend, it surprised Ruby even more. As Ruby boarded a train for New York the next day, her heart fluttered. But she was sure that she could succeed. She had a few dollars she had saved from her job at the diner, plus some money her parents had saved. The bravado, courage and folly of youth filled her. As the train took her to a new life, dark eyes watched from the platform.

Chapter Two

March 1997

Rose Cottage, Stoke Hind, UK

As with most things, Hilda's trip to the USA began with an idea. One spring morning Hilda threw back her blankets and leapt out of bed. No small feat for a seventy-seven-year-old. Sticking her head out of the window, she spied the milkman. 'Hello Fred, I'm off to America.'

Fred half dropped a pint of milk. He glanced up at Hilda's red curly hair and green sparkly eyes. Recovering, he said, 'oh, do you still want milk today?'

'Of course, dear. I'm not off now.' Hilda shivered in the early chill. 'Things to do, plans to make.' She disappeared inside. Fred placed the milk into the milk rack. Hilda popped her head back out and called, 'packing to do.' This time Fred dropped the milk, but from such a low height it landed with a satisfying clink. He stood and glared up at the now closed window. Shaking his head, he trudged away from the rose-covered cottage.

Inside, Hilda rushed around, talking to herself. 'People to call, things to organise.' Despite her multiple layers, it did not take long to dress. Purple tracksuit bottoms and a blue jumper completed her outfit. Even for the end of March, in the south of England, the temperature had not topped forty-six. Hilda still thought in Fahrenheit - chilly indeed.

She headed downstairs. In the front room Hilda gazed into the fireplace, all set up with coal ready to light. She walked out, then decided the fire took too long to get hot and so headed back into the room and struck a match. 'Perhaps central heating had some advantages,' she thought. It only took a few minutes holding a sheet of newspaper over the fire to speed up the lighting. Having started a roaring fire and put the metal guard in place, Hilda had a quick bite to eat, then headed to town.

Fly-Away Travel Agents, Stoke Hind, UK

The local travel agents were not prepared for Hilda's arrival - very few people were. Hilda knocked the manager Joyce backwards the moment she unlocked. Joyce hadn't even removed the keys from the door. Hilda bounced over to the desk and sat waiting for Joyce to recover and join her. Hilda was jumping up and down like a child. The moment Joyce sat down; Hilda said, 'America!'

'America?' asked Joyce.

'Yes dear, America, the US of A. I want to go,' said Hilda.

'Do you mean now?' Joyce typed into her computer terminal.

'Well, obviously not today dear,' said Hilda, shaking her head. Joyce stopped typing and stared at Hilda.

'Right, when are you looking to go?' Joyce sat back in her seat.

'Next week.' Hilda wiggled around in the plastic seat.

Joyce sat forward and started typing again, 'you have a visa already?'

'What's a visa?' asked Hilda.

'Permission to visit a country.'

'I need permission to go on holiday?'

'Not to go on holiday. But yes, to visit America. The quickest way is to take your passport to the American...'

Hilda cut her off. 'My passport? Oh yes, I'll need one of those, won't I?'

'You don't have a passport? Absolutely, you'll need one of those. They take longer than a week to come through, though.'

Hilda was no longer bouncing. 'How very inefficient, that won't do at all. How long will that take?'

Joyce put on her most professional sounding voice. 'Well, if you need a passport *and* a visa. Is anything booked yet?' Hilda shook her head. Joyce tried not to frown. 'I'd leave it at least twelve weeks.'

'Twelve weeks! That's a lifetime.' Hilda's green eyes lost a bit of their lustre.

'That will give you time to get everything organised. There will be hotels to book...'

Hilda interrupted Joyce. 'Oh no, I'm not going to stay in hotels. I will drive across America.'

'*You*... drive... all the way across?' No doubt Joyce had seen Hilda drive in the past. Most locals had.

'Yes,' Hilda nodded vigorously, 'in one of those big camper van things.'

'An RV?'

'That's it, an RSP.'

'An RV.'

'That's what I said.' Hilda shook her head.

'Right,' said Joyce. She whispered 'RV' under her breath.

Hilda walked out of the travel agents with a few brochures about the USA. Joyce held the door and watched her walk away. Joyce's mouth was part open, and she was shaking her head. Just as she was about to close the door, a young couple arrived. Her smile reappeared, as if a switch had been thrown.

Barkeast Bank, Stoke Hind, UK

Hilda's visit to the travel agent left her with an important question. Did she have sufficient savings? Joyce had shocked her with the costs of flights and RV hire; gone were the days when travel cost a few pounds. Mind you, Hilda had never travelled further than Wales. She headed to the Barkeast Bank and strode in, acting like she owned the place. In her view, she did. After all, it was her money; that the bank kept there. She had banked in the local bank at Stoke Hind for forty-five years. Those were the days when the branch was still The Hargreaves Farmers Union Bank. Hilda had fond memories of the large central desk. When Miss Long had sat enthroned at her desk. Peering over her glasses at any customers who dared to interrupt her important business. Whatever that was, it never seemed to involve helping customers. Those were the days before the glass and steel barriers that faced Hilda in the modern bank. Hilda could barely see the cashier through the layers of glass and metal.

Arriving in the bank, Hilda was early enough to go straight to a cashier's window. With no one yet in the bank, the cashier had turned around to sort out paperwork. Hilda coughed to draw his attention. No response. She tried a call, 'cooee!' Joe slowly turned around and asked, 'how can I help you Mrs Shilton?'

'At last, young Joe, I thought you'd gone deaf,' said Hilda.

'I was just sorting things out, ready for the day,' said Joe.

'I need to see Mr Devil.' Hilda always got his name wrong.

'You mean Mr Deville. What's it in connection with?' asked Joe.

'About my savings account.'

'More specifically?'

'To ask the balance.' Hilda shook her head.

'I can help you with that.' Joe spun around to his computer terminal and typed. All the assistants knew Hilda well.

'I beg your pardon; I've no wish to share my financial state with every whipper snapper. Especially not you, young Joe. Scrumping apples from my garden. No, I need Mr Devil, I mean Deville.'

Joe turned red and said, 'Mrs Shilton, you cannot mention my childhood every time you visit. I only took one or two apples on a dare. I was ten.'

Other customers arrived. No doubt, not wanting more childhood misdemeanours publicly uncovered. Joe said, 'I'll see if Mr Deville is free.' He popped into a back office and came back after a few minutes. 'He'll see you now.'

Mr Deville came out of a locked side door and then took Hilda through to his office. She glimpsed his messy desk and tutted. 'You really should keep your desk neater; you know. I told you last time.'

'Never mind my desk,' said Mr Deville. He still glanced at it. 'Joe said that you had an important question, only I could answer.'

'That's right, I want to know the balance in my savings account,' said Hilda.

Mr Deville huffed. 'He could have told you that.'

'I'm not having young Joe Parsons looking at my personal and private affairs. He used to throw snowballs at me,' said Hilda.

'That was when he was a child.'

'A leopard never changes his trunks.'

'Spots.'

'Spots?'

'Yes,' said Mr Deville.

After a contorted conversation, Hilda finally found out that she had enough money for her trip to the USA. She also gained advice on how best to access her cash whilst in America. As she left, she said, 'you see, young Joe wouldn't have been able to help me with travelling checkers and exchanging my rates.' She was out of earshot before Mr Deville could correct or contradict her.

Rose Cottage, Stoke Hind, UK

That evening, Hilda stretched out in her armchair, enjoying her coal fire. She had removed the fireguard to benefit from its warmth. A spark jumped on to the rug and caused yet another burn mark. The originally plain mat, now interestingly patterned by the scorch marks. Hilda mused how there was nothing like a proper fire, although they were hard work. All that preparation in the morning, the adding coal during the day and raking out the ash last thing at a night. Then it all started again the next day. But oh, they felt so snug. She glowed as brightly as the fire.

She had been sitting long enough, so she leapt up and went through to her kitchen. Returning moments later with a tray of crumpets and butter. Impaling a crumpet on a toasting fork, she held it in front of the embers. 'This was how a cold evening should be,' she thought. Once ready, she lavished butter on top. After eating the delicious treat, she picked up and glanced through one of the travel brochures. Having read a few pages, she threw the magazine back on the coffee table and picked up another. She then stared into the hearth and smiled.

Hilda glanced at the photograph of her husband Arthur on the mantlepiece and smiled. He had died after just six years of marriage. She told people 'at least I've known a great love in my life.' She never mentioned the possibility he may have cheated on her once. That was something she pushed from her mind. She lived her life focussing on the good. Not pretending sorrow didn't happen. But looking for the positive. Hilda shed tears but did not wallow in her sadness. She wanted to live life and look for adventures - find the fun. So, she never spoke of the day Arthur died. A day that had cut her to the heart. Left her with a sense of betrayal. She remembered the six years of love and happiness. Some may call her blind. But it helped her cope.

Early that evening, after returning from town, Hilda had phoned Pearl Parker, her best friend, since school days. They used to be next-door neighbours as children. In recent years, they had lost contact. But Hilda remembered all the fun they had enjoyed together on a holiday to Wales, back in 1985. So she wanted to invite Pearl on the trip to America. When Hilda phoned Pearl to ask her along on the trip, she reminded Pearl of that Welsh holiday. The two ladies had very different memories of it...

Summer 1985

West Wales

Back in 1985, Pearl was at a loose end, and had jumped at the chance of a caravan holiday. They made plans, packed up with provisions and headed for the pinnacle of West Wales, St David's in Pembrokeshire. They setup their caravan and awning at a campsite overlooking the beach of Newgale. Appropriately named, as they would find out. It was positioned on an exposed location, near a cliff edge overlooking the Atlantic. The weather lived up to the place's name. A gale howled. Hilda was inside the caravan making a cup of tea, whereas Pearl was outside using their toilet facility.

Pearl screamed as the toilet tent was ripped from around her; and she found herself sitting on a commode in the middle of a windy Welsh field. Being exposed and perched on a clifftop overlooking the turbulent Atlantic Ocean is not a situation anyone wants to be in. Wind whipped around her.

Hilda heard the commotion and popped her head out of the awning and asked, 'are you all right dear?' then noticing Pearl's lack of cover, shouted, 'oh my goodness! Your bare legs are showing, and you're nearly showing your nether regions. Cover yourself up dear, people might see.'

'Help me! The toilet tent's blown away,' Pearl shouted.

'You do make such a fuss. It's just a little breezy. I've got the kettle on. Come in when you're ready,' said Hilda. With that, she disappeared back inside the awning and into the caravan.

The campsite was almost empty, although there was a caravan twenty-five yards behind, out of her view. Pearl checked the coast was clear. She carefully extricated herself from the commode. Trying to keep decent at the same time.

***

Henry and Val Silkins sat in the caravan behind Pearl and watched the entire event with rapt fascination. Val had called Henry over when the toilet tent shot over the cliff 'That poor lady Henry, do you think we should help?'

He carefully examined the situation and said, 'noo, she's fine, she's a friend to help.'

'Her friend's gone again,' said Val, staring out of the window.

Henry shivered. 'Oooo, maybes to fetch aid?'

'Henry, that poor woman is trying to get off the khazi without flashing!'

'Ai, good luck with that, oh deary me! Tell me when to look, Val. I saw a wee bit more than I should.'

'She's decent now and off inside. Whoops, she tripped over... back up again.' Val's eyes fixed on the unfolding scene.

'I looked too soon.' Henry turned red.

***

Pearl got back up and entered the awning, which the two friends had carefully setup on their arrival. A precarious situation. The whole structure stretched and flapped. Creaking and groaning sounds surrounded her. She quickly entered the caravan where an unconcerned Hilda sat drinking a cup of tea.

'There you are. Here's your tea,' said Hilda. Passing Pearl, a steaming cup.

'Are you absolutely sure the awning won't blow away?' asked Pearl. She took the proffered cup, after first finishing making herself fully decent.

'Definitely, we hammered the pegs in solidly and it's firmly attached to this solid caravan. Don't worry.' Hilda took a bite of biscuit.

Pearl sipped her tea and sighed. Then a screeching, ripping sound filled the caravan. Followed by a loud bang and the light on the right side of the caravan increased as the awning disappeared over the clifftop.

'I'm off,' shouted Pearl, dropping her cup of tea on the table. 'We're not safe. The caravan will be next.'

'Don't worry, it's perfectly safe.' Hilda still sat enjoying her tea and biscuits.

'You said that about the toilet tent and the awning.' Pearl leapt out of the caravan. As she left, the caravan lurched with the lost weight. Hilda dropped her cup. 'Wait for me. I'm coming too.' She followed Pearl out of the door.

Hilda felt like a giant hand was pushing against her as she stepped outside. She had to lean into the gale force wind, to avoid falling backwards. She caught up with Pearl, who had only managed a few steps in the storm. They struggled up the field towards the only solid structure. A concrete toilet and washing area. The rain lashed at them, cutting through their thin clothes. Just as well it was summer, and the wind was not too cold. At the top of the hill, they sheltered in the doorway of the toilet block, and stared through the rain at their caravan.

Their temporary abode was rocking in the wind. But for all its movement, it appeared solid.

'You see, it's perfectly safe,' said Hilda, pointing at their caravan.

'I'm going to sleep elsewhere.' Pearl gripped her arms around herself.

'Where?' asked Hilda, looking at the nearly empty field and smelling the toilets.

Only three other caravans were braving the storm. None of them seemed any more stable than Hilda's.

***

Val and Henry had an excellent view of the escape. Val was straining against the glass to see them and asked Henry, 'why do you suppose they ran up there without coats?'

'Well, they've no toilet no more,' said Henry, sitting next to his wife.

'They're just in the doorway,' said Val, 'standing looking out at the field. Oh, do you think they can see us? Let's wave.'

***

At the toilet block, Pearl thought she saw a movement in a caravan. But with all the rain sweeping over the field, she decided it was her imagination. They shivered with cold, standing at the toilet block for a while. Then reluctantly walked back to their caravan. Pearl did not sleep a wink that night. Hilda slept like a baby. If a baby were to snore loudly all night.

Spring 1997

Rose Cottage, Stoke Hind, UK

As Pearl remembered the Welsh caravan holiday from twelve years earlier, she just smiled. Time is a great healer. Now that Hilda was on the phone, encouraging her to join the new 'adventure of a lifetime' in the USA, the thought was appealing. Pearl always enjoyed her times with Hilda, even the challenging ones. So, she agreed to 'join the fun,' Hilda's expression. Pearl also had an ulterior motive.

When Hilda had phoned, Pearl was reading some old letters. An open box of papers lay before her. Tears were in her eyes when the phone rang. The latest letter was dated May 15th, 1937, written by a Mr and Mrs Davies from Big D's Farm, Marlan, Ohio, USA. The box itself was high-quality workmanship, with a walnut veneer. There were decorations of flowers and butterflies that looked like a child had painted and stuck on. Her tabby, Merlin, rose from the sofa, stretched, and yawned, then strolled across to help investigate the box. He brushed against the lid. It bore the initials VW in a fancy scroll lettering on a brass plaque. Then purred and fussed.

'Merlin are you hungry again?' said Pearl. She added the box of letters to create the beginning of a pile of things to pack. Then picked up Merlin and walked towards the kitchen.

'What do you think, Merlin? A twin sister, eh? Who would have thought?' As Pearl served Merlin, his favourite gourmet cat food. 'Now don't worry, Aunty Katie next door will look after you, I'm sure.' As Merlin ate, Pearl stared out into the garden and an imaginary past.

End of May 1920

Cabot Towers, Fifth Avenue, New York, USA

At the New York home of Warren and Georgia Cabot, only one person was peaceful. Their three-year-old son, Ted, was fast asleep in his nursery. One wonders what dreams three-year-olds have. No doubt they dream of future adventures and careers - perhaps as a soldier, or a ship's captain. Being a young child that might include a stint as a pirate. Looking at his nursery floor, with its clockwork steam train, perhaps time as a train driver. It's unlikely he imagined himself heading up his father's global empire. Ah, the joys and innocence of childhood.

Warren and Georgia Cabot were far from peaceful. The polite society of which Georgia was part would not recognise her. With her red screwed-up face, glaring, blood-shot eyes, tears running through her make-up. 'Who was she?' shouted Georgia for the sixth time.

Warren carried on getting ready for The Astor's Ball. It was the season highlight. Their absence would be noted. His lack of response seemed to make Georgia even angrier. She stamped heavily across to him. Quite a feat, considering her slight stature and the fact she was barefoot. Pushing between him and the mirror in which he was admiring his attire, she shouted louder, 'who... was... she!?'

Warren stopped adjusting his newly put on bow tie and glared at her. When she began her tirade, he had already sent his valet away, along with Georgia's maid. He said calmly and slowly, 'I told you, she's no one.'

Georgia looked fit to explode. She took a deep breath and said, 'a heavily pregnant woman turns up here asking for you *by name* and you say she's *no one*.'

'She probably got my name from the society pages.' Warren smiled at his wife. A flicker of doubt crossed her face. 'I am famous, my love. Any chancer wants a bit of what we have.' He waved around at the room. Even their dressing room was opulent.

Georgia's breathing slowed. She stared at Warren, then said, 'look at me and promise that you don't know her.'

Warren stared deeply into his wife's eyes, and said, 'I promise.'

***

Later that night, after The Astor's Ball. Warren was sitting alone in his study; cigar smoke filled the air. He opened a drawer and took out some cash, half he placed into an envelope. Then rang a bell, and when a servant answered. He said, 'fetch Franklin.' A while later, a tall, darkly dressed man appeared. They had a brief exchange and Franklin left. The envelope of cash was now in his inside pocket and the remaining money in his wallet.

New York Harbour, USA

New York Harbour at night was a dreary place - even in May. The light drizzle added to the dour appearance. Crowds pushed their way towards a ship in the dock. Dock workers stowed the cargo. Those passengers able to afford first class had already boarded, their route wide, clear, and protected.

Franklin was talking to the pregnant young lady. The same one who had earlier so disturbed Georgia. Her clothes appeared to have been finely made. Yet they were muddy and dusty from days of travel on foot. The edges of her skirts frayed. Her monogrammed case bore the letters VW. Though now battered, it was of exquisite workmanship. The two were standing near the ship. After what appeared to be an argument, the lady took a ticket and the envelope of cash from him, shaking her head. She haltingly boarded the ship. Franklin stood and watched until it set sail for England. He didn't leave the dock until the ship was out of sight.

Chapter Three

May 1997

Leithly Hall, Somershire, UK

Leithly Hall was the country estate of Jayne Milford, The Duchess of Somershire. An extensive residence situated just outside Stoke Hind. Jayne was a fortunate woman. Is your husband dying a year after you marry fortunate? This was the subject Jayne was discussing with a visiting friend, Penelope Kendal. Inseparable friends since boarding school, well friends anyway. In those dim and distant days, Penelope gained the nickname Bonbon. Jayne saw her as such a sweet girl. How little we really know about our friends.

Penelope was on one of her regular visits from the USA. Where she had an extensive condo on the seafront in LA. Her current trip included visits to The Chelsea Flower Show, Royal Ascot, and Wimbledon. Her plan was to return to the USA in mid-July - she always found time to see Jayne. Jayne had offered a room at her extensive mansion for the duration of her friend's stay. Bonbon preferred to make her own arrangements, as usual.

The two ladies were sitting at a small table on the rear veranda. As they gazed out across the lawns, it afforded them extensive views of Jayne's estate. A lowered section of garden wall gave an unobstructed view from lawn to countryside. This clever and age-old technique was called a 'ha-ha.' Not because everyone laughed when someone disappeared over the hidden drop. Perhaps its name originated from the surprise one felt when first coming across the unseen edge. Bonbon was sipping a glass of white wine. Jayne held her own glass of wine and said, 'peace at last.'

'It is a lovely place you have,' said Bonbon as she enjoyed the view.

'I don't mean the place.' Jayne winked at her friend.

'Oh, I see, you mean now the duke has... marched onwards,' said Bonbon, laughing at her own joke.

'Exactly, the freedom and peace,' said Jayne. Edward was a useful husband. Jayne waved her hands around. They both laughed. 'But he preferred his own company to mine.'

'Why ever did he marry you?'

'An excellent question.' Jayne sipped her wine and watched an eagle soar high above.

Bonbon interrupted her friends' thoughts. 'Can you join me in LA again this year?'

'I thought you'd never ask.' Jayne always loved to visit Penelope's LA home. The house had spectacular views from its beachfront location. As a bonus Bonbon held lavish parties, populated by anyone who was anyone.

Unseen by either of them, Jake Vort was monitoring their activities remotely. He would describe himself as an entrepreneur. Interpol viewed him as an international jewel thief and smuggler. They only knew him as 'The Ghost.' It was his activities, rather than his person, that had been uncovered. He had not become an international jewel thief by being stupid and careless. Normally, he spent months in planning and research to find a suitable mark. His contacts gave him access to the highest echelons of society all around the world. He was careful to only use his contacts for one or two jobs each. That way, law enforcement agencies could never find a pattern.

This job was very different; unique for him. He had been commissioned to do it by a third party. A large organisation who normally handled his stolen goods approached him about it. His contact in the organisation, a lawyer, had instructed him, not asked, but instructed. He had his suspicions that the jewels were for the head of the organisation. A shady figure known as 'B.' Rumours abounded she was a woman of refined tastes. The other unusual thing about this job was the information he had received. Normally, he used bribery to gain information on the safe and house layout. With this job, they had provided him with much of that. Almost like an inside job. Could the Duchess of Somershire be pulling an insurance con? He still setup nearby the property and observed his target for a few weeks. Tapping into phone lines, recording video and audio. He had a mobile headquarters designed to look like a large caravan at a nearby location. Over time, he would find out all the extra information he needed and research to find out what was going on. He didn't want to be the one being conned.

Staring through the binoculars at the duchess, The Ghost wondered if she looked like the criminal sort. He thought about the job ahead of him. To steal twin diamonds that the duchess' late husband had inherited.

The diamonds were 'acquired' by his great-great-grandfather, George, on his 'Grand Tour' to Africa. This had been in 1780, and he'd wanted to gain some animal trophies. Things did not work out as planned.

On the second week of his expedition, he became separated from the rest of the group. He had spotted a colourful bird and stopped to admire it. No one noticed that he had fallen behind. The bird's beauty and song were so enthralling he stayed watching it, caught up in the moment. On turning back to re-join the group he could not find their tracks. Stumbling through thick jungle, he fell into a small ravine. It took him an hour to scramble out. Injured and confused, he struggled on. Night came on quicker than he expected. He climbed a tree, thinking its branches would offer safety. Clinging to the trunk in the dark, weakened by loss of blood and scared half to death, he imagined danger at every noise. He gave up and dropped to the jungle floor, running through the darkness. He reached an unseen cliff in the darkness. Below lay a fast-flowing river. Falling, he hit his head on some rocks. Darkness enveloped him, and he thought his end had come.

George awoke to the face of an angel, sunlight glowing around her hair. He thought he was in heaven. He was suffering from a combination of broken bones, loss of blood, and malaria. A young lady from a remote village had found him in the river. She chased off the birds of prey, waiting for a tasty meal. His saviour dragged him miles to her village on a makeshift pallet. By now, the rest of his party assumed he was dead. They had searched for a few days, then gave up and carried on.

Over many months, the young village girl nursed George back to health. On regaining more strength, he learned their language and customs. The young girl's name meant river walker. The tribe attributed names as children grew and formed habits and characteristics. She would often walk along the river - fishing and daydreaming. A fact he was grateful for. It had saved his life. The tribe was welcoming. They had not seen many outsiders. Ones who had ventured that far to the interior had been good to them. Unfortunately, that would change in the future - the very near future.

As time passed, they saw George as part of the tribe. They granted him the highest honour. An introduction to see their god. This was equivalent to being brought into membership of the tribe. A religious ritual kept only for those whose hearts were true. They housed their god in a cave behind a waterfall; the route marked with coloured stones. They took George along the path. He noticed that some of the coloured stones were precious gems. It brought to his mind England and how much such gems were worth in his home. His heart changed. As the tribe's leader took him into the cave, George stood spellbound at the entrance. The leader assumed George felt the honour of seeing their god. In fact, he swooned at the sight of all the gold and precious gems that studded the walls. But the thing that caused George to be overcome with avarice was the statue of their god. The god had twin uncut diamonds for eyes, glowing and shimmering a blueish colour. Even in their uncut state, they were beautiful. They called them the eyes of Hora. George became obsessed with those diamonds. Overwhelmed by a desire to possess not just them, but as much of the treasure as possible. When he had full strength, he visited the cave as often as he could. Studying and planning how to remove the gold and diamonds. The villagers thought he was such a devout man that they asked him to become one of their gods' servers, the equivalent of a priest. This gave him more opportunity to plan.

Six weeks later, George left the village with bags stuffed full of their sacred treasure. As much of the gold, the eyes of Hora, and other gems as he could carry. After weeks of trekking through the jungle, being chased by the same villagers who had saved his life, George made it to a British outpost - then onwards to his home. He claimed he had been wandering lost in the jungle all the months he was missing. The stolen gold and gems enabled him to buy Leithly Hall. A much better place than the one he left. The eyes of Hora he hid in his safe. A few times he considered having them cut, but experts told him the value may be diminished. The twin uncut diamonds were almost identical in their uncut form. The true owners, the African villagers, had seen it as a miracle. If that were the case, they were now a hidden miracle, coming out on rare occasions for the duke to admire. He was married soon after his return and they had a son. George died young, perhaps the ravages of illness, or something more hidden. He left a widow and young son. The son inherited the diamond along with a letter from his father that told its story. On his deathbed George had felt some guilt and truthfully recounted the story of diamonds origin.

The family passed the eyes of Hora diamonds down until Jayne's husband came into ownership. Along with its ownership came the letter, containing the story of its theft. This dubious origin caused each new owner to keep it hidden. On the unexpected death of her husband, the Duchess inherited the diamonds. He had never spoken of it to her, hoping to have a male heir to inherit. She had not had time to read all the paperwork in the safe, which included the letter. Thus, Jayne knew nothing of its shady past. She first saw the eyes of Hora diamonds when opening the duke's safe to check through his papers. At first, she thought they were just stones. But taking them out and holding them to the light, the shimmers and glow was astounding. She had a London valuer look at them; they were valued at £32 each million for insurance. He advised that she not have them cut before selling them, as that could reduce their value. Jayne planned to auction them as soon as possible.

Early June 1920

Train from Southampton Docks to London, UK

You will remember a heavily pregnant woman visiting Warren Cabot in New York. Even though he claimed her pregnancy had nothing to do with him, he instructed his servant Franklin to put her on a boat to Southampton. He also gave her an envelope of cash. Not the obvious signs of an innocent man. They had left this pathetic-looking figure alone to cross the Atlantic. Now in England, she was making her way to London.

Having boarded a train to London, she wished for a first-class ticket. A method of travel she was more familiar with in the recent past. But common sense had prevailed, and she was in third class. When all the money you have in the world is in an envelope, you must eek it out. That is until you can earn or find more.

The train clattered and bumped its way from Southampton docks to London, Waterloo. The sounds reminded the lady of the shouts and screams of her parents a few weeks earlier. Their only daughter's pregnancy had horrified them. Their hopes and dreams for their debutant daughter destroyed. A jostle of the train made the lady wince and screw up her face.

But the pain of memory was jostling for supremacy. Her father's words, 'you are no longer my daughter,' causing tears to run down her face. Choking soot filled the carriage, coughing added to the pain and discomfort. Her fellow passengers stared at her, but she was far away. In her mind she was walking from her home in Connecticut, a place she would never see again, towards a false hope of salvation. She had hoped in Warren Cabot, the married father of her unborn child. A vain hope. He had sent her away to England, alone. She stared out of the rain-streaked carriage window.

***

The train finally pulled into Waterloo with a bang of metal and a hiss of steam. The woman gathered up her monogrammed case. Her face was a picture of desperation and hope. London, Waterloo train station was heaving with passengers. Drips of rainwater found its way onto the platform.

The pregnant lady strode, head up, pushing through the crowds. She burst out onto the waterlogged, busy street. She had no coat or umbrella. Water hammered onto her frail body, soaking into her thin shawl, and running down her neck. She had been catapulted from her rich lifestyle wearing only the thin clothes upon her back. Planning for poor weather had never been in her remit. That was the job of her maid. She carried but few things in her hands; none of them sensible or warm. Her once carefully fashioned curls, bedraggled, hung limp, and soaked. All energy and hope finally failed her. She sank to the muddy pavement, alone, unloved, forgotten. Tears blended with the rain. Only visible because they formed lines through her soot-stained face.

She was not unseen, and love had not completely deserted her. Maternal love was building in the heart of a woman who had taken the same route across the platform. Leaving the station by the same exit, this motherly figure saw the young pregnant girl fall to the ground. Maternal love swelled and drove her to action. Walking up she said, 'can I help?' Just three simple words. With such incredible power.

The girl stared up from the muddy ground. Disbelief and hope fighting each other. 'Yes, please.' Her voice was so weak, only her mouth moving showed the response.

Seeing the swollen belly, the motherly angel reached a hand towards her and asked, 'have you no place to go?' The woman's eyes held such compassion.

'No,' said the young girl. Sobs came from deep within her soul. The kind-hearted woman took hold of her hand and lifted her to her feet, saying, 'don't cry, I'll help you.'

Kilburn Maternity Home, London, UK

The charitable woman took the pregnant young lady to the Kilburn Maternity home. It took in unmarried mothers and arranged adoptions. This was a different form of help than she may have wanted. In the 1920's, when you were single, with no support, nothing else would be offered. When the kind-hearted lady left, she looked back in sadness. Wishing she could have done more. But she had done more that the hundreds of others. Her husband would never allow her to bring an unmarried pregnant woman home. That night, the pregnant young lady safely delivered not one but two children, twin girls.

***

When the young lady had recovered and could leave, she was desperate to do something for her twin daughters. They may force her to give them up, but they must know that she loved them. Having chatted to a few other mothers in the home, she was fearful of their future. Often twins were adopted separately. She discovered she could send no letter with them, explaining about their past. Only possessions could go with them and maybe a photograph could be slipped in. Using some of her remaining money, she had three photographs taken of the twins together, one for each child and one for her. With nothing else to leave them, she left her monogrammed case and a fancy wooden box in which she had kept treasures as a child. When the twins were later adopted, the case went with one child and the decorated box with the other. When the lady left the maternity home a few days later, she was an even more forlorn sight. Her few worldly goods were now contained in a tattered cardboard box. She trudged away with no direction, no hope, no friends, and no family. They would not even keep the names she gave them.

The unmarried mother leaving her babies was Victoria Worth. She named her children Hope and Faith. Things she had not lost in all her trials. Their new families were not even told those names. They renamed the children Pearl and Ruby. The two sets of adoptive parents arrived on the same day and as we have seen, they kept in touch, despite ending up an ocean apart.

May 1997

TSU Plc, Meedham, UK

Hilda's son, William, worked at Tibbert, Styles and Unbridge (TSU) accountants. A job he first found when he lived 'at home,' as Hilda stilled called it. They were based in London when he started there, and his commute had been easy from the local London Transport train station. It took him about fifteen to twenty minutes, depending on hold ups.

After meeting and marrying Louise, they moved out to live in Meedham. His commute had increased a lot. But they loved living in Meedham. It had been a wonderful place to bring up Josh. The crime rate was the lowest in the South-East and the schools were in the top ten. Louise had got a job teaching 12-year-olds at the comprehensive school.

As TSU grew, they became a public limited company, (Plc) This led to continued growth nationally and internationally and the need for bigger offices. London real estate prices were sky high. Coincidentally, Meedham was offering incentives for companies to re-locate, which they did. William's commute was reduced massively. Not just speed, but cost.

***

Harold Styles was one of the founding partners of TSU. As the youngest and most capable, he had been elected by his colleagues as the CEO, when they voted to go public. The partners kept a majority holding to keep control.

Harold had seen a potential in William from the day he started as an office junior many years earlier. That was long before William had met Louise. In those days, William was a scrawny young man, still living with his mother in Stoke Hind. Harold took pity on him and used to invite him back home. William was happy to be noticed and get so much special attention from his boss. Harold's wife, Dorothy, would let William stay on for an evening meal.

Harold, Dorothy, and William became good friends. Seeing a natural gifting with numbers in William, Harold encouraged him to take night classes. That was how William had gone from office junior to accountant. Some at TSU Plc saw Williams' rapid rise in the company to senior department manager as favouritism. The truth involved no nepotism. Harold was always aware of that accusation and held off promoting William for as long as possible. In the end, other partners insisted William be promoted. His hard work and skill shone out. No one wanted to lose him to another company.

As TSU Plc grew, it had plans to set up offices in other countries. This included the USA. The expansion into America would have a direct impact on the whole Shilton family.

Chapter Four

Spring 1997

William & Louise Shilton's House, Meedham, UK

The Saturday, after Hilda Shilton had decided on her trip to the USA, her son William woke up in an altogether less energetic way. He opened an eye, glanced at the clock, frowned, and closed it again. His wife Louise, who was standing by the bed, gave him a nudge. There were a lot of household chores that needed doing. Lying around in bed would not get them done.

They lived in the new town of Meedham, about twenty minutes away from Hilda. Which, as William described it, was 'close enough to my mother for emergencies, and far enough away for my sanity.' As William lay in bed, being prodded and poked, he was reliving fond memories of his childhood. His mother had at least let him lie in. These were unusual youthful reminiscences. Normally, he only remembered his mother embarrassing him at every turn.

The doorbell rang and Louise went to answer it, after giving William one last prod and saying, 'get moving, sleepyhead.'

A bright and bubbly figure stood at their front door. Their son Josh had all the bounce and energy of his gran, Hilda. Added to that was a practical and well-organised nature, very unlike her. No doubt that was inherited from the lady beaming at him, full of delight. Louise gave him a hug and explained that his dad was lounging around in bed. He rushed up the stairs, shouting, 'fire!'

William leapt out of bed and went into his pre-planned fire escape mode. He was an accountant, highly organised in everything, not just numbers. He already had his emergency bag, filled with important papers, in his hand, ready to leave. Then he noticed Josh, standing by his bedroom door, doubled over in laughter.

'That's not funny,' said William. His face flushed red. 'Fire is a serious thing.'

'You just lack a sense of humour, dad,' said Josh. 'Mum wanted you up. Besides, I have news. Come and have breakfast and I'll tell you.'

While William was getting dressed, Josh helped his mum get breakfast ready. She asked him how his photographic business was doing. He told her about a big photo shoot in the USA, he had bid on. They liked his other work and sought him out, but he still had to submit his costs for their approval. When William joined them, Louise was hugging and congratulating Josh on the accolade of such an opportunity. After catching William up and receiving his more muted compliments, they sat down to enjoy breakfast. Partway through, Josh shared his news about Hilda's planned trip to the USA.

'She's doing what?' William stared at Josh in disbelief.

'Don't shoot the messenger,' said Josh. He helped himself to more toast. 'She called it "A journey of a lifetime."'

'To the USA?' asked Louise. 'She's never left the England before, has she?'

'I don't know, has she, dad?' Josh glanced at his dad while buttering his toast.

'Oh, I don't know. But never mind that. She can't, it's just not... no, I won't allow it. Not on her own. Not that far. At her age, honestly, it's not safe.' William stamped his foot.

Louise looked at him over an imaginary pair of glasses and said, 'since when do you decide what your mother does?'

'I'd love to see that,' said Josh. He had a mouthful, which caused a frown from his mum. 'Can I be a fly on the wall? Besides, she's not on her own.'

'Who's with her?' asked William.

'Her school friend,' said Josh.

'You mean Pearl?'

'I think that was her name,' said Josh. He took another bite of toast.

'Well, at least Pearl is sensible. But really, mother's too old.' William gazed at Louise; his hands outstretched in a pleading gesture.

'Since when has she ever acted her age?' asked Louise as she got up to fetch more toast.

William was silent for a while. Then his face changed. He had a beatific smile and said, 'it's all right, I have an idea. We can go with her. Keep her safe.' Louise dropped a plate and Josh spat out some toast.

'What about your job?' asked Louise, staring at her husband. 'You don't have two month's holiday.' Then glancing at the mess Josh had made; she shook her head.

'Ah, that's the genius of this,' said William. His smile even wider. 'Now my company has gone public. They plan on opening a few offices in the US. Harold's asked if I would help set them up, as he's too busy here. I wasn't keen on the idea... until now.' William glanced at Louise. She was standing staring back at him, open-mouthed. 'What do you think? It means being there for over two months. Then we just add on some holiday. You mentioned she isn't going till about July?' William looked at Josh. He nodded. 'This will be perfect timing. That's when Harold wanted me to go. It'll all tie in with your holidays as well. I knew being a teacher would come in handy.' William clapped his hands.

Louise had shaken her head part way through William's diatribe. She waved a finger at him, 'it's not all holiday, I have essays to mark, preparation to do.'

'Can't you take it with you?' asked William. 'You always wanted to go to the USA.'

Louise opened her mouth, then closed it. She looked at Josh. He smiled at her and asked, 'but how will that work?' Louise said. 'Hilda wants to travel. As if I don't know the answer.'

'The first offices are in New York, Maryland, and Chicago. She wants to cross the country. I join in bits of the trip, make sure she's all right....' said William. He stared at his feet, then continued, 'you could travel with them... keep an eye on them.'

Louise frowned and then said, 'I've always fancied going to America. But I'm not so keen on sharing a camper van with Hilda and Pearl.' Josh seemed like he was trying hard not to laugh.

'Let's give it some thought,' said William, picking up his coffee. He had a sip, while peeking at Louise.

Josh said, 'I miss out. I haven't got two months free.' Then he remembered something. 'Mind you; there's that photo contract I'm bidding on...'

Louise smiled at him. 'Absolutely; I don't want you missing out. Besides, I need some moral support. Now who's telling Hilda that we are joining her?' She and Josh laughed. William stared into his coffee cup.

Rose Cottage, Stoke Hind, UK

That same morning, Hilda was sitting in her usual armchair by the fire. She only ever sat for a few minutes at a time. Then spent the rest of her day on the go. The radio was playing tunes from the forties and fifties. A station that seemed to have been created just for her. The announcer was sluggish; he spoke with a drawl. Hilda wished he would speed up, but his music choices suited her down to the ground. Hilda tapped her feet in time to a tune. Pearl was staying with Hilda for a few days so that they could sort out a few details of the trip. She was in the kitchen washing up the breakfast things, having volunteered after seeing the slapdash way Hilda had washed the dishes the night before. She had brought Merlin for this brief trip. He was resting on the front room sofa.

On the radio, the next tune just had to be danced to. Tapping her feet just wasn't enough. Hilda pranced and danced around her small front room. She knocked into a vase; catching it, she used it as a pseudo partner. Merlin, opened one eye and glanced up. Obviously unimpressed with human dancing, he closed the eye and curled up.

Pearl popped her head in the door to ask a question, saw the scene, checked on her cat, laughed, and left Hilda to it. The question could wait. The song ended and Hilda replaced the vase. Another even more upbeat song started. Hilda kicked her legs and wished she had a partner who would throw her into the air. She contemplated picking Merlin up for a spin around the room when the phone rang - saving the poor, innocent cat. The phone had that satisfying real bell ring. The type that only came from an old British Telecom phone. None of those modern trill, electronic sounds that pass for telephone announcements these days. Hilda would have no truck with those.

Hilda danced to the phone and announced her name and number, in her best telephone voice.

'I keep telling you not to give the caller all your details,' said William.

'Why ever, should I keep that a secret from you dear?' said Hilda.

'You didn't know it was me,' said William.

'You always ring on a Saturday morning; you wait until the weekend because it's cheaper,' said Hilda.

'No reason to pay four times the cost.' This was one of William's accountancy foibles coming to the fore.

'Tight as ever,' Hilda sat down on the telephone chair.

'Just being careful with money.'

'Well, I am fine as always, lovely to hear from you, goodbye,' Hilda started to hang up.

'Wait! I wanted to ask you something,' William shouted.

'No need to shout,' said Hilda, putting the phone back to her ear. 'I'm not deaf.'

'I hear from Josh you're going to the USA.' William looked up at Josh and Louise, who were standing next to him.

'A trip of a lifetime dear,' Hilda called towards the kitchen, 'Pearl, come through, William wants to hear all about our trip.'

'What's that?' said Pearl from the kitchen.

'Come through dear,' Hilda shouted.

After Pearl had joined her, Hilda told William all about their plans. Most of which he had heard from Josh. But he listened carefully, holding the phone away from his ear so they could all hear - Hilda was loud. The minutes ticked by. Hilda explained they planned to hire an RD, which Pearl corrected was an RV. A motorised recreational vehicle, to sleep in and drive across America from Portland to Portland. She loved the idea of driving between two places with the same name. Especially as they were on opposite coasts.

William's first line of attack was to question them about driving such a large vehicle. But Pearl and Hilda had driven lorries in the war and an RV would be simple in comparison. When he suggested someone might mug them, Hilda repeated that to Pearl and they both laughed for five minutes. In the end, William just asked if he and Louise could join them, and Hilda was delighted with the suggestion. She had planned to ask them, anyway. At William's house, Josh and Louise both smiled. William looked exhausted.

From William's perspective, the one good outcome was that it distracted Louise from the Saturday chores. She headed off to plan what she needed to buy. Josh had to leave. He had a client due. William grabbed his newspaper and sat on the sofa. But Louise returned to the lounge before she left and gave William a sheet of paper. He glared at the list of things that needed sorting. As he reluctantly got up to start on it, Louise called over her shoulder, 'it's just as well we have plenty of savings. This is going to be an expensive trip.' She walked off, leaving William open-mouthed.

***

Back at Rose Cottage, Hilda and Pearl were well ahead with their planning. Pearl was better at such things, having worked all her life as an office administrator. Which was odd because Hilda had also worked for many years as a clerk at a solicitor's office. No one quite understood how she got that job, nor kept it. She only used her administrative skills professionally, like a cleaner with a messy home, or a mechanic with a car that never runs right. Hilda had a hidden talent that only came out occasionally. She had a knack for solving mysteries and murders. Fortunately, they don't happen too often – to most of us.

During the war, both ladies had a stint in the WAAF (Women's Auxiliary Air Force). Pearl had fixed and driven lorries, whilst Hilda had done various jobs, including driving. Her favourite job had been moving the toy planes, as she called them, on the enormous map. A group of women like herself had sticks with hooks on. They would use them to hook and move model planes around the map of the South Coast of England. It enabled the air commanders to visualise ongoing battles and manoeuvres. Hilda saw it as a game. Fortunately, by the time she was doing it, the war was over. They were using it for exercises. Which meant her game of who can hook the plane fastest only got her in trouble. It caused no disasters for the aircrews.

Hilda's cottage was looking much like a war planning room. Maps, leaflets, and books filled the walls and tables. All it lacked were women with little planes, rods, and hooks. One of the biggest things they had was a map of the USA stuck on a wall. They had roughly planned a route across with places ringed they wanted to visit. Hilda noticed Pearl had ringed a small town in Ohio called Marlan. 'Why have you ringed this place?' said Hilda.

'Oh, it's got a couple of interesting things to see,' said Pearl. She had her reasons. But now was not the time to share them. They had much to sort first. Next on the checklist was medical insurance.

Pearl insisted Hilda get travel insurance. This caused a disagreement between them as Hilda stated she was never unwell. There may be some truth in this. She had not visited her GP since moving to Stoke Hind forty-five years earlier. Hilda finally agreed that she needed medical travel insurance. So, Hilda phoned to buy a policy from the same place as Pearl, it did not go smoothly.

'What do you mean?' said Hilda crossly.

'You will need a medical report, because of your age,' said the customer service rep (CS Rep) for the second time.

'My age! I'm only seventy-seven and I look much younger,' said Hilda. She appealed to Pearl for support, who was subtly occupying herself with other things.

'My friend is nodding in agreement,' said Hilda. Pearl glanced up in surprise at hearing her name.

'We need an independent medical report. So, unless your friend is a GP?' said the CS Rep.

'I have lived in this house for forty-five years and never needed to see my GP. Can you say that?' asked Hilda.

'No, I certainly can't.' said the CS Rep sharply.

'There you go,' said Hilda.

'Because I am only eighteen,' said the CS Rep.

'Really? You're far too young to be answering phones. Have you finished school yet?'

'This isn't about me, it's about you. To provide you with an insurance policy, we need a medical report.' The CS Rep sounded very impatient.

It took some more convincing, and Pearl getting involved, before Hilda finally agreed to get a medical report.

Stoke Hind was just a village when Hilda and Arthur had moved there in 1952, full of excitement about their future life. Being so near to London, it had been swallowed up into the suburbs over the subsequent years. When Hilda's husband, Arthur, had died, his civil service pension had paid off the mortgage and given Hilda a small income. She needed to work part time to top it up. She wanted to buy William whatever he needed. In common with many people, William's memories were that he always lacked things as a child. Hilda's parents were both working and not available to help. They died soon after their retirement, and Hilda had no one else to fall back on. Arthur's parents were already dead.

Hilda was strong and had such an indomitable spirit, it kept her going. Even when others might have crumpled. She never gave up and kept on smiling. Perhaps she was a little too exuberant for her son. Singing and dancing, not only around the house, but in public. The characteristics of his mother, that William found so difficult and embarrassing; her tendency to laugh, sing, and dance in any situation. Were who she was and why she got through hardships. They were part of her joyous, sunny nature, which seemed oblivious to reality; and helped her cope when others failed. William knew that his mother felt the loss of his father. He occasionally saw Hilda sitting on her own, sadness in eyes. He thought there might be more to it than his father's death, but never asked. She never told him about Arthur's infidelity.

Doctors Surgery, Stoke Hind, UK

For the first time in forty-five years, Hilda was sitting in the waiting room at her doctor's surgery. She could not understand how the announcement system worked. A digital number that flashed up. A board that showed which room your doctor was in and a series of hooks to hang the number they gave you when you arrived. Hilda was utterly confused. She asked the receptionist, 'so, I go in when the display flashes?'

'No,' said the receptionist for the fifth time, 'only if it's your turn.'

'But how will I know?' asked Hilda.

After a few more attempts to explain, the receptionist decided to tell Hilda when to go through. Hilda still insisted on hanging onto her number ten card.

Hilda sat waiting for her number to come up. The display showed number eight. She looked around the room and spotted a middle-aged man who was looking nervous. He obviously needed cheering up. She always found conversation helped her, that must apply to everyone.

'You'll never guess how old I am?' said Hilda. She was smiling at him.

'No, I'm sure I wouldn't,' said the middle-aged man. He shuffled around in his seat.

'Well, have a guess,' said Hilda.

'I have no idea,' said the middle-aged man. He tried turning away from her. Obviously hoping she would get the message to leave him alone. It didn't work. His number was not too many away.

'That's not trying awfully hard, dear,' said Hilda. She leaned forward so that she could see the man more clearly.

The man glanced around briefly at the old lady next to him. Piercing green eyes twinkled at him through the thick lenses of her tortoiseshell glasses. These kinds of questions are always hard. If you guess too low, it looks silly. If you say what you really think, you risk insulting the person. The man must have aimed in the middle because he said, 'seventy maybe?'

Hilda preened herself and proudly announced, 'I'm seventy-seven.'

'Oh,' said the man. He didn't look surprised.

The waiting room was full, and the bored patients were finding this exchange helped pass the time. A man on crutches was also in the waiting room. Hilda recognised him as a neighbour. She had not noticed him on arrival but looking around now; she saw him. Hilda said, 'oh hello dear. Why are you visiting the doctor? Is your old trouble playing up?'

Other patients pricked up their ears. What was his old trouble? Unfortunately for them, he did not answer, and it left them wondering. Hilda did not leave them without entertainment for long. Although the adage 'be careful what you wish for' comes to mind. Hilda worked her way around the patients, introducing herself and asking why they were there. She addressed the room saying, 'it's so boring sitting waiting, isn't it?' nods all round, 'I am going to introduce myself and why I am here. Then we will go around the room, and you all do it.' Horrified looks from everyone.

'I am Hilda, I'm seventy-seven years old, I know I don't look it,' said Hilda. She waited a moment, but no one responded, and so she said, 'I thought I'd better have a check-up to make sure everything is working as it should.' Hilda changed to a stage whisper, 'just between you and me my waterworks are not as they were. Although that's not why I am here. I'm having a check-up for a big trip.... You're next.' She pointed at the middle-aged man.

'I'm not really wanting to...' started the indicated man.

'Nonsense, I've shown the way,' said Hilda.

'I'm here to see my doctor,' said the man. He looked at the floor as he spoke.

'Well, of course you're here to see your doctor. But we don't know your name or why? That's what we all want to know?' A few nods of agreement around the room confirmed Hilda's assertion.

'I'm a private person,' whispered the man.

'Private, eh? Things not working, right?' said Hilda. She sat on the edge of her seat. Others in the waiting room also sat forward.

'Well, yes, I don't share things publicly,' said the man. He frowned at Hilda.

'Bowels, is it?' said Hilda.

'No, it's not!'

Hilda moved her mouth without vocalising, 'Is it your personal bits?'

'What?'

Hilda tried again. 'Down there?' she pointed.

'What are you saying?' The middle-aged man's mouth was wide.

'Your bits and pieces. Is it your bits and pieces?' said Hilda loudly. 'Oh, I'm sorry dear, that's very inappropriate of me.'

'Yes, it is,' said the middle-aged man.

'I'm sorry you're having trouble in that area,' said Hilda. She tried to sound soothing; but failed.

'I mean, yes, it is inappropriate of you,' the middle-aged man turned away and folded his arms over his chest.

There were a few sighs of relief when Hilda was called by the receptionist. Some looked ready to leave before Hilda reached them in her game. Others were watching the board, perhaps praying their turn to see the doctor would come quickly.

Hilda headed out of the waiting room and searched around for her room number. She had an appointment with Dr Langhill in room two. Corridors headed in three directions and signs pointing each way with lists of rooms on each. Hilda glanced at the first corridor. It did not have a Dr Langhill room two. She checked the second, still no sign. She reasoned that the third must be right and headed up without checking. She passed four doors, none of which were Dr Langhill's room two. At the end stood the Treatment Room with a number two written above it. It seemed obvious to her that this must be his room. After all, none of the others were correct. As its occupant expected her, Hilda just walked straight in. The sight of a neighbour greeted her, standing in just his underpants - the nurse was next to him. Hilda was unperturbed and asked. 'Where's Dr Langhill?'

'In his room, of course,' said the nurse. 'Could you please leave?'

'Right oh dear,' said Hilda. She glanced at her neighbour, 'oh hello, nice to see you again.'

Hilda stepped out of the door, then popped her head back in and said, 'where is his room? I can't find it?'

'Just next to reception. Now leave,' said the nurse.

'That explains it, cheerio,' said Hilda.

By the time Hilda made her way back down the corridor, Dr Langhill had come out of his room to look for her. He was in the waiting room, hearing how she had left ages ago. Among other things, about her.

Dr Langhill looked up and said, 'ah! There you are, Mrs Shilton. We were about to send out a search party.'

'You have a very confusing layout here,' said Hilda. She pointed to the corridors.

Dr Langhill looked at the large sign with his name and room number on next to reception, shrugged and said, 'this way Mrs Shilton.'

Once in his consulting room, Dr Langhill set about taking a medical history for the insurance form. His computer had little information on her.

'Really, one should come in for regular check-ups, especially once you get to your age, Mrs Shilton.' Dr Langhill was looking at his computer while he spoke.

'At my age, I am not old, you know,' said Hilda. She stared at Dr Langhill in disgust.

'Quite so. I just mean that we need to monitor you,' said Dr Langhill. He looked at Hilda, and seeing her crossness, just smiled.

'Why?' asked Hilda.

'To make sure that your blood pressure is not too high and that you have all the vaccinations you need,' said Dr Langhill. He was now fully concentrating on Hilda.

'Why is the pressure of my blood important? You make it sound like car tyres. Next, you'll be agreeing with my son that I shouldn't drive. When I am perfectly safe,' said Hilda.

'Why does he think that?' said Dr Langhill. He glanced back at his computer.

'He seemed to think I was getting dangerous. Such a nonsense really. It was all the fault of the ice-cream van,' said Hilda. She stared at the ceiling, remembering.

'What ice-cream van?' said Dr Langhill.

'The ice-cream van that was parked by the side of the road, do keep up dear.'

'How was an ice-cream van that was parked, responsible for you having problems?' asked Dr Langhill.

'It crashed into me off course,' said Hilda, shaking her head.

'A parked ice-cream van crashed into you?' asked the doctor.

'Oh yes, one minute I was driving along minding my own business and the next minute there were ice cream and ice lollies everywhere. I say it's a wonder no one was hurt.'

'Yes, absolutely. But you said it was parked... Stationary?'

'Are you sure you're a doctor?'

'It sounds to me like your son may have been right about you not driving anymore,' said Dr Langhill. He made a note on his computer.

'Men always gang up against us poor, defenceless women. An ice-cream van smashes into me, and everyone thinks I should stop driving. You really are unfair,' said Hilda. She seemed almost ready to cry; but she was an excellent actress.

'We are not ganging up on you, Mrs Shilton. Just sounds like a sensible move. Perhaps you should think about it.'

'Well, I can't stop driving. Pearl and I are going to be driving an RV across America.'

Dr Langhill sat open-mouthed, staring at Hilda. Then he said, 'um, maybe you need to be less hasty about that. We need to complete a medical after all. There may well be reasons you should be careful.'

'I told you men gang up on us poor, defenceless women,' said Hilda.

'It's nothing like that,' said the GP, 'we just need to check out your health for the insurance. Now if you go behind that screen and strip down to your underwear, I will examine you.' He got up and pointed at the examination area.

'I beg your pardon, young man! I will do no such thing. I've heard of people like you, getting women to strip down to their naky shaggy,' said Hilda, still sitting.

'No, Mrs Shilton, I just need to listen to your heart and lungs. It's all part of the examination. I will have a female nurse here as well.'

'Will you still be here?' said Hilda firmly.

'Well, yes, of course, I will do the exam,' said the doctor. He sat back down and leant forward towards Hilda.

'No, absolutely not. First, you try to ban me from driving. Now you want to have your wicked way with me.'

'I think we may need to find you a female doctor.' Dr Langhill turned back to his computer and made more notes.

'Female doctor, my goodness. Such new-fangled notions. If I had realised you had such things, I would have asked for one.'

'Yes, we do, looking at the date of your flight that needs sorting soon. Meanwhile, I will request some blood tests and you can re book to come back and see Dr Terral. Nice to meet you. Goodbye,' said Dr Langhill.

'Oh, is that it?' said Hilda.

'Well, unless there's anything else?' said Dr Langhill, looking up.

'No, I suppose not, goodbye,' said Hilda. She accidentally left her umbrella on the floor by her chair. When Hilda walked past the waiting room, another neighbour was just hobbling towards Dr Langhill's door. Hilda called at reception to change doctors and book a blood test and then headed out. She realised she had forgotten her umbrella when she saw the rain outside. Hilda headed back to Dr Langhill's room and walked straight in saying, 'sorry, I forgot my umbrella.'

Hilda's neighbour had his bottom on display as the doctor examined his piles. Dr Langhill looked up, shocked, and said, 'Mrs Shilton, this is very unacceptable. Please go.'

'Ooo, my goodness, I'm coming over all peculiar.' Walking out of the door Hilda realised she still did not have her umbrella, so she again barged back in. Her neighbour was just pulling up his trousers. 'Sorry, still forget the umbrella,' said Hilda as she picked up the umbrella. On leaving, she waved at the astonished faces of the doctor and neighbour.

It took a return trip to see Dr Terral for Hilda to get her medical sorted. They passed her as fit to travel and drive. No doubt her neighbour would have been relieved that he had no appointment that day.

Rose Cottage, Stoke Hind, UK

Back home, when Hilda recounted her medical tales to Pearl, she found her less responsive than usual - no laughter and no reprimands. Pearl had other things on her mind. She sat on the sofa, stroking Merlin and staring out of the window. A few times, Pearl started to say something to Hilda, then stopped. Hilda was not very tuned into people's emotions. As her mother was fond of saying, 'a watch knows where it's going.' Although Hilda never understood why she should copy a timepiece. Perhaps Hilda should also listen more carefully, as other people most likely heard her mother say, 'watch where you're going.' But Hilda was not observant when it came to how others were feeling. She often missed the subtle mood changes in others. But even Hilda occasionally noticed things. One day she said to Pearl, 'what's the matter?'

'Nothing,' said Pearl. The impromptu question quite surprised her.

'You've been acting oddly,' said Hilda.

Pearl denied any such strange behaviour. She wanted to finish reading the box of letters first and then tell Hilda the entire story. That night she read the end of a letter dated September 1937. Ginny Davies, Big D Farm, Marlan, Ohio had written it.

'... Ed's been out working day. You'll remember me saying about harvest time. This one is the worst.

I agree with you about telling the girls about each other. But what about the adoption and their mother? We need to find a way to tell them about all that.

I did what you asked and visited our local library. It's too small to hold national newspapers. I asked about how to find out about folks who went missing in the 1920's. The girl just looked at me like I was crazy. Perhaps we'd be best not telling them just yet. How did you get on at your end?

I must get on. Ruby and Ed will be back soon. Ruby has a dance tonight. That girl's head is in the clouds.

All my best Ginny'

Pearl searched through the box. This was the last one Ginny had sent. She sat and thought through everything she had read over the last week. There were gaps that needed filling, but she knew enough to tell Hilda; when she got a chance.

TSU Plc. Meedham, UK

One Monday morning, William was in Harold's office, chatting about the US trip. Harold had kept his office in the same Victorian style as his previous one in London. The walls were dark wood panelled. A selection of oil paintings adorned the walls, each illuminated from above by brass lights. The antique desk and chair came from his previous office.

As William sat in Harold's office updating him, Harold smiled. He'd hoped William would lead the start-ups in the US. Harold had been over there for the initial setup with his friend and business partner, Larry Campbell. But he needed a trusted employee to continue with the next stage.

Harold nodded as he chatted to William. 'I'm so glad you can oversee the operations.'

'It suits us too, as I told you. I wasn't happy with Hilda going alone,' said William.

Harold reminded William of the time he'd met his friend Larry Campbell. William had met Larry a couple of years earlier. Larry was Harold's friend from university and the future CEO of TSU Corp. As a multi-millionaire business mogul, Larry was just the person they needed as part of the US operation. William had embarrassing memories of their meeting and was hoping he did not have to see too much of Larry in America. Little did he know of the big part Larry's family would play on their trip.

Having sorted out all the details that were needed, William headed home. Everything was coming together exactly as planned.

Chapter Five

Summer 1931

Marlan, Ohio, USA

Ruby was eleven years old in the summer of 1931. Six years before the awful night when she would discover her adoptive parents dead on the kitchen floor. In 1931, such an idea seemed ludicrous. Who would want to kill them? They were poor farmers, nothing made them stand out from their neighbours. They were recent immigrants, ordinary people. Such things do not lead to murder, do they? Considering the state of the American economy in the thirties, their family life was idyllic.

On the long hot summers, Ruby would play out with her friends in her pa's cornfields. One evening, six youngsters lay in a field, tired from chasing and leaping around. Their mom's had told them to be back by supper or risk a hiding. They lay in a circle, hidden in the corn, bent stalks forming their makeshift camp. Together, as they rested in the warm evening sun, they felt brave. No one wanted to break up the group. They all felt cosy lying there. As they enjoyed the camaraderie of youth, the sun disappeared behind the towering crop. Crickets chirped, and in the distance, a horse whinnied. Flies chased each other above the kids' heads.

Childhood distorts memories, some it encases in a cosy glow, others it hides away. In the future, this memory lay buried deep within the psyche of them all. But as the children lay enjoying the evening warmth, they knew nothing of that future. The words of their moms forgotten; ignored. Ellie, the youngest, cracked first. She had chores to do before supper. Perhaps her mom was the fiercest or Ellie was the weakest. The other five all teased her in that cruel way children master from a young age. Ellie shouted at them as she left. Tears formed white lines on her dusty face. They never saw her again... alive.

Two days later, a neighbour found her. Her youth was gone, torn away by death. 'An accident,' 'lost her way,' folks said. 'I kept warning bout that old well shaft.' The Sheriff shook his head sagely as he spoke. But as Ruby thought about that fateful day, it made no sense. The old well was in the opposite direction of her house. Why would she go there? She was heading home, too scared of a hiding from her mom.

The night Ellie disappeared. Ruby had been heading home. The remaining five children had split up soon after Ellie left. They all remembered the warnings from their mom's soon after Ellie's departure. As Ruby trudged home, she saw a lad she recognised from school. He came from the direction of the well. Despite the darkness, she felt sure it was Orville Stanley, except for the lack of a limp. He always limped. Perhaps she saw someone a bit like him. She couldn't be sure in the half light. Not sure enough to tell anyone. His clothes looked torn and stained dark. She walked faster, eager to get home. It had been after Jill's murder that Ruby's friends always walked home with her at night. Safety in numbers, they all felt a bit unnerved by it. Even though it was called an accident.

The events of that day also affected how the kids treated Orville. No one liked him anyway. They all avoided him even before that. It just got worse. He smelt strange, looked odd, walked weirdly, cripples did that.

The more Ruby thought about that night, the more she wondered if it could have been Orville. He always limped. Days later, she worked up the courage and told her parents about seeing him that day - nothing happened. The sheriff had pronounced it an accident. Her parents chose not to confuse things. Ruby instinctively felt the sheriff had it wrong.

The years went by, then Ruby's parents were killed. Two murders in a small town, even six years apart. Such things just don't happen. After her parent's death, Ruby fled to New York in search of a new life. Marlan no longer felt safe.

May 1997

Josh Shilton's Photographic Studio, Meedham High Street, UK

Hilda was in Meedham doing some shopping, ready for her big adventure. As she walked up the High Street, she popped in to see her grandson, Josh, at his photographic studio. She arrived part way through a photo shoot. She did not know the meaning of arriving quietly. After disrupting the ongoing photo shoot. Hilda settled into a seat with a drink and Josh continued. He was photographing a middle-aged woman. She wanted a portrait picture for her husband. Some people would call it a glamour shot, but that term could be misunderstood. What she wanted was a classy portrait of her looking good for her husband. She had seen the exact type of shot that she wanted Josh to replicate. A head and shoulders in soft focus; the model was bare shouldered. In the example photo, the model was beautiful and very slim or should we say flat. To say that the client was average looking would be the kindest description. Josh had another issue. His customer was large, in every regard, bulging in every direction.

Josh had asked his female assistant to help the client get ready. The client lacked any suitable off the shoulder outfits, in her size. So, Josh asked his assistant to create a makeshift one. This was not the best idea, especially now that Hilda was around. The photo shoot started well. The rather large client was setup in front of the backdrop and the lights arranged. A soft-focus filter helped. Josh took a test shot with an instant camera. He viewed the result and adjusted the lights, then added a stronger soft-focus filter. These were the days before digital. The next test appeared to be acceptable. At this point everything went wrong.

Hilda felt she had sat still long enough. Besides, she had finished her coffee and had plenty of bounce. Getting up, she walked over to join Josh. She stood behind him and tried to imagine what the finished photograph would be like. It was just not good enough, and she said, 'this just won't do, it's almost indecent dear.' She went over to the client, took hold of the makeshift covering, and pulled upwards. The covering was a sheet of material wrapped under the woman's arms. It stretched down to below her knees and was safety pinned at the back. The effect for a bare shoulder photo looked good. The customer was too well endowed to be contained easily in such a makeshift affair. Josh's assistant had not designed the covering for rough handling. Rather than making the customer more decent, pulling on the material had the opposite effect. Yanking the covering upward caused the safety pins to pop undone, and it left the covering in Hilda's hands. The client was left in an embarrassing situation.

***

Later, Josh was doing his best to look seriously at his gran, but he kept smirking. Hilda could not see that she had done anything wrong. She felt no blame for the lady ending up topless. Whose silly idea had it been to use such a flimsy covering, after all? After being hurriedly covered by his assistant, the client had rushed through to the changing room. Perhaps not surprisingly, she had left without wanting to finish her photo shoot. Now that his assistant had gone to lunch, and the shop was closed, Josh could catch up with his gran.

'They don't make safety pins like they used to,' said Hilda. She searched her bag. 'I have a couple of good strong ones in my bag, if you want. You never know when your elastic will give out. You don't want to lose your…' Hilda mouthed a word that made Josh blush.

'No! you keep those just in case you need them gran,' said Josh.

'Yes, thank you, dear. I have been caught out needing them in the past,' said Hilda.

Josh burst out laughing. Hilda stared at him in astonishment and said, 'are you quite all right dear? Is it the shock? I suppose you haven't seen a half-naked woman before.'

Josh laughed even louder. Hilda got up and walked over to him, gently patting his hands, and saying, 'there, there.'

'You really are a hoot gran, you brightened up a dull day. Although I do feel sorry for my client. I hope she isn't too traumatised.'

'While I'm here, is there anything else I can do to help?' said Hilda. For some reason, Josh bent double in laughter and tears ran down his face.

Antique Shop, High Street, Meedham, UK

Having left Josh to get ready for his afternoon clients, without her help, Hilda headed off further along the High Street. As she passed an antiques shop, she saw some watercolour paintings in the window, so she headed inside to examine them. They were all watercolours by travellers on their grand tours in the 17th and 18th century. Hilda could just picture herself, whipping out her sketch pad or easel and creating a quick masterpiece. Her pictures adorning art galleries and museums; family, friends, and art critics lauding her amazing paintings. Realism was not one of her greatest strengths. As her birthday was coming up, Hilda decided to ask her family for art lessons and materials.

She mentioned her idea to William on their next phone call. He said, 'art lessons, really? Why?'

Hilda said, 'so that I can paint and draw on the trip.'

'But are you artistic?' said William, and then relenting he agreed, 'of course we'll buy you art lessons, if that's what you want.' He walked through to the other room. Louise was singing and sorting out some things ready to pack. She looked bright and was dancing. William stopped and stared.

Louise saw her husband staring at her and said, 'oh, hello, you look like you have news?'

'Umm, ah yes,' said William. He watched Louise bounce around the room. 'My mother wants art lessons.'

'Wonderful, great idea.'

William grunted an acknowledgment and went back into the front room to find his newspaper, shaking his head.

Night School, Meedham, UK

A week later, Hilda was at a local night school. The timing had worked out just right for their six-week course before her trip to the USA. She walked into the busy reception area; new students of all ages were milling around. A sign that read: 'New students enrol here.' After a brief wait, she stood in front of a young lady who said, 'which class are you wanting to sign up for?'

'Ah, now, let me see. I did know, dear,' said Hilda. She had forgotten to bring the prospectus.

'There is a queue. Do you want to take a copy of the prospectus and look through it over there?' asked the receptionist.

Hilda spotted a poster on the wall that read: 'Life drawing.' She vaguely remembered wanting something about 'life'. It may also have had the word 'still' in it. 'But surely that couldn't be important, still, was such a small word.' She thought.

'That's the one, the life drawing class dear,' said Hilda, pointing at the poster. She wondered why the poster had a scantily clad lady on it. After all, still life was fruit and vegetables. But adverts these days are provocative. The receptionist booked Hilda onto the course and directed her.

A mixed group headed down the corridor to the same class, although she was the oldest. The others knew each other and chatted away happily. Hilda walked behind the group, clutching the drawing pad and pencils that Josh had bought her. Her excitement was building.

When they all reached the classroom, the teacher was already waiting. Ms Watkins was a 46-year-old skilled artist. In the middle of the room were two fur covered chaise lounges. They were at a 45-degree angle to each other, pointing outwards. Around the room, were set out a semi-circle of easels, facing the chaise lounges. Hilda searched around and was wondering where the fruit or flowers were hiding.

'Welcome everyone, I'm Ms Watkins and I have deliberately not told you which sex model will be on which chair. You need to be able to draw both, so find a seat and get set up,' said Ms Watkins. The students found seats behind the easels. All except Hilda, who was puzzled. She walked over to the teacher and said, 'Miss Watkins, I have a question.'

'Ms' said Ms Watkins.

'What?' asked Hilda, 'did you say Mrs or was that Muzz?'

'Ms, it means neither Mrs nor Miss.'

'Don't you know if you're married?' Hilda put her head to one side.

'I am perfectly cognisant of my marital status; I merely choose not to publicise it.'

'I understood some of that. Could you just go over it again, dear?'

'We only have one and a half hours and I want to get started. So, no I can't,' said Ms Watkins. She turned to an adjacent door, and said, 'OK, Jacqui, Henry, you're up, come on through.'

Everyone looked towards the door. Two people walked through. A young man in his late twenties, muscular, with short dark hair and rugged features. Next to him was a woman in her thirties, with shoulder length curly brown hair. She was attractive and well proportioned. They were wearing knee length robes and slippers, but nothing else. Jacqui walked to the left-hand chair and Henry to the right. After a moment of silent anticipation, the two of them dropped their robes and sat on the chairs, slipping out of their slippers. Henry stretched his muscular naked form out in such a way that his left leg was bent and his right leg flat as he lay on his right. This meant it fully displayed him to everyone on that side of the room, including Hilda. Meanwhile Jacqui had laid herself out on the opposite chair showing her buxom beauty to that side of the room.

Hilda stood in silence for a moment, looking at Henry's manly form. Then, as if propelled by a giant spring, she leapt into action. Grabbing the recently discarded robes, she threw one over Henry and one over Jacqui.

'They're in their naky shaggy, can't anyone else see this?' said Hilda. She glanced at each potential artist. She came to the tutor and said, 'Miss Watkins, I'm not surprised you're confused about marriage, if you let this sort of thing go on. Has no one taught you about the birds and butterflies?'

Meanwhile, the models had again removed their robes, so that as Hilda turned around, she was looking down at a naked Jacqui spread before her.

'Oh, my goodness,' Hilda said, wafting herself with her hand, 'it's like being in a ginalogical ward.'

One of the other students, who had laughed at Hilda's antics, said, 'I think you mean gynaecological ward.'

'Whatever ward we are on,' said Hilda. 'Put those away, young lady. Don't you know there are men in this room?'

Hilda glanced around and noticed that most of the other students were drawing. She said, 'they're drawing your bits and pieces dear, have you no shame? If my mother was still alive, she'd die of shock.'

Hilda then went over to Henry and said, 'I haven't seen anything like this since my dear Arthur died.' Then as she took in his naked body longer. 'I haven't seen *anything* like this before. Cover yourself up, young man. There are ladies present. At my age I might have a heart attack any minute, or at the very least have an attack of the vapours. My mother was always talking about an attack of the vapours. I have no idea what it is, but I feel I may have one any minute.' She wafted herself with her sketch pad.

Ms Watkins was getting impatient. She said, 'will you please stop interfering with the models? Either sit down and draw them or leave.'

'I am a refined lady. I do not draw nude models. No person of refinement would,' said Hilda. She stood tall.

'Michelangelo did,' said another student.

'I don't care what your friends get up to,' said Hilda. She searched around for the culprit, unsuccessfully.

'He's a famous artist who painted the Sistine Chapel,' said the same student. Hilda glimpsed him.

Hilda glared at the offending student and said, 'what your Italian friend Micky Di Angelo does for a living doesn't interest me. I just know when something is wrong. Drawing nudes is wrong.' All this time, Hilda had been standing in front of Henry.

Ms Watkins said to Hilda, 'why don't you leave then? You don't seem in any hurry.'

'My son and daughter-in-law bought me these art lessons. Maybe I should go and do a still life. Where is the still life class?' said Hilda.

Ms Watkins glanced at her papers and said, 'room 5F.'

'Room 5F,' said Hilda, 'is that far away?' She still stood where she was, her head to one side.

Rose Cottage, Stoke Hind, UK

That weekend at her house, Hilda was sitting on the sofa. Josh and William had popped round to see how things had gone with her first art class. Louise was back at home, marking schoolwork. A teacher's work is never done.

Hilda had a large bag next to her. Josh said, 'when do we get to see your artwork?'

Hilda was smiling and kicking her legs in anticipation. She stared at William and Josh and said, 'remember, I am only a beginner, so don't expect a masterpiece.'

'Come on, stop dragging it out,' said William. He stood in front of her, next to Josh.

Hilda picked up the bag and pulled out the drawing pad. She proudly held it up for her son and grandson to enjoy. They spent a while studying the picture, then turned their heads to one side, then the other. They pursed their lips, frowned, and stared. Laid out on the page was a naïve, pencil drawing, of a naked woman. One part of their brains was obviously trying to see the expected still life of fruit and veg. But Jacqui's, naked body would not resolve into a fruit bowl, even as poorly drawn as it was, no matter how hard their brains tried.

Hilda had stayed in the life class but felt unable to draw a picture of Henry. So, instead, she had drawn Jacqui. What Hilda lacked in artistic skill; she made up for in passion. Eventually Josh said, 'that's not a bowl of fruit.'

William's eyes went wide, and he said, 'that's a nude woman.'

'Yes, that's right, she's called Jacqui, she was a nice young lady. I bumped into her in town the other day. She was telling me I'm a bohemian,' said Hilda, smiling.

'A bohemian, you? Do you even know what that means?' said Josh.

'Something to do with art. Jacqui was explaining it,' said Hilda.

'But, but,' William said, or rather stammered. 'What will Rev Pugh say, or Mrs Pugh, for that matter? What about the fellows at the golf club? Oh, I can't bear it. You really are the limit sometimes.' William's mouth opened wide, and he stared off into space.

'You worry about things far too much, just like your father. You'll give yourself high blood like him,' said Hilda. She waved a reprimanding finger at her son.

'Pressure,' said William in a distant voice.

'Pressure? Pressure what?' said Hilda.

'I'll give myself high blood pressure, like father,' said William. He sounded robotic.

'Oh, I don't think he had that. I'm sure it had something to do with his blood,' said Hilda, shaking her head.

'It was his blood. High blood pressure,' said William. He started to re-focus.

'Yes, just what I said,' said Hilda.

'But you... never mind,' said William. He went over to a chair and sat down heavily.

'Some things are best left, dad,' said Josh. He also sat down.

'Don't get in such a tizzy. Remember what your grandfather used to say? Neither a worrier nor borrower be,' said Hilda. She was looking proudly at her own picture.

'Lender nor borrower,' said William. He was fully alert now and looked cross.

'What's that got to do with worrying?' said Hilda. She stared at her son in puzzlement.

'Exactly,' said William. 'It's got nothing to do with worrying.'

'You're getting strange in your old age, William. Your cousin Tim went the same way,' said Hilda.

'I am not strange; I am not strange,' said William.

'It's not from my side. Tim was on your father's mother's side,' said Hilda.

'There is nothing odd about me.' William's eyes stared wildly. 'Nothing odd at all.' His voice rose to a high pitch. Josh walked over to him and patted him on the back. William looked up at Josh, pleading.

'You just go for a little lie down. I'm sure you'll feel better soon,' said Hilda in a calm and quiet voice.

'It's you who is going around painting nudes in your old age,' said William. He jumped up, pushing Josh aside, and walked around in a tiny circle. The room was only small.

'Why did you paint a nude gran? It seems most unlike you,' said Josh.

'I did no such thing,' said Hilda.

'But you're holding up the picture gran,' said Josh.

'And you're saying I've lost the plot?' said William. He had stopped circling and was standing, panting, in a corner.

'I did a drawing, not a painting,' said Hilda. She held the drawing up proudly.

'The issue isn't the medium. It's the fact that you have a picture of a nude,' said William loudly.

'I certainly didn't go to any seances, so I met no mediums,' said Hilda.

'Dad wasn't meaning that kind of medium. He meant pencil or paint, artistic medium,' said Josh. He looked at his dad anxiously, who was panting hard.

'He really should be clear, then. I hate it when people aren't clear. Do you know at school the number of times I got the cane because the teacher wasn't clear? It's very unfair. They shouldn't blame me if the teacher doesn't explain things properly. Miss Wentworth, my old headmistress, has a lot to answer for. She caned me so many times for things that were not my fault. It was all because the teacher didn't explain properly,' said Hilda.

'I'm sure your old head teacher has a lot to answer for. But what about the painting, I mean drawing?' said Josh.

'You see, people are always mixing things up. It's confusing. Is it any wonder I get things wrong?' said Hilda.

'Please, please, please. Just tell us why? Just tell us why?' said William. He sank back into a chair and hung his head. His breathing slowing.

'Calm down, dear. Apparently, there's an Italian chap called Micky Di Angelo who paints in a toilet. He is incredibly famous, and he even paints nudes on toilet cisterns. They never explained why, but apparently everyone knows him, and they tell me that makes it all right. Anyway, the teacher, who doesn't know whether she's married, explained that drawing nude people is a good idea. So, as I was there, and you'd paid for the lessons, and I had my pencils and drawing pad I thought I would join in. Besides, it was a long way to class 5f, I've only got little legs. I am seventy-seven, you know, dear. But you'll be pleased to know I enjoyed it so much. I'm going back next week. I thought I'd draw Henry next time.'

Josh and William looked at each other in amazement. Then Josh said, 'Henry? Is that a male model?'

'Yes, of course it is. Henry would be an odd name for a lady. He's an extremely nice young man,' said Hilda.

'Nude?' said Josh.

'Of course. What else? It is a life class. Really, the men in this family are such prudes. Louise will understand,' said Hilda.

William looks at Hilda in horror and said, 'I don't know what to say.'

'There's a first,' said Hilda. She switched on the TV. A programme on Greccio-Roman art was playing. Ancient nude pictures were on screen and the narrator was talking about classical artists. Hilda gave a sweeping gesture towards the TV screen and said, 'you see, I'm just being classy.'

July 1997

Leithly Hall, Somershire, UK

At the Duchess of Somershire's country home, all was quiet. She was in Los Angeles with her friend, Bonbon. Jake Vort, AKA 'The Ghost,' crept like a panther across the lawn; because that is what burglars do. He arrived on the veranda, where only a few weeks ago the duchess and her friend Penelope had been drinking wine. A CCTV camera was pointing at him from each direction. He seemed unconcerned. Within a few minutes, Jake had made it inside, up the stairs, and stood before the safe. The safe had been hidden behind a picture in what had once been the duke's bedroom. Although such an obvious place hardly counts as hidden. Jake passed several CCTV cameras on route to the poor hiding place. No alarms were ringing, silent or out loud. His inside information was proving accurate. He checked his watch. Thirty minutes till the next security patrol car came by. He opened the safe by using the number. Which seemed very odd. No need for high-tech equipment, explosives, or stethoscopes. Why didn't all burglars do that? Maybe they did not all have access to the number. They ought to try this method. It looked much easier and far less messy.

***

After Jake had removed the diamonds and replaced them with very realistic fakes. He did his usual thing. At least it had become usual recently. He was feeling invincible. He removed his mask and stared at his new prize. The blue glow of the uncut stones shone on his face as he stared into their depths, one in each hand. For a while, he stood, lost in their beauty. He had always preferred uncut diamonds. There was something real and rare about them. Then he securely placed them in his bag and closed the safe, putting his mask back on before leaving.

He would delete all the CCTV footage before he left. It normally took a few weeks or months before a victim discovered one of his thefts. The owner would eventually realise they now had a fake. Only vague clues about the thefts were ever found. A tire track in a lane at one country house, a stranger seen entering the grounds of another. One time, they found a footprint in the garden; but it could have been anyone's. The only clues to Jake's existence were from the sale of the stolen items. No surprise then that Interpol had nicknamed Jake 'The Ghost' and no wonder he had become overconfident.

Jake headed back to his waiting transport. Next part of the plan was always the hardest. Getting the diamonds out of the country undetected. In this case into the USA.

Chapter Six

July 1997

Rose Cottage, Stoke Hind, UK

Hilda had a problem sitting still at the best of times. With their holiday to the USA drawing near, she was like a spinning top. Pearl and William were the cool heads in the group, the planners. William decided he would phone a few days before the trip to check all was on track. Unfortunately, he spoke to Hilda, even though Pearl was there. Why didn't he ask to speak to Pearl? A question he would be sure to ask himself soon enough.

Hilda decided it would be good enough to relay the call to Pearl, who sat with pen and paper ticking things off. William was sitting in his home office, checking his list. First and most important was the place to which they were flying - not something to get wrong. It has often been noted that you read what you expect to read. Many people also hear what they expect to hear. William told Hilda, Portland, Maine, Hilda heard Portland, Oregon. That may have been partly because she was dancing around with the phone in her hand. Whatever the reason, she said to Pearl just one word, 'Portland.'

Pearl was a thorough person, so she asked, 'that is Portland, Oregon?'

Hilda did a twirl and asked, 'what dear?'

'I'm checking it's Portland, Oregon?' asked Pearl.

'Of course,' said Hilda, trying a bit of tap dancing.

William could hear some sounds. But he also heard Hilda confirm the destination. He ticked off the arrival point: Portland, Maine.

With that simple misunderstanding, the scene was set for the two groups to arrive on opposite sides of America. Pearl's plan had been that they would meet in Portland, Oregon, on the West coast. Then she and Hilda would pick up their Recreational Vehicle (RV), a large motor caravan; and Louise join them on their trip East, towards Portland, Maine. Meanwhile, William would catch up with them as often as possible. On hearing the phone call, Pearl was unaware that William was working in reverse.

William had a specific deadline for his trip, a start date for TSU Corp., New York. The new jewel in the crown of the American arm of TSU Plc. Because Hilda had delayed her medical, they were not ready till the next day. The two groups set off a day apart, unknowingly heading to opposite sides of America.

Their perfect plan ruined before it started. Still, had it not been for the confusion, all the good things that happened would have been missed as well. Then again, they would also have avoided the problems. In the end, things worked out exactly as they should. Life is a rich patchwork of light and dark.

Josh Shilton's Photographic Studio, Meedham, UK

The next morning, Josh arrived at his photographic studio and started work. About 9:30am a courier delivered an envelope from the USA. He stared at it, then slowly opened it. He put it down as his first client arrived. It is possible they did not receive his undivided attention. After they left, he again picked up the envelope. Having read it, he stared at it for a long time. Then he picked up the phone and dialled a number. A receptionist said, 'TSU Plc, how can I help you?'

'Can I speak to William Shilton, please?'

'Who shall I say is calling?'

'His son.'

Heathrow Airport, Longford, UK

On the day after Josh received his news, William and Louise were at the airport. They arrived in a fluster. Louise spent an hour trying to get William moving. He was not an early morning person. It was bad enough having a 7am flight, but the fact they needed to be a few hours before that was too much for him. They had stayed in an airport hotel to make it easier, in theory. But the guests next to them had kept them awake till late. They finally arrived at the security gate queue. Louise asked William, 'did you have to?'

'I've heard they can do a free upgrade,' said William.

'Fine, but once she refused,' said Louise.

'There's no harm in persistence.'

'Ten minutes?' said Louise loudly. A passing young lad looked up at her.

'Yes, well, perhaps I'm tense about the journey,' said William.

As they passed through the security gate, they were dealt with by the same staff who would handle Hilda the following day. There was one difference: they had a much shorter interaction with them than she would. They were cleared through to the departure lounge and found a seat. William turned to Louise and said, 'I've just remembered. He got it.'

'Who got what?' asked Louise.

William sat on the edge of his seat. 'Our son got the photo shoot in the US, the one he bid on. He's still waiting to hear about a second one that's too hush-hush to tell me about.'

'Really? That's amazing. What a shame he can't come over with us,' said Louise.

'He'll be there in the next week or two. He isn't sure of the exact dates or location. That's still being sorted. I gave him my office contact details, so he can let me know.' William looked like a kid in a sweetshop.

'How exciting! He also has the hotel details,' said Louise.

'Oh, why did you give him that?' William looked like he found an empty sweetshop.

'I wanted him to keep in touch,' said Louise.

The wait for their plane seemed to zip by, and they boarded their flight for Washington Dulles. On arrival, William and Louise hardly had time to notice they were at an airport. Probably because they were so tired. But let's give the luggage staff some credit. Their bags arrived quickly, and immigration decided that the couple standing before them was genuine. William had an entire explanation ready to justify their extended stay. But they were just waved through. It was an anti-climax. The interconnecting flight to Portland International was on a tight time window and they made the flight on time.

Portland International Airport, Maine, USA

It was after arriving at Portland International Airport that William and Louise had the customs gauntlet to run. The customs lady watched them walk through the green zone; she had the eyes of a hawk. Louise strolled casually, but William seemed to have a problem with his legs. He acted almost drunk, but then he was exhausted. His eyes kept flicking towards the customs desk, but she let them through; she must have thought he was too obvious to be a smuggler. Their longest hold-up was queueing for a taxi to get to the train station.

They had a lengthy train ride into Portland itself. William had watched too many American thrillers. He expected to be robbed at knifepoint or have someone pull a gun. When the man sitting opposite, put his hand inside his jacket, to get his wallet, William stuck his hands up. Realising his mistake, he tried to turn it into a yawn and stretch. The man looked at William oddly for the rest of the journey.

William was exhausted and ready for the journey to end. But Louise found the journey more uplifting. A young man had helped lift her bags onto the train and sat chatting to her for the first three stops. She was sorry he got off so soon. Especially when he said on leaving, 'no way you've gotten a grown-up son.' Louise had a noticeably lighter step as she left the train.

Rose Cottage, Stoke Hind, UK

The day before their flight, Pearl and Hilda were almost fully packed and ready. Their flight was the next afternoon. Pearl was in the other room sorting a couple of things. Hilda was in the lounge looking for a few missing art materials to pack, important not to forget those. She might not get to paint any nudes in America, but the scenery would be amazing. The phone rang, and she answered in her usual manner, giving all her personal details. William's warnings had been a waste of time.

At a call centre in Manchester, Terry scribbled a note of her name and location. He had just rung random numbers, finally; he had a bite.

He spoke breezily. 'Good morning, Hilda, I'm Terry. We're offering five free hearing aids to residents in the Stoke Hinds area.'

'I only have two ears, dear,' said Hilda.

'I mean, five lots of hearing aids, to different households. Each has up to two, depending on your hearing need,' said Terry.

'That's exceedingly kind, free hearing aids.' Hilda sat down; it seemed like this call could take a while.

Terry started his patter. 'Yes, and they are the latest, high tech, super small, hearing aids. Almost invisible in your ear.'

'The wonders of modern science,' said Hilda.

Pearl walked into the room to see if it was Katie phoning about Merlin. When she saw Hilda chatting away on the phone, she turned to leave. Hilda looked up and said, 'this will interest you, Pearl, your hearing is terrible.'

Pearl said, 'What?'

'You see, I told you.'

'Is there someone else there who needs a hearing aid?' asked Terry.

'You said you were only giving them to five households,' said Hilda, sharply.

'Isn't the lady I heard in your household?' asked Terry.

'Certainly not. She's a friend,' said Hilda.

'But presumably, she is from Stoke Hinds?'

'No!'

'Oh, well, let's get on, shall we?' said Terry. He glanced back at his notes.

Hilda had some thoughts. She spoke aloud when thinking. 'I do hope you aren't going to offer one to Colonel Huntingdon. He's rich enough to buy one himself, besides he's a bit crosspatch.' Terry was scribbling notes as Hilda spoke. 'I think you should give one to little Miss Runcie. The poor old dear.' Hilda sighed. 'Mind you, there are the Sanders Twins, we mustn't forget them, must we? Although, now I come to think of it, it's best not to talk about them, isn't it?' She carried on chatting about various people in the town. Terry furiously scribbled notes of their names and circumstances.

Pearl asked Hilda who she was talking to. Hilda said, 'it's about free hearing aids dear.'

'That's very unlikely,' said Pearl. 'I'd hang up.'

'My friend says that I should hang up,' said Hilda to Terry.

'Do you always do as she says?' asked Terry. He was looking at his growing list of information with a smile. He had an extensive list of people to call.

'No, although she is a good friend, and very sensible,' said Hilda, glancing at Pearl and smiling. Pearl smiled back.

'I think it's only right to mention that my hearing is exceptionally good. Unlike Pearl's,' said Hilda. Pearl stopped smiling. She indicated Hilda should put the phone down. Hilda turned away and said to Terry, 'will that be a problem, the fact I can hear well?'

'Of course not,' said Terry. His smile was growing broad. He filled in some order details on his computer screen to save time later. 'In fact, Hilda, it's a positive advantage.'

'Really?' said Hilda. 'Why's that?'

'Oh yes, you see, if you start out with good hearing, then these amazing hearing aids will make it even better. Think of it like this: you will get super hearing.'

'Super hearing?' said Hilda. She liked the sound of that. Pearl was shaking her head.

'Yes absolutely, you'll be able to hear things you miss out on now,' said Terry. He filled in Hilda's name and phone number. Now he needed her address and bank details for the payment.

'How exciting,' said Hilda. She stared out of the window. 'I'll be able to listen in to people, like in those spy movies.'

'Possibly,' said Terry cautiously. Perhaps remembering a reprimand he received last week from his supervisor. He had exaggerated the capabilities of their hearing aids. 'That's the kind of thing. Now all I need to do is to sort out the delivery of these wonderful hearing aids. Can I take your address and bank details?'

'My bank details, why ever do you need that, for something free?' said Hilda. Pearl was looking at Hilda, shaking her head fast and moving towards the phone.

'There's an initial deposit, and then there's a monthly cost for the batteries and maintenance. Plus, there's a consultation fee. Someone must come out and check your hearing to make sure we give you the correct aid. After all, you wouldn't want the wrong one, would you?' asked Terry. The phone seemed to go dead. 'Hello, Hilda, hello.' He studied the list of names she had given him and searched for them, one by one. None of them came up. What he did not know was that Hilda got people's names wrong. The one she got right, Colonel Huntingdon, was ex-directory. Terry screwed up his notes and deleted what he had already typed on his computer.

In Hilda's lounge, Pearl was explaining about the techniques used to trick people into buying things they did not need. These so called 'free' products, which were just high-pressure selling. Hilda nodded sagely and seemed to understand. It remained to be seen if the warnings were heeded.

Heathrow Airport, Longford, UK

The next day Hilda and Pearl were at Heathrow Airport. They arrived early as instructed, allowing time for security and check-in. They had an afternoon flight.

Jake Vort, AKA 'The Ghost,' was at the airport, watching for a suitable, unwitting 'mark' to take his stolen diamonds through customs. This method had worked well in the past and seemed his best option for the diamonds. His buyer wanted a speedy delivery. Jake watched the passengers arrive. His 'patsy' needed to be unlikely to be stopped by customs in the USA. After patiently waiting for an hour. Hilda and Pearl walked past him. Hilda seemed to be his ideal subject. She not only looked like an innocent old lady, but she looked like someone the customs staff would just want to get rid of fast. Those of us who know, and love Hilda, may well have warned him to search for another, more suitable mark. But then again, should crime be easy? Should crime pay?

Jake moved with the speed and skill of a magician. He walked towards and bumped into Hilda. She glanced at him in surprise. The evil deed was done. The diamonds were now deep inside her handbag. How do criminals do that?

Following the brush with Jake, Hilda had carried on to the security gate. She was now in a disagreement with the security staff manning it. The same ones William and Louise had met so briefly the day before. Hilda was not keen to give up her handbag to be searched. It contained personal things she did not want anyone rummaging through. Little did she or they know it also contained two stolen, multimillion-pound diamonds. Once the security man had finally wrestled her bag from her, he searched it under Hilda's watchful eye. There was nothing of interest to him. It puzzled him why she had spare elastic, safety pins, and plastic bags. Be prepared was Hilda's watch word. The diamonds were concealed in an innocent jar of face cream. Hilda had glanced away when he examined the jar, distracted by a commotion on the other aisle and so she missed this addition to her bag. Just as well. The cream was not a brand she used. Far too expensive.

Next came the battle of the metal detection arch. She did not want to walk through a giant magnetic arch. The security man explained it would check for any metal objects, which did not reassure her. After a lengthy argument with the man on duty, she insisted on speaking to a female operative. When a woman came out, Hilda took her to one side and asked, 'what about my...' then mouthed the word 'bra?'

The operative smiled and said, 'don't worry, that won't cause a problem.'

'But it's *underwired*,' said Hilda. She studied the operative up and down, examining the appropriate area. 'I realise it isn't an issue for *you*. But there is a *lot* of wire in mine. Some of us have a greater need for support than others.'

The operative frowned at Hilda and said, 'it will *not* set the machine off.'

'On your head, be it,' said Hilda, cautiously walking through the arch. No alarms went off, so she shrugged, picked up her handbag, and walked off, muttering, 'obviously faulty equipment.'

Jake followed Hilda through. He had no argument with the staff and was cleared to pursue Hilda in the departure area. He sat watching her. Sitting in the departure lounge, waiting, Hilda was getting bored. But perhaps not as bored as the young lad sitting next to her. He and his family had arrived two hours earlier; their flight was delayed. The toddlers' parents had run out of ideas to amuse him. They lay back, exhausted. They were regretting the decision to fly with a youngster; he was amusing himself. The young lad ran around the area in between the two rows of seats, making car noises and accidentally treading on passengers' toes. Most of whom were understanding when they saw the age of the transgressor.

Hilda sat down just as the young lad was resting between bouts of active play. He turned to her and screwed up his face. She smiled and then hid behind her bag. Appearing suddenly and shouting 'peak-a-boo.' This was not a game he had seen before; his parents were too up to date for such things. The young lad was startled and then amused. His mother saw what was happening and was about to stop this strange woman when her husband put his hand on her shoulder, seeing an opportunity for respite. The mother held back and watched events unfold. Hilda continued her game of peekaboo. But the child quickly grew bored and decided he needed to run around again.

Any form of movement was always more attractive to Hilda than sitting still. Seeing the toddler running around, she joined in. But she showed him a new game - aeroplanes. Holding her arms out beside her, she made aeroplane noises, and then ran around in the gap between the two rows of chairs. Watching her for a moment, the youngster joined in. Whilst the seated passengers had been forgiving of a 2-year-old treading on their toes, they were less understanding when Hilda did so. Whether this was because of her age or weight, who can say? This brought the game to an abrupt halt. Hilda left a sea of red faces; feet being rubbed and rude remarks.

Pearl suggested that they have a meal in a nearby restaurant. They left the disgruntled parents to amuse their own child again - not to mention the angry mob. Jake had been sitting far enough away to save his feet. He now sat in the restaurant. Everything was going to plan for him - so far.

Eventually, Hilda and Pearl's flight was called, and they boarded the plane heading to Denver, Colorado. Jake had a seat three rows behind them. Immigration always happens at your first point of landing in the USA, so Hilda and Louise faced this in Denver. For William and Louise, it had been simple. He had over-prepared and been surprised at not being questioned; the reverse was true for Hilda. She was in a separate queue to Pearl, who went straight through. Expecting the same smooth process herself, Hilda arrived in front of the immigration officer and announced her arrival by saying, 'howdy.' She assumed that was the local parlance, then she handed over her passport. She held out her hand, ready to take it straight back. But the officer looked at the passport and then up at Hilda, and asked, 'Is this your passport?'

'Of course, dear, I would hardly have given you someone else's.'

The immigration officer stared at the picture and back at Hilda and asked, 'where were you born?'

'At home,' said Hilda.

The officer frowned and asked, 'where was your home?'

'Oh, I'm sorry, Kilburn, London,' said Hilda.

'I need to check this passport. Come with me.' The officer took Hilda into a back room.

Jake had hung back from going through immigration himself. He wanted to check all was well with his 'mark.' He got worried when security led Hilda into the back room. Normally, his chosen 'carriers' sailed through immigration and customs. This was not how things were supposed to go. He realised he would seem suspicious waiting too long and so continued through immigration himself. As per usual, they quizzed him closely. He must have a guilty face; they found nothing. He went and sat near Pearl in the internal transfer area. They were both waiting patiently for Hilda. Customs would not be until the final airport. But Jake was monitoring Hilda at every stage.

Meanwhile, in the backroom, Hilda was being investigated by the immigration officer. It was all her own fault. When Hilda had her passport photo taken, she had read the instructions carefully. No smiling and wear glasses where necessary, not as a fashion accessory. Perhaps she didn't read carefully after all. Hilda decided she wanted to appear at her best for such an important photo. When out shopping, she had seen a makeover offer in a department store. It had surprised the girl in the store that Hilda wanted the top-level transformation. But the makeover cost a lot, and she was on commission, so she did it anyway. Hilda's face was completely transformed; almost unrecognisable. The make-up comprised a base layer to cover wrinkles and blemishes. Then the tonal layer to give shape to her cheekbones. Finally detailing of eyebrows, lips, and lashes, the effect was a new woman, not ideal for a passport photo.

To complete the effect, Hilda put on her best glasses. Ones she only wore for parties and ballroom dancing. After the photo she went back to the shop and asked that they remove the make-up. The assistant was incredulous that Hilda had paid so much, for something used such a brief time.

This fancy passport photo caused all the problems. The officer had taken Hilda to have a new photo taken. He then took her passport through to the back in order that it could be entered into a special machine and compared with the photo they took of Hilda. The machine looked at facial angles rather than being fooled by makeup; it passed the photo as being Hilda. Normally, this machine came into its own spotting people trying to use makeup to look like a person on a stolen passport. Not people who had a complete makeover for their passport photo.

'OK, you are free to go,' said the officer. He handed Hilda her passport. 'I don't know what you did in this photo?'

'Nice, isn't it dear?' said Hilda. She grinned as she accepted her proffered passport.

'Yes... no... what I was saying...,' said the officer. He sounded confused.

'Thank you, all this fuss. Anyone would think you found a bomb in my bag,' said Hilda rather foolishly.

'You have a bomb?' asked the distracted officer. He grabbed his radio and called an alert. Armed officers appeared and surrounded Hilda.

'Where's the bomb?' said one of them, who acted as the one in charge.

'What bomb?' said Hilda, looking confused.

'The one you just said you had,' said the first officer.

'I said you would think I had a bomb,' said Hilda. She wondered what all the fuss was about.

'Do you have a bomb?' said the senior officer.

'No, of course not,' said Hilda, shaking her head.

'You mustn't joke about things like that,' said the senior officer sternly.

'You really are a serious lot,' said Hilda. She looked as innocent as a newborn babe.

'This is a serious matter; promise you won't do that again and we'll say no more about it,' said the senior officer, staring hard at Hilda.

'I promise,' said Hilda. She stared at her feet.

'OK, you can go, ma'am,' said the senior officer.

'Well, I must find Pearl,' said Hilda.

When Hilda found Pearl, she just explained that the officers were slow for her. Neglecting to mention her part in the hold-up.

Portland International Airport, Oregon, USA

On finally arriving in Portland, they had customs to clear. Jake only took one small carry-on bag and cleared customs fast, then waited outside the doors to arrivals. Hilda and Pearl had to wait for their luggage to be unloaded and arrive at the carousel before they could go through customs. They were not stopped.

Life would be so simple if Jake had repeated the magic trick of bumping into Hilda and this time taking the diamonds back. Life is not simple; the best laid plans always go wrong. As Jake moved towards Hilda to bump into her, a man who was pushing his luggage trolley tripped. His trolley veered left into Jake, catching him on his right side. Jake was winded, and his right leg hurt badly enough to stop him in his tracks. He turned and shouted at the man pushing the trolley. Hilda and Pearl glanced at the disturbance but continued to the exit. By the time Jake turned back around, they were exiting through the revolving doors.

He half ran and half hobbled after them. As he reached the outside, they were getting into a taxi. He pushed an old man out of the way and got in the next one, saying, 'follow that taxi.'

The driver peered over his shoulder and laughed. Jake said, 'follow that taxi and I'll give you $500 on top of the fare.' The taxi took up the chase.

***

Portland was a surprise to Hilda and Pearl. As the taxi took them to the hotel, Hilda said, 'are you sure we are not back in England?' The rain was so heavy that they could not see much out of the taxi window. Had they been able to, then the wide roads and distinctive style of buildings would have given a lie to that notion. The rain did not bother Jake. He just wanted to catch their taxi. But the heavy downpour made it hard for his driver to see the car in front. Despite his best efforts, and the promised $500 made those efforts good, he lost the other taxi.

Jake couldn't believe his bad luck. He asked the driver to pull over and wait. Getting out, he walked a short way off and screamed. Feeling better he headed back to the taxi. It had gone. The driver forwent the fare rather than have a crazy man in his cab. Jake felt relieved that he at least had his bag over his shoulder. But it took him a long time to walk to an intersection and then find a main road.

Jake found another taxi and headed to his favourite hotel in Portland. Arriving exhausted and fed up, he collapsed into a disturbed sleep. Dreaming of old ladies ten feet tall teasing him with strings of diamonds.

Chapter Seven

July 1997

Tower Hotel, Portland, Oregon, USA

Arriving at the Tower Hotel in Portland, Hilda and Pearl headed to their rooms and unpacked. That night at the evening meal, they realised they were in a different Portland than William and Louise. They had planned to all have a table together. Pearl checked with reception and found no Mr and Mrs Shilton at their hotel. William and Louise discovered the mistake about the same time. They were both staying in hotels called The Tower, but in different Portland's. After their evening meal, William asked reception for the number of The Tower Hotel, Portland, Oregon, and tracked Hilda down.

There had a speaker phone conversation between the four of them. Hilda told William, 'It's an easy mistake for you to make.' Fortunately, he had drunk a few glasses of wine with his meal and was feeling mellow. Plus, Louise was patting his back in a soothing manner. She was feeling rather pleased not to be joining Hilda and Pearl in the RV.

In the end they agreed the best course of action was for each group to drive towards the middle of America and meet in St Louis. The place was Hilda's idea. She loved the 1944 Christmas Musical, 'Meet me in St Louis.' This gave Hilda and Pearl the longer drive, but that worked out about right timing wise. William had a lot of work to fit in before he could even set off.

***

The day before, when Jake's taxi had lost his quarry, he took a room at his usual Portland Hotel - The Tower. Life is full of coincidences. He was in a room one floor down from Hilda. No doubt he found her dancing above him a nuisance, if only he knew who's not so light feet were tapping away above. The hotel was large. Even the meals were in an enormous ballroom with hundreds of people eating at a time. Unless something unusual happened, they were unlikely to meet. Hilda should be safe.

TSU Corp Office, New York, USA

On his first day of work in the USA, William pulled up in a taxi at the new TSU Corporation offices in New York. He stood and gazed up at the towering glass office block, set in a sea of skyscrapers. William felt hung over; lack of sleep and the time difference were telling on his body. If only he had planned a day or two to recover from jetlag. Instead, he was straight to work the day after he had arrived. Everyone had told him that travelling west would not be a problem - especially Harold. Who argues with their boss? Perhaps William just needed more sleep than most people did.

William strode into the lobby. Perhaps strode is a bit strong. His legs were feeling wobbly from exhaustion. He managed to reach the semi-circular reception desk. The young man sitting behind it dealt with the small queue. On eventually being served, William asked for directions to TSU Corporation. The young man checked his list and asked, 'who?'

'TSU Corporation,' said William. 'They've just moved in.'

The young man checked again, then phoned a supervisor. He made a few monosyllabic comments on the phone, hung up and asked, 'name?'

'I told you, TSU,' said William.

'Your name,' said the young man. He stared at William as if he was foolish.

'Oh, William Shilton.'

'Elevator seven, floor eight-five, office nine,' said then the young man. Then glanced behind William, ready to deal with the next person.

***

William waited for the elevator. His eyes closed for a moment; a binging sound from the doors woke him. He stepped in with several others and leaned on the back wall. His eyes closed again. In theory, he was only in the US to act as a figurehead for the fresh staff. A representative of the parent company. Although he would have plenty of paperwork to do as well. A few weeks earlier, Harold had visited the USA. His time had involved meeting up with Larry, his friend and business partner. In between catching up and socialising, they had chosen offices, interviewed, and employed staff. Larry would be the CEO of the American operation; he was already a multi-millionaire and trusted by Harold.

***

While William was zooming up in the express elevator, the core staff for TSU, had already arrived. Karen, Ray, and Tom, the staff Harold and Larry had employed, gathered around the coffee machine. They were discussing the new company. All three were experienced accountants. Karen was to be the general manager of this office. Ray and Tom were the managers.

Ray was leaning on a sideboard in a makeshift break room, coffee in hand. He glanced at Karen and asked, 'what gives, bringing in a British guy?'

'It's a UK company,' said Karen.

'I know that. We had those old guys, along for the interviews. Don't they trust you to run it now?' asked Ray.

'Those old guys; were the CEO from the UK and the new CEO for over here,' said Karen. 'Haven't you read up on the company you work for?'

Tom looked at Ray and said, 'you've never worked for a British Company before, have you?'

'No... you?' said Ray.

'Yep, they're hands-on. They probably still see us as a colony,' said Tom, laughing. He put his empty cup down on the side.

'Where have you worked before? You wash your own cups here,' said Karen. She pointed at the sink.

'Had disposable in the last place.' Tom slowly picked up his cup, and half-heartedly washed it. 'Just the three of us to run everything?'

'For now,' said Karen. As she was speaking, William staggered out of the elevator. He bashed into a pile of boxes in the hallway and sent them flying. They heard the crash from the room they were in.

'Boss is here,' said Ray, sniggering.

Karen rushed out to greet him, 'you, OK? We haven't unpacked yet.'

'I'm fine, just hadn't seen them,' said William. He was unsteady on his feet. Karen righted the immense pile of empty boxes.

Introductions were made, and William had a strong coffee. Then they all sat down in what would become Karen's office. At that point it just had a desk, a few chairs, and boxes in it. William was so phased out by tiredness that he sat silently. Karen led the meeting, and he just observed. Karen was obviously well chosen by Harold, as she quickly organised a plan of action. Not just for that day, but a strategy for the company. William nodded and seemed happy; his eyes closed occasionally. The plan was to sort the office out over the next couple of days. Employ a general assistant to do the filing and answer the phone. Meanwhile, Karen organised Tom to get set up ready for the initial audits. Within a few days, the office was ready for business and William was finding his feet working alongside Karen. She helped him understand the difference between working methods and laws in the US compared to the UK. She was a great guide in all the tasks he had in finalising the company registration and articles of incorporation.

Tallmart Store, Portland, Oregon, USA

While William had been finding his feet in New York, Hilda and Pearl had also been busy. Following their day of rest and before picking up the RV, they picked up a few supplies. In all the movies they had watched, people always went to gigantic out-of-town stores. What Hilda would call a supermarket or even a hypermarket. In the US, they just called it a store. So, they got a taxi to a huge Tallmart store nearby. On route to the store, the rain had stopped, the first time since they arrived. This gave them a view of the distant, tree-covered mountains.

When they reached the store, they found it sold everything from ice-creams to nappies, prescriptions to furniture, and clothing to guns. Walking in the door, Hilda turned to Pearl and said, 'first, I want to buy a cowboy hat and I want your help.'

'Oh, I was going to look at the clothes.' Pearl's shoulders slumped.

'But I need you,' said Hilda. She took Pearl by the arm.

Pearl allowed herself to be led.

As Hilda pulled her along, Pearl looked longingly towards the clothes section. Then they wandered around looking for hats, finding them on a back wall. Hilda went straight to the cowboy hats. An assistant was nearby. He had moved to Portland from a rural part of Texas a year earlier. The store manager asked him to keep a particular eye on the cowboy hats, an area of expertise for him. Hilda picked up two, one in each hand, and looked puzzled.

The assistant stepped in and said, 'how do you ya do ma'am, I will help all I can.' He touched his hat in greeting.

'I need help to find the right hat,' said Hilda.

'Now, what type do ya need?' asked the assistant.

'Now don't be silly, young man. That was what I asked you. How do I know what type I need?' said Hilda.

'Right you are. Let's see now. Will you be riding?' The assistant pointed at one section of hats.

'Bicycles?' asked Hilda.

The assistant looked puzzled and said, 'horses.'

'Horses? Why ever would I do that?' Hilda shook her head.

'I'll take that as a no. Will you be riding in a coupé?'

'A coup? I'm not a hen,' said Hilda.

'No, a coupé ma'am, it's an open-top car,' said the assistant.

'Why would they open the top of a car?' Hilda glanced at Pearl for support. She just shrugged.

'I guess not. What about country and western?' The assistant pointed to another section of hats.

'Country and western what?' asked Hilda.

'Dancing, will you be dancing?' said the assistant. Hilda's ears pricked up.

'Oh yes, absolutely,' said Hilda. She did a little twirl to show her prowess.

The assistant seemed confused. Then said, 'now we're gettin somewhere. How bout packin, do you want crushable or solid?'

'I want a hat, like the cowboys wear,' said Hilda.

'Yes, I know that. But you can git them, so they crush down for packin' or solid. Them crushable ones are popular.'

'Oh, I see. Let's get one that crushes it's bound to get a few knocks and bumps. I am a bit accident prone, aren't I, Pearl?' said Hilda. Pearl nodded her head. After they had chosen a suitable hat, they headed to the clothes section.

Hilda decided she would also like some Western Style clothing. But after looking at a few items, Hilda got bored and left Pearl to it. She came back later for a quick purchase. Hilda was curious to explore the gun section she had noticed on the way in. They sell guns in UK sporting goods shops, a much more limited range. Here they seemed incongruous in the middle of a supermarket right next to the pharmacy and food. They sold everything from bazookas to semi-automatic rifles. Obviously, deer moved fast in Oregon. You must need to fire at them rapidly or explode whole groups of them. On arrival at the counter, there were no customers. A young man stood behind it, looking expectantly at Hilda. Being his first day, he had gone through all the training and background checks and appeared nervous about putting them into practice. He was supposed to check residency before anything else. But when Hilda approached him and asked, 'do you have the gun James Bond uses?'

He was flustered and said, 'that's a Walter PPK, I'm sorry ma'am we don't carry that. Is there another gun I can interest you in?'

'What about a six shooter?' Hilda remembered the Westerns she enjoyed.

'Would that be a Colt 45?' asked the junior assistant. He took one out of the cabinet and showed Hilda. He should have asked for her ID.

'That's it, can I hold it?'

The gun was unloaded, but the assistant went through his usual safety double checks. At least he remembered to do that. On handing the gun to Hilda, she almost dropped it. Guns are much heavier than they seem in the movies. She adjusted to its weight, lifted it up, and swung it around.

'Don't point it at folk, keep the gun pointing down,' said the assistant. A flash of panic crossed his face. He said, 'I need to take that back from you. Do you have any ID?'

Hilda was having far too much fun. She waved it around and started re living various movies. She spun around towards a passing woman, and said, 'on the floor, sucker, or I'll shoot.' A line she'd remembered from a movie.

Unfortunately for Hilda, her target was an off-duty police officer. She was close enough to Hilda to grab the gun and hand cuff her before she knew what had happened.

***

An announcement on the speaker system brought Pearl to the information desk. There she found Hilda and the off-duty police officer. She was no longer handcuffed but looked embarrassed. On arrival the police officer questioned Pearl, saying, 'I need confirmation you know this woman. She says you have her passport?'

'Oh golly, what's Hilda done?' asked Pearl.

'All in good time. Can you show me some ID?' said the police officer.

'Yes, of course,' said Pearl. She handed Hilda her bag, so that Hilda could find her passport. 'She asked me to hold her bag so that she would have her hands free. I hope that's all right, officer?'

'That's fine, for now,' said the police officer. She stared at Hilda, looking through her bag so slowly. 'If you could just get a move on.' Hilda found her passport, and the officer checked it carefully. She also wanted to check her driving license as her passport photo looked nothing like her.

'That appears to be in order. There was a little misunderstanding,' said the police officer to Pearl. Then the officer stared at Hilda and said, 'I think you have learnt not to play with guns, even unloaded ones, haven't you, ma'am? We can leave it at that, this time.' A machine at the back of the shop distracted Hilda.

'What's that?' said Hilda.

'You won't be doing this again,' said the officer more loudly.

'Oh no, no, never again,' said Hilda, not really paying attention.

'Alright, you can get along,' said the police officer.

'I really must find out what dry ice is,' said Hilda. She strode off to the dry ice machine, leaving Pearl standing with the officer, apologising for her friend.

When Pearl caught up with Hilda at the machine, she was talking to an assistant who was explaining about dry ice.

'Why does everyone call me ma'am?' said Hilda.

Pearl was very flustered by the police enquiries. She was in no mood for nonsense and said, 'what?! You realise that they could have arrested you back there? And what's all that with your passport photo?'

Hilda carried on as if nothing had happened and said, 'yes, yes, never mind, he's another one kept calling me ma'am. I came over to ask about dry ice and this young man says it frozen CO something or other.'

'CO^2, ma'am,' said the store assistant.

'You see,' said Hilda. 'Stop calling me ma'am.'

Hilda found out that frozen CO^2 had uses as an extra cold ice. But that it also produced a smoky/steamy special effect if put in water. She had to buy some to try it out. She bought a big, insulated box full and tongs to handle it with. Pearl just shook her head in astonishment.

After finishing their shopping in a less eventful way, they headed back to the hotel with the frozen CO^2, some new clothes, and a hat. Pearl bought a postcard to send to her neighbour Katie. Although Hilda pointed out that everything she wrote was addressed to Merlin.

They decided that after they picked up the RV, the next day, they would come back and load up with food and supplies. Just as well, the shop had such a large car park, and they did not monitor its poor use.

Tower Hotel, Portland, Oregon, USA

Back in her hotel room, Hilda half-filled the bath with water and tipped in all the dry ice. She over-estimated the amount to put in, and the amount of water. The smoke effect started out just like in the movies, creeping out of the small bathroom and along the floor. She danced through it dramatically, as she had seen in music concerts on the TV. Then the smoke effect went higher, filling the entire room.

CO^2, if it fills a room, is quite dangerous. Hilda found she was coughing from the elevated level of CO^2. So, she tried to open the windows, but they were sealed. She then opened her door. The CO^2 poured out into the hallway and off in both directions. The hotel had CCTV and the operator, seeing what seemed like smoke, he set off the fire alarm. He assumed that the detectors on that floor were faulty. The position of the cameras was such that he could not see which room the smoke was coming from, just as well for Hilda.

The hotel emptied into the car parks; multiple fire trucks were called. The police and other emergency units surrounded the hotel. Fortunately for Hilda, by the time the firefighters reached the corridor outside her room, no CO^2 vapour remained. The automatic door closing system had shut her room door. No evidence came to light about the source of the smoke. They put it down as a mystery, or a trick of the light. Once the fire service gave the all-clear, Hilda re-entered the hotel more sheepishly than she left it. Hopefully, she had learnt not to repeat that experiment. She saw a bit of dry ice left in the pot, looked at a cup of water, then shrugged.

***

Jake Vort had gained a bit of valuable information from the false alarm. Whilst standing in the car park, he had seen Hilda, but she did not have her handbag. He followed her back to her room and noted the number. There were too many people around for him to force his way in. As morning broke, Jake went back to his room to await nighttime and plan how to regain his diamonds.

***

It was nighttime. Jake pushed the passkey in the door slot and walked into Hilda's room saying, 'room service,' there was no reply. He walked in further. A mound in the bed was snoring. A bag stood on the side table. He crept up to the bag. With the light off, he was working by shapes. Rummaging in the bag, he found a jar and turned to leave. A voice from the bed called out. He spun around, struck the figure with a bludgeon, then ran from the room, jar clutched victoriously in hand.

RV Adventure Hire Centre, Portland, Oregon, USA

Earlier that same day, the day Jake entered what had been Hilda's room. She and Pearl had checked out of the hotel and headed off to pick up their RV.

Truth really is stranger than fiction. It's one of those odd things that somehow two lots of people often get confused with each other. Of course, it is not helped when they have the same name. Mr and Mrs Shilton, locals from Portland, Oregon, had booked a small camper van from the same hire company as Hilda Shilton.

The manager of the local branch of the RV Adventure Hire Centre was waiting to welcome Mr and Mrs Shilton. They were due in at 9am but running late. Just to add to the confusion, Hilda and Pearl were running early.

The manager looked at what he assumed to be an odd-looking married couple walking towards him. This was seventeen years before same-sex marriages in Oregon. Once they reached him, he said, 'hi folks, on this fine morning.'

'Hello dear,' said Hilda, waving as she walked towards him.

Pearl was a few steps behind; looking at the huge Recreational Vehicle (RV) she took to be theirs. The manager led the way into a prefabricated office building on the extensive lot. He indicated a couple of chairs for them to take while he sat behind a cluttered desk. A noisy fan acted as the only cooling system in the airless office.

The manager was confused. He re-checked his paperwork. In black and white was printed Mr and Mrs Shilton. Then back up at the couple in front of him. Well, he might be confused. Neither of them was lacking in the chest department. It was hard to see either of them as a potential man. The manager was not easily prejudiced against people. Perhaps one of them had sex reassignment surgery. He glanced from one to the other, and then decided who was Mr Shilton. He addressed Hilda, saying, 'could you please sign here, Mr Shilton?'

Pearl looked out the window at the large vehicle they were about to hire. So, she did not hear the comment, nor did she read the paperwork. Hilda was her usual daydreaming self, and just assumed she had miss-heard him. She never read paperwork before she signed it, much to Pearl and William's disgust. With a flourish, Hilda signed the wrong document. It was not all Hilda's fault; the manager should have checked Hilda's identification documents. That way, he would have seen that she was the wrong person. He was far too distracted by the whole situation and merely glanced down at the UK driving licence, which should have been a red flag to him. The Mr and Mrs Shilton he was expecting were American. The information about the UK licence lodged somewhere in his subconscious to come back later.

The manager led the ladies outside to the small camper van that Mr and Mrs Shilton from Oregon had hired. They walked straight past the large RV that was reserved for Mrs Hilda Shilton. This surprised Pearl, as she had been staring at it for some time from the office. It was the only large RV left on the lot. The company didn't have many of them for hire at such a popular time of year. Pearl assumed she must have the wrong vehicle, so she followed the manager and Hilda.

The manager had already taken Hilda inside the small camper van. Hilda did not know what to expect from an RV, but she had expected something a tad bigger. She stood in the middle and stretched out her arms. Her hands touched each side of the camper van. Turning sideways, she asked the manager to move out of the way. Her arms reached most of the way up and down the van. By this point Pearl had stepped into the van. Hilda said, 'it's much smaller than I was expecting, dear. Be cosy for our trip.'

Pearl looked around the interior, shaking her head. She said to the manager, 'this is what you call an RV 3800 super deluxe X5?'

'Oh no, that's the van next to this,' he said, pointing to the other van.

'So why are you showing us this one?' asked Pearl.

'This is the one you're hiring,' he said, shrugging.

Pearl took out the paperwork from her bag and showed the manager the confirmation of the RV 3800 super deluxe X5. As he checked the paperwork, the name of the hirer, Mrs Hilda Shilton, seemed to jump out at him. His subconscious recalled reading her driving licence. Realising his mistake, the manager ushered them back into the office to sign the correct paperwork and shred the other paperwork. He had just completed this and sent them on their way in their RV 3800 super deluxe X5, when the delayed Mr and Mrs Shilton arrived. They would never know about the mix up nor about their namesake driving across America.

Curiously, they were distantly related to Hilda. The Mr John Shilton, who picked up the small camper van, was the several times great grandson of James Shilton Esq, a distant relation of Hilda's. A tobacco merchant who had settled in America back in the 17th century. Not exactly a close relation, but a relative, nevertheless. One they would never meet. Ah, the vagaries of life. How many times do we pass or nearly meet distant relations?

Tower Hotel, Portland, Oregon, USA

Back in his room, Jake stared at the jar he had grabbed from what had once been Hilda's hotel room. The poor lady who now occupied that room would suffer a nasty bruise; she had also lost an expensive jar of face cream. As Jake studied the jar, he was puzzled; it was not the same make as the one he had put in Hilda's bag. A rummage around its contents confirmed that fact: no diamonds, just expensive face cream. He threw it in the bin, angrily. Slowly, he realised he had been too late. Hilda had already left. He knew her name from her luggage label. She had been a means to carry his diamonds through customs. A means that had failed. She was still carrying his diamonds, unbeknown to her and, much to Jake's frustration.

Jake had some luck. The staff member who had checked Hilda out at the front desk fancied a bit of extra cash. They remembered calling a taxi to take Hilda and Pearl to the RV centre. Jake's hopes rose, and he set off on their trail. On arrival at the RV centre, Jake flashed his false FBI ID badge - it worked a treat. Jake had paid for the forgery a few years earlier and found it very useful. Within a few minutes, he was chasing Hilda and Pearl along the I-84.

Chapter Eight

July 1997

Tallmart Store, Portland, Oregon, USA

The day before Jake started chasing Hilda and Pearl and unaware of any such future possibility; the ladies headed back to Tallmart. They bought their provisions and carefully loaded them; well, Pearl was the careful one. Hilda just wanted to get going. Already three days into their American stay and not having left Oregon. Hilda and Pearl finally set off on their grand adventure. Had Hilda thought about it, she would have remembered all the places she wanted to visit in the Portland area. Instead, they headed off out of the city and across America. Poor old Portland ended up as a place they only remembered for its hotel, store and hire centre. Oh yes, and the rain.

They set off, heading towards Interstate 84 (I-84), not dissimilar to a British motorway. If you ignore the difference in service stations, road width, road signs, the way they do road works – not very similar at all, really. When they were back in England, a friend asked, 'why didn't you travel on Route 66?'

After Hilda had stopped singing, she said, 'maybe next holiday.' Pearl was with her, and she turned white. Maybe she was less keen to repeat the adventures.

But let's not end the holiday early. They have only just set-off. They are travelling across the US of A, Pearl driving and Hilda map reading. It is uncertain which way around would have worked best; but that way was a disaster. Hilda held the map out in front of her and spoke confidently. This gave Pearl a greater sense of confidence than was justified.

As they were heading down a residential road with no obvious exit, Pearl pulled up by the side of the road. She looked across at Hilda, and asked, 'where are we?'

'Route I-84 dear,' said Hilda confidently.

'Really? Then why does it have houses on either side and no way through? I saw a road name back there, and it was not I-84,' said Pearl.

'Umm, maybe I've made a tiny mistake. If you could just turn around?' said Hilda.

Pearl looked at the road and the length of their RV. Even though American residential roads are wide by UK standards, a turn would not be easy. So, she asked Hilda to get out and help her back into a side road, ready to turn. Hilda leapt out and headed to the road they needed to back into. A middle-aged man was in his front yard. He was wondering why a large RV had parked so near to his front yard. Hilda explained to him in her usual way, which involved much hand movement. Unfortunately, Pearl could not see the man, and mistook Hilda's hand movements for directions to her. She started backing up.

As is often the way with such accidents of fate, Hilda's hand movements guided her perfectly onto the man's wide driveway. He stood looking in utter horror. Although he admired the way Pearl had backed so perfectly into his drive. Nothing scratched or damaged. Pearl waited, but Hilda didn't get back in, so she turned off the engine and went to investigate. Hilda was chatting to the man; he was looking quite relaxed and happy; he even invited them inside. Which was an unusual thing to do in those parts. It turned out he was British too, and happy to meet some fellow Brits. Although as they drank coffee and chatted about where in Britain he was from. It seemed his English heritage was from four generations earlier. When they told him where they were from, he asked if they knew Manchester well, that was where his family originated from. Pearl explained Manchester was about four hours from their home, which he thought that was quite close. He also said Manchester sounded a small place. Surely everyone knew each other.

When they were ready to leave, Pearl decided it would be better if she map read for the next part of their journey. They got back into the RV and Hilda had her first try at driving on an American road. The man might have preferred if that had not started in his front yard. The RV had power steering, which made it very easy to turn. Hilda had driven heavy vehicles in the WAAF, but not with power steering. She threw the steering wheel hard, left before Pearl could warn her of its responsive nature. The man's bushes were flattened by the RV. As Hilda waved at him from her open window, she thought his wave seemed to involve his fists; most odd. He shouted something, but she was too far away to hear, just as well. But she shouted 'goodbye' from her window. It's at times like this, we can consider it fortunate, that our doctors do not monitor our every activity. Hilda's GP may have felt justified being concerned about her driving had they witnessed the destruction. He may well have seen an echo of the ice-cream van incident.

Hilda and Pearl found I-84 with only minor incidents. We shall not dwell upon her minor traffic infringements. After all, the police vehicle that she cut in front of ignored it. Perhaps just as well, they had a more urgent call to answer. The lights Hilda drove through had only just that moment turned red. As for the one time she drove on the wrong side of the road. Anyone can make a mistake. That seemed to be the meaning of all the hand signals other drivers gave her. No doubt waving her on.

Hilda finally got the hang of driving in America; she was enjoying herself. Pearl had regained some colour and was breathing more evenly. Hilda found driving on the highway in an RV so brilliant. She was high up; the roads were wide. She felt like she was in a road movie.

Then she noticed the CB radio. She had never used one before, but it didn't look hard. Pressing the big button on the side of the hand mic, Hilda said, 'hello big buddy, come on dear.' Pearl looked up from the map and asked, 'what are you doing?'

'Just seeing if there are any smoky bears out there, we need to avoid,' said Hilda.

Pearl looked out of the window. Searching for furry type bears, and said, 'I can't see any.'

'Well, you wouldn't. I am asking my fellow truckers if any are ahead. Or if there's a bear trap,' said Hilda. She enjoyed acting out old movies. 'Breaker, breaker, we are on our way to the windy city. In need of a watering hole.' Pearl was open-mouthed.

'10-4 big buddy come on,' said Hilda.

Perhaps fortunately for everyone, Hilda had not switched the CB radio on. She sang trucking songs at the top of her voice into the microphone. In her mind she was entertaining the other CB users. With no response, she soon grew bored and hung the mic back on its hook.

They drove along past the Columbia River. Hilda imagined herself in a wagon with four oxen, crossing the plains, ready to find a new homestead. She was sitting up front, Ned, her husband, sat beside her. The three children finding space amongst the sacks of supplies. All their worldly possessions in the covered back part of the wagon, the oxen were pulling well. Ned was hot and dusty. She checked on the kids, making sure they were managing with all the bumps and rattling. Looking in front, she could see the trail of other wagons heading West to their new home. Hilda thought her husband needed a drink and asked, 'ready for some water Ned?'

'Who's, Ned?' asked Pearl.

Coming out of her daydream, just as well, when driving a large and heavy vehicle. Hilda, quick thinking as ever, and said, 'slip of the tongue. I meant Pearl.'

'You're driving. I need to sort the drinks. Are you ready for a break?' asked Pearl. They stopped for their first rest at Boardman. Swapping drivers and having a snack.

Their first proper stop was not much further on, at a Native American Reservation Museum and shop. Hilda had a picture in her mind of the Indians she had seen in Westerns. It surprised her to discover the history of Native Americans, and how they had been mistreated by early settlers. This did not stop her from asking how to do an Indian rain dance. They were patient with her, treating her as an elderly person who was not with it, close to the truth. She also bought some beaded clothing as a present for Louise.

She set up outside the shop to do her first bit of drawing. Her picture was of an older lady in native clothing, sitting by the shop door, demonstrating her craft. Hilda sat for ages studying, drawing, and concentrating. Later, Pearl held the picture up in several directions before she could work out what it depicted. Hilda explained she was still learning. She filed it away in her book of sketches. Beginning to feel like one of those Victorian grand tour artists. There must have been a few who couldn't draw.

Not much further on, they setup for their first night in the RV. The campsite disappointed them. They had pictured camping out in the wilds. This one stood right on the edge of a town, near a school playing field. But it meant they could walk to a nearby shop to get fresh supplies. It all felt so different to the UK, more spaced out, wide roads, the buildings flat roofed and many prefabricated, advertising signs everywhere.

That evening, they wanted a pre-prepared meal. So, they found what they saw as a café and Hilda asked for chips with her main course. She handed back the pack of crisps they gave her in disgust. Eventually, she came to realise what she called chips; they called French fries, or fries. Which did not stop her from correcting various assistants when she asked for things. Typically, she would say something like, 'I want chips with mine, what you wrongly call fries.'

***

As they were setting off after their first overnight stop, Jake set off from Portland in pursuit of them. He knew the vehicle they were driving, and they were starting out along the I-84. Hilda and Pearl were oblivious to the fact they were being chased. Jake was driving a much faster vehicle, so he could start catching them up.

Utah, USA

A few days in, Hilda and Pearl were doing well on their travels. They had reached Utah. About a quarter of the way across the vast continent of America. It's a state which has few people but a lot of land. Mountains and flat lands, deserts, and a huge Salt Lake. On the west is Nevada, above is Idaho and Wyoming, east is Colorado and below it is Arizona. A lot of the state is so far above sea level, it takes time to acclimatise. They even sell canisters of oxygen in some shops, which Hilda had to buy and try out. Although she was not suffering from any oxygen starvation. She just liked the idea. Hilda has a childlike fascination with anything new. Many people misunderstand her. They assume that her love of simple fun comes from a lack of deep feelings or a simplicity of character. But she is a person of great love and compassion. Not intellectually clever, a fact her teachers unanimously agreed with. Perhaps not the most intuitive, something her family and friends often noted. But she sensed pain in others and always looked to bring joy into their lives.

Hilda had noticed from the first phone call to Pearl that she was not her normal self. Something was occupying her mind. Most people, upon noticing that, would ask, 'what's wrong?' Not Hilda, her approach was to cheer her friend up. Bring her out of herself and leave her to express her feelings in her own time. Others may judge how effective that was as a method. In Hilda's eyes, the CO^2 creating smoke at the Portland Tower Hotel was a bit of fun. A way to help Pearl unwind and enjoy herself. But Pearl had not enjoyed standing outside in the drizzle. In Utah, Hilda thought Pearl would enjoy an impromptu impersonation of Darth Vader. So, she wore an oxygen mask and made raspy, gasping sounds. Pearl rushed up to her to check she was alright. Perhaps Hilda's future ideas will be more effective and help Pearl share whatever was on her mind.

The Shooting Star Bar, Huntsville, Utah, USA

Looking on a tourist map, Hilda discovered another enjoyable idea. A visit to Huntsville, a town that looked like it came straight out of an old western movie. It had a bar called The Shooting Star, where customers had written on dollar bills and pinned them to the ceiling. Hilda added her own note to a bill and asked a tall man to pin it up for her. Short of standing on stepladders, she would never have reached. Pearl and Hilda sat out back and drank bottles of Budweiser. They found it hard to see what the appeal of that larger was. They gave up on it and ordered an orange juice and lemonade. Judging by the look on Pearl's face, she was not enjoying the visit so far.

A jukebox sat in the corner. Hilda treated the few customers to an impromptu sing along of 'Take me home, country road.' Some folk headed home during it, perhaps taking the hint. Pearl grabbed Hilda before she started another song. The bar tender thanked her on the way out and Pearl gave him a half smile; was that enjoyment or resignation?

They set off again along the dusty roads, with Hilda driving. She had a habit of drifting off into daydreams. Not a way to concentrate on a long trip. Hilda could almost see the cowboys of old rounding up their steers in the dust of the flatlands. It was the old west, and she was at their ranch on the prairie with her two kids inside. She had left the stew and coffee on the iron stove. While she headed out to the well and started pumping the handle, filling her wooden bucket. Standing for a moment in the sweltering heat, she wiped her brow with her apron. The noise and dust in the distance told her Ned was coming. A herd of cows appeared. Ned was at the rear with two other cowboys, driving them forward. Hilda realised it was not her imagination. There were cowboys, modern day ones. They were riding through the herds of cattle, kicking up dust and wearing their Stetsons. She wondered if they were crushable ones like hers. She needed to keep more focused on driving and do less daydreaming. A thought Pearl would have totally agreed with.

A campsite, Utah, USA

That night, Hilda and Pearl parked their huge RV in a remote campsite. All around were views of shrub, distant mountains, and a barren landscape. There were only five other motor homes on the site, all well-spaced out. Two were as large as theirs, one was even bigger. The largest one looked set up with everything its two owners would ever need. A kayak on top, trail bikes attached to the back. They had set up an area outside the van for eating alfresco. Makeshift windbreaks enclosed it, within which were a grill, tables, and chairs. A canopy extended from the top of the van to give the entire area protection from the sun.

Hilda and Pearl's RV had three sleeping compartments. One at the front, one in the middle, and one at the back. The one at the front could convert into a sitting/eating area and was just behind the driver's cabin. The one in the middle was next to the kitchen and the one in the back was next to the shower/restroom cubicle. Hilda slept at the back and Pearl in the middle. The RV had its own inbuilt LPG gas for cooking and to heat the hot water. It also operated the small fridge. The RV had a built-in water tank and a septic tank. Enough for 2-3 days between refill/emptying, depending how careful they were. Batteries powered the lights, but they often liked to sit in the dark and look up at the stars. Or create a small fire to sit round on a chilly night. They used folding chairs and a table to sit outside. Pearl was glad she thought to pack blankets for their knees, as the evenings were cold. The first evening at the campsite, they sat by an open fire. Pearl said, 'isn't this like girl guides?'

Hilda thought back for a moment. She remembered the rain of her last time camping with girl guides in England. She looked around. Although it was chilly at night in such a desert-like place, it was also dry. She stared into the fire, crackling brightly, and over at their neighbours in the huge RV. It smelt like they were cooking steaks. The odours wafting over were delicious. Hilda peered up at the canopy of stars above, ending at the distant mountains. She turned to Pearl and said, 'you remember girl guides differently to me.'

Pearl laughed, and they sat staring into the fire. They were both thinking back to their girl guide days.

May 1930

St Mary's Church Hall, Kilburn, London, UK

Pearl and Hilda had been great friends since childhood. So, when they first started as girl guides, they went to their first meeting together. Neither wanted to admit to their mothers they were afraid and there was strength in numbers. The church hall, where meetings were usually held, had changed just for that one night. All the regulars were told. As Hilda and Pearl were going along to join, they knew nothing of this. A first aid training group had swapped with guides after a mix up on their speaker's schedule. The guides were happy to meet outside that evening. They were out in the woods, learning to start fires; at least that was the plan.

Arriving at St Mary's church hall, Hilda pushed open the outer door and investigated the entrance lobby. No one was there. Pearl followed, and they stood listening. They could hear voices in the main hall, but it was not as boisterous as they expected for a girl guides meeting. Hilda led the way, pushing open the inner door. The lady giving the talk on 'dealing with minor cuts' looked up. The fact she had stopped talking and was looking at the door caused the fifteen people in the room to turn around. Everyone wanted to see the reason for the disturbance.

The trainer asked, 'can I help?'

'St Mary's?' said Hilda. She was going through a phase of abbreviating everything.

'That's right, take a seat,' said the trainer. She pointed to some seats. Both groups began with St Mary's, the St Mary's Guide Troop, and the St Mary's First Aiders.

Hilda and Pearl sat in the front row. As usual, that row had been left empty. They watched, listened, and became increasingly surprised. They had not expected this from a Girl Guide meeting. The trainer showed what to do with a minor cut. She believed in bringing in a bit of realism. A volunteer had a blood-coloured mix in a skin-coloured pouch stuck on their arm. The trainer had explained about this just before Hilda and Pearl arrived. Now the trainer punctured the pouch with a knife. The effect was dramatic - faux blood spurted everywhere.

Pearl was squeamish about blood, and she squealed. Hilda thought it great and got up for a closer look. Maybe this was where Hilda gained her fascination with murder. Or at least with gore.

Five minutes later; they realised they were in the wrong meeting. When the trainer handed out leaflets headed, St Mary's First Aiders. Pearl was out of the door as fast as her feet would carry her. She would entertain none of Hilda's suggestions that they join the first aid group instead of guides.

***

The First Aid trainer had told them where to find the guides, so they were now headed through the woods. On route Pearl recovered from the shock of seeing the false blood. Hilda took her mind off it, by hiding behind trees and leaping out, shouting, boo! They eventually found the guide troop.

The group of fourteen girl guides and two leaders were sitting around a pile of sticks and branches. One leader was next to the inert pile of wood, talking. It was difficult to see her clearly because of their large wide-brimmed hats. But she was speaking loud enough to be heard, '.... repeatedly like this. As you can see, causing heat to build up. Umm, normally heat builds up,' said the guide leader.

There seemed to be some giggling from the girls. Then the other leader called for order and the leader next to the sticks said, 'sometimes, you must try a second time...... or a third.... or even a fourth.'

More giggling and another reprimand. The leader by the sticks sounded cross when she said, 'well, you see the principal of lighting a fire with two sticks. I think we will use matches this time, for speed. After all, we want to cook something on the fire, don't we girls?' A cheer went up.

Hilda and Pearl considered jumping out and surprising the troop with a loud boo! But in the end, they walked up to them and introduced themselves. The leader next to the fire was glad for the distraction.

July 1997

A campsite, Utah, USA

As Hilda sat by the fire in Utah, these were her recollections of guiding. It is unlikely Pearl was recollecting the same events as she was snoring happily in her chair. Hilda woke her up, so she could go to bed.

Next morning as Pearl served breakfast. Hilda lifted her hands to eat, Pearl cried out. Hilda's right hand had a swollen red area in the centre. It seemed to swell more as they watched it. Her entire hand turned red and grew larger. In panic they left the breakfast and drove to the nearest hospital. An emergency hospital trip may not seem like a fortunate thing, but for them, it turned out to be.

***

As Hilda and Pearl headed into town looking for a hospital, Jake was driving towards their campsite, looking for them. He had finally caught them up, having checked a few other sites. On arrival, he pretended he was looking for his elderly aunts. He asked the campsite owner about them. He was told they had booked in the night before and pointed to their pitch. The owner had not seen them rush off to the hospital. Hilda and Pearl's pitch looked like The Mary Celeste, a table set for breakfast, chairs pushed back in a hurry, bowls of uneaten cereal on the table, hot tea steaming. Their RV had gone. Perhaps they were on to him and had seen him coming. These two were cleverer than he had expected, no doubt leaving the table to fool him into thinking they would return. Jake headed to his car and kicked the tyre. His buyer was getting impatient. Jake needed the diamonds. He headed into the nearby town to find a motel and a phone, planning his excuses on route. He passed the hospital they were in but didn't notice their RV in the large car park.

A hospital, Utah, USA

Hilda and Pearl arrived in that same town a little earlier. They stopped at the first hospital they found, parking the RV in a distant corner of the car park, then rushed over to the emergency department. There was a reception desk, which they assumed was to tell of Hilda's medical need. Being their first encounter with an American medical system, it surprised them that the first questions were all about payment. Fortunately, the paperwork was Pearl's forte. Many years as an administrator had equipped her well. She had all the medical insurance details to hand and sorted things fast.

Hilda was feeling relieved to be in a hospital. Having not used a toilet in the RV; her first need was to find one there. She expected a long wait to see a doctor and so headed straight to a WC. Pearl sat nearby in the waiting area. Hilda was mistaken. A nurse sought her out the moment she entered the restroom. A bite that causes swelling is an urgent emergency. It suggests an allergic reaction that could lead to further complications. The staff were keen to assess Hilda as soon as possible. Hearing her friend's name called, Pearl pointed at the restroom door. The nurse stood outside and said, 'hi! in there.'

'Hello out there,' said Hilda. It surprised her to hear a voice calling.

'Hello,' said the nurse, adapting to Hilda's style of greeting.
'Who is it?' asked Hilda.
'Just checking, you're, OK?' said the nurse.
'Yes, thank you.'
'I'm here if ya need me.' The nurse waited outside.

Hilda finished her necessary use of the facility and then looked around. She was unsure how to operate the hand dryer, and said, 'hello out there.'

'Hi!' said the nurse.

'I'm not quite sure how to dry my hands,' said Hilda.

The nurse studied her notes. It did not mention any mental health issues. Although it gave her age. 'OK, let me in,' said the nurse.

'How exceedingly kind, dear,' said Hilda as she let the nurse in.

Having been shown how to use what to Hilda was an unnecessarily complicated dryer. They progressed to a side room. The nurse had introduced herself as Hilda's personal nurse for the duration of her stay. It impressed Pearl and Hilda to have a nurse dedicated only to her. Although it took a while before

Hilda realised, she was a nurse, not a toilet attendant. After just five minutes a young lady appeared, who introduced herself as Hilda's personal physician. Although that did not seem to include looking at her lumbago, which disappointed Hilda. She came and went throughout their stay.

The diagnosis was that Hilda had suffered an allergic reaction to a spider bite. They nearly had to sedate Pearl on hearing that news. She was an arachnophobe. The treatment was a series of intravenous anti-biotics. The swelling gradually went down, and it left Hilda with a red mark on her hand. She was told to call at a doctor's clinic in a day or two, to check that all was OK. They also gave her a prescription for anti-biotic tablets.

***

Back at the campsite, the manager told them a relative had been by looking for them. Neither of them could understand who that could be. William and Louise were on the other side of the country. They assumed it was a mistake. That night Pearl performed a miraculous act, she juggled a torch, a grab stick, and a rolled-up magazine. Then she searched every nook and cranny of the RV. Not the smallest part was left unexamined for spiders. Even so, she slept under a mosquito net with the light on. Not exactly slept, more kept a nervous watch on every corner of her sleeping area. There was not a chance that a spider was going to get near her.

A Motel, Utah, USA

Jake found a motel room in town. He called the contact for his buyer to explain the delay. The contact told him he would pass on the message, but expect her to be unhappy, *very unhappy*. That is what Jake expected. His buyer was head of an international crime syndicate. He had heard rumours she arranged hits freely; he had better not fail her. Patience was not something she was known for. He remembered all the tales of people disappearing when she was unhappy with their work. Why had he taken this job? Then he remembered. His wife, Laura, thought it sounded a lucrative payout. He liked to please his wife, but she wasn't the one who'd have to face the consequences if he didn't get the diamonds back. He slept fitfully that night.

Chapter Nine

July 1997

A Motel, Utah, USA

The next morning, Jake woke in his hotel, feeling jaded. His buyer's contact had called back and passed on a message. The words were ringing in his head. Had kept him awake: 'You failed to get the diamonds back from an old woman? I have a message from B. Do you want to be replaced?'

For replaced, read terminated. Jake had stammered, made excuses, and eventually promised prompt action. He now knew for certain, something he had previously guessed, that he was working for the notorious underworld boss, B. She was not a woman to be crossed.

Jake thought about the task ahead. He was a professional, and he only had to get the diamonds back from an old woman. He could do this easily, of course he could. She was a mere old woman; he was a master criminal. Why did that not make him feel better? There was a large map of the USA spread across the bed. Staring at the map would not get the diamonds back, 'think, Jake, think.'

The RV Hire Company owner had told Jake that Hilda planned 'a trip of a lifetime' across America and that her destination was Portland, Maryland. She had regaled the hotel receptionist with her travel plans. Plans the receptionist had passed on to Jake. He stared at the map hard. First, he drew a straight line between those two Portland's – Oregon and Maryland. He studied what places the line crossed. Then checked all the big things to see between them. He circled a few. They had gone off track from a straight line already. The nearest to where they were now was Yellowstone; he ringed that a few times. Surely, they would not miss that. The hotel receptionist had mentioned Hilda's love of bears. She kept talking about Winnie the Pooh. Even told him he looked cuddly, like a teddy bear. Yellowstone did not have Winnie the Pooh, but it had bears. Jake felt a rise of hope.

A campsite, Utah, USA

In the middle of the night, Pearl was having difficulty sleeping. She got up to make a cup of tea, while also checking the area for any eight-legged creatures. The noise caused Hilda to get up. All the excitement of the day meant that Hilda was not sleeping well either. They sat drinking tea, a single fluorescent light over the sink giving a soft light to the van. Hilda pulled back a curtain. Outside, all was so dark that they could see a blanket of stars laid out above them. - no streetlights to mask the view.

Pearl didn't fancy the idea of sitting outside by a fire, as they had the night before. She was now obsessed with spiders; she imagined they were sitting in the scrubland waiting to pounce on her from the darkness, armies of them planning an attack.

So instead, they stayed in the RV and switched off the light. After a while their eyes adjusted, and even more stars became visible. They sat in silence for a while, then Pearl wanted the light back on just in case anything had crawled in under cover of darkness. She imagined crawling sensations on her skin. Hilda wanted to take her mind off spiders. So, she reminded Pearl of their school days at Miss Wentworth's Academy. They shared stories, laughed, and shook their heads. School was quite different in the 1930's.

June 1934

Miss Wentworth's Academy, Kilburn, London, UK

Their classroom was utilitarian by modern standards. The teacher stood in front of a large chalkboard. Tall sash windows to her right gave onto a view of a small, paved playing area, part walled. The left-hand wall contained maps, shelves, and pictures. In front of the teacher were ten desks, each inset with ink pots, all but one occupied by a thirteen or fourteen-year-old girl - the missing girl had a cold. All the young girls were concentrating on the teacher; except one. The teacher addressed this errant child, saying, 'Hilda Shilton, if I have to call your name one more time, I will send you to the Headmistress.'

'Yes, miss,' said fourteen-year-old Hilda. She sat up straight. This was her last term at school. She did not want the cane... again, four times was quite enough.

Miss Wentworth's Academy for Young Ladies was a private school. One that Hilda's father had insisted she attend. He wanted an excellent education for his only child. He could just afford to send her there. Fortunately for Hilda, they lived close enough for her to be a 'day girl,' the idea of boarding had never appealed to her. The Academy taught forty girls and about half boarded - an old-fashioned school. Miss Wentworth, the owner, and headmistress was only in her thirties, and yet behaved more like a Victorian school mistress. Perhaps because her parents had been very strait-laced Victorian's. Meaner minded people, bent on gossip, whispered about her being left standing at the altar, on her wedding day. The pain turning her against men and making her very stern. Hilda had never seen her smile. Although there may have been one time, she smiled. When the history tutor gave her a box of chocolates for Christmas. But it was so fleeting, Pearl claimed Hilda imagined it, and maybe she had.

In the classroom pressure was mounting on poor Hilda. The teacher stared at her young charge and said, 'Hilda, we are waiting.'

Hilda looked up blankly and then across at Pearl. Judging by her expression, Pearl was suffering some pain in her face. Then Hilda realised she was trying to mouth a word to her. What was it? 'Re.' But re what? Maybe it was 'We,' no that could not be right, was she saying 'Me?' Now she was pointing at a book, the textbook they were studying. Slowly a light bulb switched on in Hilda's brain.

'Ah, yes Miss. You're right. We are studying this book and I am enjoying it very much,' said Hilda. She looked immensely proud of herself. Pearl's eyes shot up to the ceiling.

***

A little later, sitting outside Miss Wentworth's office, Hilda was still trying to work out why she had been sent there. Maybe she had not been positive enough about the textbook? The teacher had just pointed at the door and said to Hilda, 'go and see Miss Wentworth immediately. You can explain to her why.'

Pearl had said quietly, 'it was read,' as she passed her, whatever that meant.

The door to Miss Wentworth's study opened and a tall lady walked out and said to Hilda, 'you again, Miss Shilton. This is becoming too regular an occurrence.'

The headmistress stood above Hilda, dressed in her long black academic gown. It seemed too austere. Blonde curly hair flowed down to her shoulders. She said, 'come through to my office and explain what mischief you have been up to this time.'

When they were, let us not say, comfortably seated, in the office, Hilda said, 'you see Miss Wentworth. I am not entirely sure why I am here. There may have been a mistake.'

Miss Wentworth flicked a blonde curl from her left cheek. Then peered across the top of her glasses, and said, 'why is it that every time you are here you think there has been a mistake? This is your last term. You are soon to be leaving this academy. It was my earnest wish that you would have left it a shining example of young womanhood. Shaped by the rigours of the academic and practical teaching that you have absorbed here. Instead, I feel you are leaving untouched by our influence.'

Hilda unconsciously rubbed her posterior. She remembered the influential touch of Miss Wentworth's cane, and said, 'no, that's not true, Miss Wentworth. I have imbibed a lot here.'

Then she thought that was not the best word. The last time she sat here was after being caught drinking a glass of sherry from the staff room. Only her father's pleas had prevented expulsion. 'I have learnt many things and will take those lessons with me into life. I have felt the *touch* of your influence.' Hilda thought she had certainly learnt to be more careful when 'borrowing' a drink. That she would be much more selective about friends. There were certain school friends she would trust again. Certainly not when it came to hiding tuck in her desk. Pearl was the only one she could trust in this school.

Miss Wentworth picked up the cane and gave it a few practice swishes. Then seeming to change her mind; she put it down and said, 'I don't think another caning will help you.'

'No, I, I, I agree, ab, ab, absolutely.' Hilda stammered.

Miss Wentworth picked the cane back up and said, 'on the other hand, examples need to be made.'

***

At lunchtime Pearl was looking out for Hilda. She spotted her hobbling across the dining room and said, 'there you are. How did it go with old Sourpuss?'

Pearl offered her a seat. Hilda hesitated, then decided to stand. She said, 'I thought I was going to get away with it, but no such luck.'

Pearl shook her head and said, 'why didn't you understand me? I was saying read the next bit in the textbook.'

'Well, anyway, it's too late now,' said Hilda crossly. 'Oh, don't look now, Raggedy Ann's staring at us.' She was being rather unfair about an immaculate and tidy fellow schoolgirl.

Naming her after a character in a children's book, 'The magical land of Noom.' But then Ann had told tales on Hilda.

'She's not staring, just in a bad mood. I heard her mother has made her board from next term,' said Pearl.

'Just desserts, I say. It was her who told on me last time,' said Hilda, sticking her tongue out at Ann.

Pearl and Hilda headed off towards the tuck shop, a treat to cheer Hilda up after the caning.

July 1997

A campsite, Utah, USA

In the Utah campsite, Hilda and Pearl were both sighing at their shared school memories. It had worked to distract Pearl from her anxiety about spiders. She got up and fetched the pretty wooden box with the flowers, butterflies, and a monogrammed VW. As she sat down at the table and put the box in front of her, a ray of sunlight burst through the window and across the table.

Hilda smiled at Pearl and said, 'morning has broken dear, time to get breakfast, then get going.'

Pearl looked at the box she had just fetched, then at Hilda and said, 'I just had something I wanted to share first...'

Hilda was on her feet, bashing pans and plates. She was a noisy cook with two functioning hands, even more noisy with an injured hand.

'Let me do that,' said Pearl as she got up, leaving the box on the table.

'Oh, well, if you want to, was there something you wanted to say?' asked Hilda.

'Another time,' said Pearl.

Hilda noticed the wooden box and said, 'that box looks beautiful. Was it a gift?' Hilda smiled at her friend. Pearl opened her mouth to speak. A bang on the door interrupted them. Hilda answered it and found a slightly built lady standing in the doorway. She was shaking and anxious. Her head jerked around every few seconds. Hilda invited her inside. She entered cautiously, looking for something. The lady saw Pearl's box on the table. She stared at it, fascinated, and commented on its beauty and the VW monogram. Pearl looked at her strangely and cleared the box away into her compartment. Hilda had the lady sit down. Eventually, she explained her early morning call. She was from one of the other camper vans. She and her husband were travelling together after they lost everything a few weeks back: his job, the house, their furniture. He could not cope with the loss and started drinking. The slightly built woman kept repeating what a lovely, gentle, and caring man he was. Hilda noticed bruises on the woman's face. They became clearer as the sun rose and filled the interior of their RV. When Hilda asked her about them, she just repeated what a lovely man her husband was. Eventually, the woman got around to asking for a lift to the next town. She was planning on getting a Greyhound bus to her sister's place. She had noticed that Hilda and Pearl seemed kind-looking and were two women travelling without men, which made her feel safe. They agreed to take her to safety, setting off before breakfast. They could stop later to eat. Hilda felt there was something about her that seemed off.

All the distractions had taken away the opportunity for Hilda to find out the contents of the hand-crafted box, which would have to wait for another time. The well-being of a fellow traveller came first. They arrived at the town in plenty of time for the bus. The woman had sat at the back of the RV when they were driving. 'I don't want to be seen,' she'd said. On arriving Pearl had gone back to fetch her and found her rummaging through the box of letters.

'What are you doing?' shouted Pearl.

The woman dropped the box, pushed past Pearl and was out of the RV before Pearl could react. Later, Hilda told Pearl that she saw the woman jump into a waiting vehicle. One that had been following them. It took off at speed. Hilda wished she had acted on her suspicions. When they reported it to the local sheriff, it turned out that the woman was a known con artist. She played the victim, looking for help. Then grabbed anything of value. No doubt she assumed Pearl's fancy box contained jewels. When Hilda heard that the fancy box Pearl had produced the night before contained letters, she was keen to see them. With all the stress of the attempted burglary, Pearl needed time to recover first.

July 1997

New York, USA

While Hilda and Pearl were progressing on their tour across America. William and Louise were having a very different experience. They were still in New York City. William was busy working at the TSU Corp offices. It was all boring paperwork to other people. But his eyes shone every night when he told Louise about his day. Louise found William's tales of accountancy heaven extremely boring. She had to find ways to occupy herself each day while he worked. At first, she had gone out sightseeing alone. Then she remembered she had a second cousin, Marlene, living in the suburbs of New York. Marlene had three kids and worked as a realtor. She never had time to explore the city. So, she was delighted to hear from Louise. A visiting cousin gave her the excuse she needed for some fun, and so she grabbed it.

The two cousins hit it off straight away, feeling like long-lost sisters. Both only had brothers and decided that they must keep in touch afterwards. Marlene had an idea for their first day. She said, 'how about something different? I have a friend who can help. I'll call her and we can do something non touristy.'

Louise was happy to try something different. Marlene kept the details secret, and Louise acted like a kid in a sweet shop. On the day of the adventure, they set off on a contorted journey. But it did not take them to a new and exciting place. Louise felt disappointed to find they were at The Metropolitan Museum of Art. She could have gone there as a tourist. The promise had been to go somewhere special. Marlene soon put her mind at rest with promises that it would not be ordinary. As they arrived at the reception area, they asked for a staff member. She arranged visitor badges and took them to non-public areas, to view collections, never seen by the public. That was special. Louise loved art and art history. Their guide told them fascinating stories about the artwork's discoveries. She shocked them with the true tales behind some of the museum's most famous pieces. Then took them to the workshops to watch conservators restoring valuable artwork. It all spellbound Louise. At lunchtime they went on the roof, not the Met café roof garden. This was far better, more exclusive.

There was a small area where the staff sat and had their pack ups. There were magnificent views over Central Park.

That night at the hotel, Louise wasn't at all interested in William's tales of the new computer system. Even when he explained how fast it could add up columns of numbers, nor how efficient that would make audits. All Louise wanted to do was tell William about an Egyptian Scarab she had watched being cleaned. That moment when the curator realised its age and relevance. William did not look impressed. But Louise's' eyes shone.

***

Meanwhile, Josh had arrived in New York. Although he told his dad about meeting up in New York, he did not say when or where. It suited his mischievous nature to surprise his parents. On arriving, Josh booked into their hotel, the room right next to them. He had asked his mum about her room number on his previous call. Pretending that a friend had stayed there and found some rooms better than others. Once he booked in and unpacked, he rang his parents' room. Louise answered and put the call on speaker. Josh asked about the weather they were having and asked if their room was nice. Louise said to Josh, 'yes, until about five minutes ago, when the person in the room next to us started banging on the wall.'

'What!' said Josh. 'What kind of banging?'

'How many kinds are there?' asked William.

'Oh yes, I can hear the banging. It almost sounds like Morse code. Didn't you learn morse code dad?' asked Josh.

'I'm rusty now. Let me try,' said William.

'I'll write it down,' said Louise. She fetched a pad and pen, taking note of the dots and dashes.

William translated. 'That's i, then t, then s, then space, then j, then o, s, h. That doesn't make sense.' He looked puzzled.

Louise broke out in a big smile and said, 'come through here, you little rascal.'

William looked confused for a moment, and then he smiled. There was a knock at the connecting door. On opening it, Josh stood there beaming. They had a family hug, and they chatted, catching up. It shocked Josh to hear that his gran was on the opposite side of America, but not surprised. They headed out for a meal and had a fun evening. William insisted they did not stay out too late, as he had work in the morning.

TSU Corp Office, New York, USA

Next day, William was at the TSU Corp offices, whereas Josh had a day free to spend with his mum. They spent the morning exploring together. Then turned up unannounced at Williams' offices in the afternoon. Louise had three reasons: first, she wanted to spend an afternoon exploring with Josh and William. That idea appealed to the general manager, Karen. William was complicating things for her. Much as he was enjoying himself with paperwork and computers. She was finding he got in the way. William was happy to join his family; he had achieved all he needed that morning. Second, Louise was running out of dollars and travellers' cheques. William had access to their travel funds. This was turning out to be an expensive trip. Third was a desire to see the office William kept talking about. Louise was not impressed, because it had yet to be fully set up.

Once William, Louise, and Josh set off, William asked to visit Central Park. He always liked the look of in films. But it disappointed him when they got there and explored. Louise loved the huge rock gardens and the lake, especially the bridges. William kept making comparisons to Kew Gardens or various National Trust places in the UK. He preferred their formality. Josh followed him around doing impersonations. Playing a grumpy, and stuck-up presenter that they often watched on TV. Josh walked up to a bush, and waved an arm nonchalantly towards it and said, 'as you can see, it is lacking any aesthetic beauty. It's intrinsically worthless and hardly worth my breath talking about it, so I won't bother describing it.'

He then walked up to a rock, turned his nose up and said, 'whatever can one say about a rock?' William saw the funny side and joined in the laughter. He also allowed himself to be drawn into a game of frisbee, which got them all out of breath, but laughing.

Next, William wanted to go to The Empire State Building. On arrival they queued for the elevator for ages and then travelled up to the viewing platform. Why were things so much busier in real life? They had to wait a while until they could get to the edge and use a fixed pair of binoculars. They were fortunate that it was a cloudless day. Although they couldn't see forever, they could see a long way. Josh said, 'look, over there.'

Which prompted William to try staring through the binoculars. But he saw nothing. Josh feigned surprise and stared through them. Then, looking at his dad said, 'you mean you couldn't see that giant ape being buzzed by planes?'

William was not amused, but Louise giggled like a schoolgirl. After some more exploration and Louise convincing William to re-fill her financial coffers. They headed back to the hotel, dropping Josh at the train station on the way. He had a flight to catch to his next photo shoot. He was doing an interior shoot at Camp David for a UK magazine. It was the hush - hush contract he had won. He could tell them, but they had to keep it quiet till it was published.

***

Next day in the New York office, William was finishing all he needed to do, much to Karen's relief. He was finally ready to move on. Before William left the office, he phoned his boss and friend, Harold, to say that all was going well and to update him on progress. They kept the call short as they were both accountants and it was an international phone call. William also made a call to Larry for an ongoing update. After all, Larry was going to be the CEO of the US operation.

Having given Karen his next hotel contact details, he left her and moved to Chicago. She filed his contact details appropriately and carried on building up the New York office. The TSU New York office grew to be one of its most profitable and largest branches in the TSU Plc worldwide company. William came to boast of that as because of his foundational influence. It had more to do with Karen's hard work and strong leadership and the team she gathered.

Chicago, Illinois, USA

There is a well-known song called 'Chicago.' Hilda loved it and often sang it. What a pity that she would miss visiting 'that toddling town' because, as the song says, you can 'Bet your bottom dollar you have some fun in Chicago.' Still, given William's dislike of dancing, he might have preferred to avoid it, too. Ah well, William had two week's work in Chicago, so he had to go. Louise was planning a boat trip around The Great Lakes. There were no hidden relatives to explore the area with, so she was less keen on Chicago. Exploring a place on your own is not such fun.

A Medical Centre, Montana, USA

A few days after the spider bite, Hilda had to attend a local medical centre and be seen by a doctor. It was all part of the treatment programme laid out by the ER doctor. They would give her a clean bill of health and send her on her way. She arrived at the modern glass fronted building and went across to the reception desk. The young man on duty was only seventeen. This was a week of work experience. He checked her details and discovered an omission, so he said, 'there's no date of birth. How old are you?'

'Seventy-seven,' said Hilda.

'That old!'

Hilda was not pleased that he had considered her old and so after giving her date of birth and said, 'age is only a number,'

'Yes, but a large one,' said the young man. It was just as well his manager had been called away.

Hilda stared at him, hard, then she tapped one toe. It made a satisfying clicking sound on the hard floor. Enjoying the rhythmic beat, she tapped her other toe. Once she had the beat going well, she tap danced away from the desk and over to the waiting area. The young man watched her spring lightly away.

The surprised look on his face seemed to say maybe age was just a number after all. Or maybe he had just never seen such a sight in his life before. The people in the waiting room had equally surprised looks on their faces. But whether they were contemplating the relativity of numbers and age is anyone's guess. A two-year-old boy pointed at Hilda and jabbed his mother's leg. She was already watching and told him to play with his toys.

Hilda descended on to a chair in the waiting room. She was about to start a conversation with her fellow patients when she was called through to the doctor. Had those from her GP surgery in England been there, they would have felt jealous.

The doctor was happy that all remnants of the spider bite had cleared up and Hilda was fully fit. The doctor was impressed that someone of Hilda's age had recovered so quickly. It had taken the doctor a while to recover when Hilda tap danced into her consulting room. That was not the usual way her patients arrived.

Camp David, Maryland, USA

At almost the exact moment Hilda was impressing the doctor, Josh was at Camp David, doing a photo shoot. Oddly enough, he was doing something there that would have a direct effect on his gran later. He would not be the only Shilton to visit Camp David. Nor was he the only one to cause some dramatic changes to its layout.

CHAPTER TEN

July 1997

Montana to Yellowstone, USA

Jake may have been a criminal, but he was also an excellent judge of people's motivations. Perhaps that's what made him an effective thief; he understood what drove people. His judgement that Hilda would want to visit Yellowstone National Park was exactly right. Hilda loved teddy bears, in fact bears of all sorts, Paddington, Winnie the Pooh, they were all so cuddly. Obviously, if they were cuddly in books, they must be like that in real life, only more so.

Having guessed this was their destination. Jake had gone on ahead and chatted to all the RV campsite owners in the area. Bribing them to call him when his 'quarry' arrived.

Hilda and Pearl had a seven-hour drive from their RV campsite in Montana, to Yellowstone. So, they decided it made sense to stop overnight on route. They chose a small campsite near some shops, so that they could stock up on provisions.

Costabuck Coffee House

Having shopped, they noticed a Costabuck Coffee Shop. Having not yet tried one, Hilda was keen to see what all the fuss was about. She stood outside for a while staring at the sign and said to Pearl, 'I thought it was a coffee shop?'

'It is, let's go in,' said Pearl.

'What's all this?' asked Hilda, waving at the sign. 'It looks like a red king.'

'It's just a logo, the queue is building up, can we go in?'

'A wavy red King?'

'Yes, now let's go in.' Pearl pushed open the door, and a lady walked in ahead of them, nodding a thanks to Pearl for holding the door. Hilda stood firm staring at the sign. Eventually, she huffed and headed inside.

After entering, Hilda told Pearl to find a seat while she queued for a coffee – her treat. It was a long queue, at least four extra people had joined it while Hilda was looking at the sign outside. She said, 'red King,' under her breath, causing a little girl who was holding her mum's hand to stare up at her through wide eyes. She eventually reached the counter. The Barista looked at her expectantly. Hilda was ready with her order and said, 'two coffees please, white no sugar. We are sweet enough already, dear.'

The Barista stared blankly at Hilda and asked, 'is that mocha, cappuccino, frappe, macchiato...?'

'I want a coffee dear, not a machine,' said Hilda. She lent on the counter.

'I was asking what coffee you wanted,' said the Barista. A smile plastered on her face.

'No, you weren't young lady.' Hilda drew herself up to her full five feet four inches. 'You asked if I wanted a machineo.'

'Macchiato,' said the Barista.

'You see, you did it again.' Hilda glanced around at others in the queue for agreement. They did not seem happy at the delay.

A man in the queue looked impatient. Having parked his delivery van in an illegal place. He was keeping an eye out for the parking enforcement officer. Behind him, two young ladies were chatting about what a long wait they were having. One of them was nudged from behind and shouted, 'Hey! who shoved?'

The young lady looked around. An off-duty parks officer was innocently staring at the ceiling.

'Was it you?' asked the lady. She stared at the officer until he finally acknowledged her. 'Accident, sorry,' he said, then glanced at the floor.

'Yeah, sure,' said the lady, turning back to her friend.

'Can't trust anyone,' said her friend.

The parks officer glanced around him. He appeared to be looking for sympathy. The young girl's mother was behind him, holding her daughter's hand. She shook her head.

At the front of the queue, Hilda, the cause of all their woes, was still arguing with the Barista.

'... type of coffee,' said the Barista. Her smile was looking more forced.

'Well, if you tell me some types of coffee, I can choose. You just keep speaking Italian,' said Hilda.

'Come on,' said the illegally parked man. 'Just give her a plain white.'

Hilda stared at him in shock and said, 'I beg your pardon, young man. I came here for a coffee because Pearl has heard of this place. I have no wish to have something plain.'

The man opened his mouth to speak. Then a traffic enforcement officer took an interest in his van outside. He ran out to move it. Hilda called to his departing back, 'and so you might run away, young man. How very rude.' She turned back to the Barista. Who said, 'let me decide for you.'

'Decide... for me!' said Hilda, horrified. 'I don't think so. I am an independent woman. I'll have you know that Emma Plankhurst counted me as a friend.'

'Who's Emma Plankhurst?' asked the Barista.

'Don't tell me you have never heard of women's libations?' Hilda shook her head sadly.

'Libations? isn't that a drink offering, to a god?' asked the Barista.

'Offerings to the gods? Whatever next? I should have known a place with a red king would be a little odd,' said Hilda.

'Perhaps you mean women's liberation,' said the off-duty parks officer.

Hilda looked around and asked him, 'just what would a man know on the subject?' People in the queue were forgetting about their coffee and listening to Hilda.

'I studied Emily *Pankhurst* and the women's liberation movement, at college,' said the officer.

The two young women turned to stare at the officer. Hilda thought for a moment and then said, 'Pankhurst, Plankhurst, all I know is we were good friends.'

'Really?' said the officer. 'You don't seem old enough. She died in 1928.'

'Oh... did she,' said Hilda. 'Well, I've certainly read about her, anyway. So, I feel like I know her.' She gained confidence.

'Does anyone actually want a coffee?' asked the Barista.

A few people shouted yes. Hilda shouted over them all and held her arms out to bar them saying, 'no queue jumping, you haven't made mine yet.'

'But you haven't told me what you want,' said the Barista. She sounded impatient.

'Two coffees, white, no sugar,' said Hilda, feeling pleased with herself.

'Coming up,' said the Barista. A resigned look on her face. She promptly made two plain whites with no sugar.

'Now that wasn't hard, was it dear?' said Hilda. She took her coffees over to Pearl, leaving a hassled Barista to deal with the impatient queue.

Hilda sipped her coffee and said, 'no, no, no.' She stared at it disgustedly.

'What's the matter?' asked Pearl, drinking her coffee.

'It's no good, no good at all,' said Hilda. She couldn't understand why everyone raved over these coffees. The parks officer could hear her complaining from the queue. After he had bought his coffee. He foolishly did the gallant thing. Really, he should have learnt a lesson whilst in the queue. Walking over to Hilda, he asked, 'can I be of help?' He bowed slightly.

Hilda glanced up in surprise and asked him, 'are you able to make a decent cup of coffee?'

'I can, but I don't think the Barista would like me taking her job.' He glanced down at Hilda's coffee quizzically.

'Oh, then I guess you can't help.' Hilda wafted her hand dramatically and looked away.

'Can I join you both and hear the problem?' Asked the officer.

'I suppose so,' said Hilda.

The officer sat down heavily and asked, 'OK, what can I do?'

'I don't think you can.' Hilda stared forlornly towards the window.

'Don't give up that easy,' said the officer.

Hilda sighed and said, 'if you really want to help?'

'Of course I do,' said the officer.

'Well in that case,' said Hilda, pushing her coffee towards him. 'Can you tell that lady I don't like it and want my money back?'

The officer sat silent for a moment, staring at Hilda's coffee cup, then said, 'not really what I meant.'

'If it's too much trouble…,' said Hilda. She hung her head.

'Now, I didn't say that,' said the officer. He checked the coffee counter. The barista was serving a group of smartly dressed young men. 'Might need to hang on a minute.' He may well have regretted his offer of help; he was not known as a bold man.

'I am feeling dreadfully thirsty,' said Hilda. She licked her lips for effect.

Pearl seemed to find it extremely hard not to burst out laughing. The officer looked from Hilda to the busy counter and back. Then the darkness lifted from his face, and he said, 'I have a plan. Let me buy you a brand-new coffee and a treat for you both. A cookie or cupcake. If you want one?' The officer glanced hesitantly at Pearl, and she nodded vigorously.

Hilda jumped up and down on the seat clapping her hands and said, 'oh! How delightful. I did so fancy a cake, but the coffees were so expensive, dear. I thought the lady had charged me for six cups.'

The officer nodded in agreement.

'Now let me see,' said Hilda. She leapt up and walked to the counter to view the selection of sweet treats. 'Excuse me, I can't see,' she pushed past one of the smartly dressed young men, who was just receiving his coffee.

'Hey!' said the confused man as he moved.

Hilda walked up and down the glass cabinet, pushing in front of several of the group of men who had been ordering coffees. They were about to hold an impromptu business meeting in the coffee shop. At last, Hilda found a perfect treat and suggested it to Pearl, who agreed on the same. Pearl returned to their table. The business executives paid for their coffees and sat at a table next to Pearl. Having reached the barista and told her which cupcakes they wanted, the officer asked, 'and which coffee?'

'Well, certainly not the same again,' said Hilda.

The officer simplified the process and ordered a latte. Surprisingly, Hilda made no comment. Probably because she was reading a poster on the wall about Bear World. Her mind imagined what a brilliant place that must be. She could see herself meeting Paddington.

'Are you coming?' asked the officer, waking Hilda from her daydream.

They returned to their table, where Pearl was waiting. The group of business executives were laughing and joking on the table next to them. It delighted Hilda as she took a large bite of her cupcake. After finishing her first mouthful she said to the officer, 'didn't you fancy a cake?'

'No, no,' said the officer. He had. But he couldn't afford the additional coffee and two cupcakes and one for himself. He had a lot of expenses that month. Ever since his wife had left him and sued him for alimony, money was tight.

'You're missing a treat,' Hilda said, taking a second bite. Pearl nodded in agreement.

The business executives became noisy as they socialised. Their raucous laughter and loud talking disturbed Hilda. She stared across at them in annoyance, then looking at the officer, she said, 'some people are so inconsiderate.'

Costabuck was always noisy and busy. The officer said, 'yes, I suppose it is.'

'Laughing and shouting, without a care in the world,' said Hilda, 'While us genteel folk are trying to have a quiet coffee.'

The officer's cheeks turn red. One of the young business executives heard Hilda's loud comment and turned around 'it's a free country lady.'

'I'm sorry...' said the parks officer.

'Don't apologise for me,' said Hilda, interrupting him. 'This gentleman was just saying how loud you all were.'

The young man looked at the officer and said, 'what's your problem?'

'I, I, well, you see...' said the officer, stuttering.

'He thinks you are all being very rude,' said Hilda, helpfully.

The other young men at the table had all turned around and were now looking at the poor off duty parks officer. One of them said, 'lighten up, would you? We have a stressful job and need a bit of fun before we get down to work.'

Hilda stared hard at them and said, 'well, I think the problem this gentleman has is that you were doing it too loudly.'

'Who does he think he is?' said another of the men.

'I would have been more tolerant, of course. But I think he may have a point,' said Hilda. She took a sip of her coffee.

The officer shuffled in his seat and glowed bright red. Hilda ate some more of her cupcake. She seemed unaware of the trouble she had caused. She then finished her coffee while the men continued to berate the parks officer.

'This coffee is much better than the last,' said Hilda after she finished her cupcake. 'I enjoyed it very much. Thank you, dear.'

'That's OK,' said a rather distracted parks officer. The men had risen and were walking towards him.

'Well, we must be going. Goodbye and thank you for the coffee and cake,' said Hilda. She and Pearl left the table.

As Hilda and Pearl headed out of the shop, the group of young men were standing around the officer. He was waving his hands, so Hilda waved back.

Yellowstone National Park, USA

Hilda and Pearl arrived at Yellowstone the next day and camped in one of its many campsites. The owner reported to Jake at a nearby hotel and received his promised payment. Hilda and Pearl planned to explore the park on a bus tour that set off from the town of West Yellowstone. Whilst booking tickets in town, they discovered a trip to Bear World. Hilda could make her dreams of cuddling bears come true. They booked that trip for the following day. By the time Jake received information on their location and arrived at their campsite, they had gone into town to enjoy the first trip. He followed and got onto the same bus. Outsmarting two old women would not be hard after all. His confidence was growing.

***

The scale of Yellowstone National Park is mind-boggling. The park covers three and a half thousand square miles. It extends into three states, although most of it is in Wyoming. Hilda and Pearl set off on the Yellowstone National Park tour. The distances, the heights of the mountains, the sheer scale of the place struck them. Driving along in the bus, it seemed as if delights appeared around every corner. A river with overhanging trees, a spectacular waterfall, or a multi-coloured mud lake. So many wonders to take in. There were wide expanses of grassland leading to the base of snow-topped mountains.

***

Jake sat at the back of the bus; he was biding his time; waiting till the end of the tour. That way, if anything went wrong, he could make a quick exit. The coach pulled over at the side of the road regularly. That meant passengers could disembark to view the various delights. At one stop, a field of bison greeted the coach, which Hilda told the tour guide were actually buffalo.

As Hilda stood by the edge of a vast landscape at the base of a mountain, she watched the buffalo. They were not, 'a vast herd as far as the eye could see,' as they had been when the early settlers were there. She saw perhaps a hundred dotted around the foothills, but her mind's eye filled in the rest. In her imagination she was sitting in her tepee. One of the other women called to her from outside, saying, 'Dances-At-Anytime, come and see.' She got up from stirring a pot of stew, pushed back the flap of her tepee, and stepped outside. The searing sun caused her to squint. On the horizon a dust cloud rose, and thunder shook the ground. Male warriors mounted their horses, Dances-At-Anytime joined the other women to encourage them. The warriors headed towards the passing herd of bison; spears ready. Dances-At-Anytime wondered if a dance would bring good fortune and started to sing and dance.

'What are you doing?' asked Pearl, staring at Hilda.

'Nothing,' said Hilda, continuing to dance.

'Really?' said Pearl. She wandered back to the tour bus, leaving Hilda to finish her dance and song. A small group of onlookers had gathered, taking photos of her rather than the scenery. They must have assumed she was part of the entertainment.

Their next stop was at Old Faithful. It was an impressive sight watching the steaming tower of water fountain into the air at regular intervals. When Hilda heard about the workers in the eighteen and nineteen hundreds, hanging their washing to clean in the hot steaming water. Hilda was delighted and said, 'my smalls need a steam clean dear.'

'I don't think the park officers would be happy seeing your smalls flying around the park,' said Pearl. She grabbed Hilda as she headed towards the steaming fountain, holding out some of her underwear.

'You're such a spoilsport,' said Hilda.

The tour moved on around the vast park. There was a tour guide who gave them information on the route around. He told them, although the wild bears lived higher in the mountains, they did venture into the lower regions. The food that humans left lying around attracted them and so they should be careful when walking around in open areas. They were also given lots of safety advice about bears. Hilda must have missed it all, because she said to the tour guide, 'I'm looking forward to meeting Paddington.' She had her marmalade sandwiches with her. He thought she was joking, but he didn't know Hilda.

The tour bus stopped at various hot mud springs. The surface of some appeared like another planet. Blues and greens mixed in with the brown muds, bubbling and flowing in strange patterns. Boardwalks spanned the larger ones so that visitors could walk out over them. The experience was like nothing either of them had ever seen before. They had walked on wooden raised platforms before in the UK, but those were over wetland areas covered in reeds. The experience of walking over bubbling multicoloured mud was something out of this world. Hilda always enjoyed films about aliens and other planets. As she walked over these platforms, she imagined herself to be on another planet. On a distant frontier. She was wearing a space suit, so she walked clunkily across the platform. Pearl wondered why Hilda was walking so strangely. In Hilda's mind, she saw a monster rising out of the mud. She shouted, 'monster!'

The whole tour party turned to Hilda in surprise. One or two of them asked, 'where?' Pearl just shook her head. Hilda decided she'd better hold back from the rest of the group.

They explored that area of the park for some time. Pearl returned to the tour bus with the group and waited for Hilda; and waited. After about ten minutes, the bus driver was ready to leave. Hilda was still nowhere in sight. Pearl asked if she could check Hilda was safe. She must have remembered the warning about bears.

The bus driver told her to make a quick check. She headed to where she had last seen Hilda. Then returned to say, 'I can't find her anywhere.'

The bus driver, Pearl, and a couple of others, including Jake, all set off. They asked everyone and looked everywhere they could think of. At last, they found a clue, Hilda's blue bonnet was floating on the boiling mud lake. No one had seen or heard anything. Although one little girl thought she heard an old lady cry out about ten minutes earlier. She had told her mum, who had suggested she was imagining it. She apologised for not taking her daughter seriously. Pearl stood looking at the bonnet, mouth open. Jake looked horrified. Hilda had her bag on her when last seen. The diamonds had gone forever. The bus driver went to fetch a park ranger.

'Poor Hilda, I hope she didn't suffer,' said Pearl. A few tears ran down her cheeks. She looked almost as upset as Jake. He looked like a man heading to the gallows.

The surface mud bubbled, and gas rose into the air. Pearl shook her head and said, 'this is terrible.' She turned to Jake and said, 'what will I say to her family?' He was white as a sheet and shaking.

The bus driver returned with a couple of park rangers carrying poles. They started to prod and poke the mud. One of them hooked Hilda's hat from the surface and brought it to Pearl. She held it and looked sadly at the reminder of a woman so full of life; now gone.

'The last thing we have to remember her by,' said Pearl.

'Is... there... nothing... else?' asked Jake, in between sobs.

'Like what?' said the park ranger. He looked at Jake oddly.

'A bag...' said Jake in a high-pitched voice.

The park ranger shook his head. Pearl was hugging Hilda's hat, weeping. But she was nowhere near as upset as Jake looked.

'Thank goodness you rescued my hat dear,' said Hilda as she walked up. 'I have just been searching for a stick to grab it. Took me ages to find this.' Hilda had a wooden fence post in her hand.

'Hilda! we were all worried sick,' said Pearl. She hugged Hilda.

'Thank goodness you're alive,' said Jake, joining in the hug, much to Hilda and Pearl's shock.

'It's good to see you as well. Do I know you?' asked Hilda after the hug, staring at Jake.

'I get easily emotional,' said Jake. He was stretching around Hilda. A strong and long strap attached her bag to her opposite side.

'Oh dear, my hat's ruined. I wonder if the mud will wash out?' said Hilda, she took her hat back from Pearl.

Jake was still trying to reach Hilda's bag.

'Where's your other shoe?' asked Pearl.

'I tried to walk out on the mud and get my hat. But my foot got stuck, and I lost my shoe.'

'You mustn't walk on the mud, ma'am,' said one of the park rangers.

Hilda spun around to face them, just as Jake had positioned himself to grab her bag, thus spinning the bag away from him. She said to the ranger, 'Ah, you say that now. Next, you'll be telling me I shouldn't pull up the fence posts.' She waved the fence post around. She accidentally hit Jake with it. No one noticed. He sat down, winded.

The Park Rangers seemed panicked and said to Hilda, 'where did you get that from?'

'Oh, I don't know, over there somewhere. Near a sign that had something about teddy bears,' said Hilda.

There was an almost unanimous chorus of: 'What!'

Just as Jake got up again, everyone rushed off towards the bus.

Bear World, Near Yellowstone, USA

The next morning Hilda tried to make up for her behaviour, not that she really thought she had done anything wrong. She made breakfast and called Pearl through. After a while Pearl appeared, sat down heavily on the bench seat, and stared at the plate of bacon, tomatoes, and scrambled eggs on toast. Hilda had worked hard finding and cooking her favourite. Pearl looked up and said, 'I suppose you think this makes it all right?'

'No dear,' said Hilda, eating her breakfast. 'I just wanted to give you a treat.'

'I thought you were dead!' said Pearl. She stared at her breakfast and licked her lips. 'Finding your hat in that boiling mud lake.'

'I keep saying I'm sorry,' said Hilda. She cut a piece of bacon. Speared through it and lifted it towards her mouth. 'We have a trip to Bear World today.'

Pearl frowned at Hilda, then watched as Hilda chewed her forkful of delicious food. Looking back at her own plate, she had a few mouthfuls. Then after a while she sighed and said, 'I suppose you didn't plan to cause me anxiety.'

'Of course, I didn't,' said Hilda, picking up her cup of tea.

***

When Hilda and Pearl arrived at the bear sanctuary, they found it delightful. There were small pens where they could see orphaned bear cubs. Hilda asked how easy they were to keep. The staff were answering her questions when they gradually realised that she meant for her to keep in her own house. She was most disappointed to be told that she could not keep a wild bear at home in England. The sanctuary also had full grown bears, moose, elk, bison, and deer. It was a bit like a zoo or a wildlife park.

They then got on a double-decker tour bus. It took visitors around an extensive paddock where the larger bears roamed. Pearl sat looking out at the bears. Some of the bus passengers threw food out to the bears from the safety of the top of the bus. This encouraged bears to come near to the bus and gave perfect photo opportunities.

***

Jake had overheard Hilda and Pearl talk about Bear World and secured a last-minute ticket. He was pinning his hopes on today, after missing grabbing the diamonds the day before. Pearl and Hilda were opposite him on the bus, at least Pearl was. Jake had become pre-occupied by the bears and taken a few photos to show his wife. When he turned around, Hilda had disappeared.

Pearl got her camera out and started taking photos of the bears. They were interested not only in the food but in something nearer the bus out of her sight. A roaming patrol car came towards them at speed. Two armed rangers leapt from the vehicle and approached their bus. One said firmly, 'ma'am, please get back on the bus. They're wild animals.'

Hilda's voice said, 'it's all right dear. They're enjoying their marmalade sandwiches, just like Paddington bear would.'

Outside the bus, the bears were indeed enjoying their marmalade sandwiches. Ones that Hilda had made especially. The two keepers were getting anxious that the bears might decide Hilda seemed like a tasty alternative. After they finished their marmalade sandwiches. They were trying to coral the bears away from Hilda. She did not make it easy for them, and it took quite a while. Once Hilda was safely back on the bus. The tour was abruptly ended. Much to everyone's disgust. Then Hilda and Pearl were asked to leave before Jake got anywhere near them.

Hilda was not the easy target he had expected. He headed back to his hotel and made further plans. Ones that would not and could not fail. 'She is just an old lady,' he kept repeating that mantra.

A campsite at Yellowstone National Park, USA

Back at their campsite, Pearl was saying crossly to Hilda, 'I thought you'd caused enough trouble yesterday with bears.'

'I don't know what all the fuss is about. I thought everyone knew bears loved marmalade sandwiches,' said Hilda. She was sitting in their dining area, with her arms crossed. Hilda could not understand the to-do Pearl was making about teddy bears. She checked in her bag and discovered she had one marmalade sandwich left. She took it out and said, 'do you want half?'

Pearl just stared at her wide eyed. Then, as Hilda munched on the sandwich, Pearl burst out laughing.

***

When Jake was at Hilda and Pearl's campsite earlier, he had attached a tracker to their RV. It sent an electronic signal to a device he carried; its range was several miles. He didn't want to lose them again. Once he was back in his hotel room, he set about making phone calls. He would enlist some specialist support. Obviously, he just needed a bit of help – a fallback plan. Meanwhile, he would follow them and look for an opportunity to arise. Surely his luck would change soon.

CHAPTER ELEVEN

July 1997

Colorado, USA

After what Hilda saw as her initial success of drawing at the beginning of their trip, she was keen to do much more, this time with watercolour paints. That was what the Victorian's had used most. If she was going to have a full selection of artworks to display in England. She would need watercolour paintings. No doubt the art critics back home were waiting in eager anticipation for Hilda's return.

When Pearl and Hilda reached Colorado, the scenery was breathtaking. Hilda pulled up at a viewing point. Pearl put the kettle on, and Hilda got out, painting equipment in hand. She carefully studied the scene before her, but it lacked something. Realising the something it lacked was people, Hilda set off in search of the missing component for her masterpiece. It was early in the morning and the parking area for the viewpoint was deserted, so she headed into the rocky desert. Only Hilda could tell you why she expected to find people in the wilderness. Most of us would think the word desert meant deserted,

Colorado is well-used by film companies. Not just for westerns, but for many other types of movies. As Hilda rounded an outcrop, she came upon a strange sight; an alien sat upon a rock, relaxing. At least, it must be an alien, as it was a green man-like being with large, multi-faceted eyes. It had no hair visible, no ears, and only long, claw-like fingers extended from its arms. At the end of rather long legs were large, webbed feet.

Hilda had realised for a while that aliens must have visited earth, that much was obvious to her. She watched the more positive Sci-Fi films and series. The ones where aliens come in peace and want humans to join inter-galactic communities. Seeing this alien sitting harmlessly and happily on a rock backed up her ideas. It was not causing any trouble and had no obvious gun. She strode over to the alien, held up a hand in the universal sign of peace. You know the one used in all the movies and said, 'welcome to earth dear, I'm Hilda.'

The actor inside the alien costume looked out at Hilda and spoke. At least he tried to answer her. But as a non-speaking extra, the wardrobe designer had not created his costume, with speaking in mind. That would be added later in post-production. So, what Hilda heard was, 'Immmnn...nnn...tt...aaa' and other muffled sounds. Which she took to be his alien language.

Hilda spoke loudly and slowly. She waved her arms. The obvious way to communicate with anyone who speaks another language. 'Sorry, I don't understand you.'

'Nnnn... oo.. I I...,' said the actor.

'I think the best idea is if you come with me,' said Hilda. She took his clawed hand. 'I'll introduce you to my friend Pearl. She's good at languages and would love to meet you.' That last part was a little optimistic.

The alien/actor allowed himself to be dragged by Hilda. They headed around the rocks towards the car park. As it was early morning, only their RV was parked there. The film company had parked out in the wilderness. Meanwhile, one of the film crew had come to fetch the actor and found he was missing. They returned to report the fact. He was only young and lacked initiative.

In the RV, Pearl was just picking up a cup of tea. Glaring red eyes, set in a green face, appeared at the window. She screamed and dropped her cup on the table. Hilda's smiling face appeared next, and she waved cheerily. Perhaps she should have done things in reverse. The door of the RV opened, and Hilda said, 'no need to panic dear, this is an alien friend of mine. I need you to translate.' Maybe this was a little late.

Pearl was not in a suitable state to translate anything. Hilda had been mistaken about her loving to meet an alien. Pearl was trying to squash herself into a corner of the RV, and had her eyes screwed tightly closed. She kept saying over and over, 'this is a dream; this is a dream.'

A posse of security and other film staff came racing across the car park. They had spotted their errant actor next to the RV. On arrival; it took some convincing before Hilda would accept; he was not an actual alien. She still muttered about government cover-ups and Area 51 after they left.

She knew all about Area 51, Josh had told her in one of his more mischievous moments. Pearl was still muttering, 'this is a dream.' Her nerves took a while to calm down. Hilda led her; eyes closed to the passenger seat and drove off. They were part way to the next town before Pearl fully opened her eyes. Looking across at Hilda singing along to a tune on the radio as she drove; Pearl wondered if she had just dreamt it after all. Hilda explained later, but it made no sense.

A Campsite, Colorado, USA

Two nights later, Hilda and Pearl parked in a campsite out in the wilds, a large open, desert like area, with mountain views all around. The facilities on site were basic, but they had all they needed in the RV, and they had stocked up in the last town. Their neighbour was in a beat-up old waggon, that he was living in it after losing his job. He was late sixties. They sat chatting about his time in the army, fighting in the Korean war. It had changed him, physically and mentally. He showed them that his left leg was a prosthetic from the knee down. Mentally, he had never settled back into his job as a doctor stateside. The things he had seen over in Korea had been so terrible.

He had started drinking, messed up an operation, and been struck off. Lost his house, his wife left him, ended up on the streets. Hilda and Pearl were in tears, hearing all that had happened to him. He said, 'hang in there, little ladies, there is light at the end of the tunnel.'

He was on the street, drinking whatever he could get hold of. Then a group of do-gooders, as he called them, had come by each day. He had shouted at them, spat at them, but they sat with him, listened to him, had time for him. They bought him food and found him shelter. Turned out they were from a local Christian church. He called them God botherers at first. Then, over the months of getting to know them, he saw they had a peace he wanted.

He explained he asked the group about the peace they had and how he could get it. Then they told him something life changing. That 'you don't get peace and joy through Christianity by seeking peace and joy.' When he asked them to explain, they told him, 'Just seek Jesus. Peace and joy are incidental.' They told him about Jesus' words in John's Gospel

Chapter 14 verse 27, "Peace I leave with you; my peace, I give you. I do not give to you as the world gives. Do not let your hearts be troubled and do not be afraid." 'Remember that when you get stressed.' The man said that his peace, his happiness, was through Jesus. He now travelled the country, telling other people about that. He had never been happier than he was now he had nothing. All his hope was in Jesus.

Pearl and Hilda went to bed that night with a lot to think about. Hilda was not known for thinking much about anything. Next day they wanted to ask Simon some more questions, but he had moved on. Pearl told Hilda that she was used to seeing preachers standing on street corners shouting at her she was going to hell. This man had been different. He never mentioned hell once. There was a godly light and peace about him. They both knew that what he said was true.

***

After they left the campsite, Hilda drove first. Pearl was map reading again. They had been driving along for about an hour, when Hilda said, 'oh, my goodness, there's someone on top of that car.'

Pearl looked up from the map. Passing them the other way was a convoy. A police car headed the four cars, then came a pickup truck. On the back of which, there appeared to be a young man standing. He was facing backwards, looking through a camera towards a sporty-looking car. Behind the car, at some distance, was another police car. Hilda pulled over to the side of the road, and once the convoy had gone by, she got out. Pearl joined her on the almost deserted road.

'That was Josh, standing in the car,' said Hilda, staring in disbelief.

'Your grandson, Josh? Are you sure?' asked Pearl.

'I'm going to be, get back in,' said Hilda, leaping back into the RV. She did a U turn, then chased the convoy.

The Police officer driving the car at the rear of the convoy was just saying to his partner how relaxing their assignment was. Then he caught sight of something moving. An RV was overtaking them fast.

'Can't they read the sign on the back?' said his partner as he watched them overtake.

'Plenty of idiots around,' said the officer, driving. He turned on the lights and siren, then he pulled up next to Hilda and Pearl. His partner spoke into the speaker system. 'Police pull over.'

Hilda had been so focussed on trying to catch Josh that she didn't notice the lights or siren. It wasn't until the police car was alongside, and the speaker announcement came Hilda woke from her reverie. 'What's that!' she said, swerving towards the overtaking police car.

Pearl grabbed the wheel in time to prevent an accident and said, 'you're being told to pull over by the police.'

'I've not done anything wrong,' said Hilda.

After a few minutes, they were all parked by the roadside. The other drivers had seen the excitement in their rear-view mirrors, stopped and turned around. Josh had explained who the interlopers were and got Hilda off with a stern warning. Now he was chatting to them.

'I got a commission taking photos of a sports car. I've already met up with dad and mum in New York. They told me you got separated,' said Josh.

'Yes, things got a little confusing. I think either Pearl or your father got confused,' said Hilda. Fortunately, Pearl was not in earshot. She loved sports cars and was having a close look at the car Josh was photographing.

'I must get on, but I am staying at a motel nearby. Where are you going to park that thing?' said Josh, pointing at the RV. 'We can meet later.'

***

After work, he came to visit them at the campsite. They were sitting around a small portable BBQ that Pearl had bought. Hilda spotted a stick on the ground and fancied using it to put the marshmallows she had bought on. As she was about to pick it up, Josh shouted, 'stop!'

'Whatever's the matter dear,' said Hilda, staring at him.

'That's not a stick. It's a snake,' said Josh.

Pearl was almost as afraid of snakes as spiders. She ran into the RV and stayed there. It was going to take a while to get her back outside again. She had only just ventured out after the spider incident. They had to take her meal inside. Other campers nearby explained that the snake they had found was harmless, but she would not come back out that night.

Hilda had a great time catching up with Josh. When he left, he shouted goodbye to Pearl, who was still inside the RV. Next time he would see them would be in England.

Chicago, Illinois, USA

William and Louise had arrived in Chicago about the time that Hilda and Irene were still in Colorado meeting Josh. These places look so close on a map, just inches away. But America is such an immense country and distances take so long to cover. It is no wonder many Americans travel internally by plane.

William headed in to meet the staff of the Chicago branch of TSU while Louise explored the harbour of Lake Michigan, looking for a last-minute cruise deal. All the ones that advertised in shops and at the travel agents were too expensive for her budget. The high-cost disappointed Louise and she went for a walk along the harbour front just to take in the sights and sounds. As she explored, she saw a chalkboard set up near the end. Far away from the major thoroughfare and the harbour master's office. Written on it was: 'Views of the Lakes Luxury Cruises,' it was cheap and had availability. Louise really fancied a cruise of the lake, but the small boat next to the sign did not look in good condition. A man in a captain's hat was standing by the board. He was shouting, 'best value cruise you'll find.'

'Is it your boat?' asked Louise.

'Yes indeed, a fine and sound boat she is too,' said Captain Len.

'Umm, doesn't look it,' said Louise.

'Looks can be deceptive. She's tatty on top, but sound and strong where it counts,' said Captain Len.

'I think I'll leave it,' said Louise, turning to go.

'Tell you what, lovely lady, a special deal, just for you, half price,' said the captain.

Louise stopped and stared at the boat and said, 'you're sure it's safe?'

'Yes siree, fully seaworthy and up to the latest standards. She has all the certificates.' If he had been Pinocchio, his nose would have grown.

Louise reluctantly agreed and boarded the boat. Her desire to cruise the lake overcoming her common sense. There were only four passengers, plus the crew of two, on the boat. The boat set off five minutes early. It seemed related to an official-looking man heading at speed along the dock. But Captain Len said to them, 'all's on board, no need to wait.'

Although it seemed strange that the official-looking chap was waving at them angrily from the dock. He was the harbour master and had been tipped off about Len's unofficial cruise.

As the boat headed into the lake, the waves got higher. It's surprising how much like a sea Lake Michigan can be on a windy day, waves crashing at the boat side. Fortunately, it was summer, as the lake can be icy in winter. The turbulent waves breached the deck and soaked the passengers. Captain Len told the passengers not to panic. Louise shivered as the thin coat she was wearing became saturated. From the shore, the harbour master could see the boat was in trouble, not a surprise. From his vantage point, the boat was more under the water than above it; he called the coastguard.

TSU Corp Office, Chicago, USA

William was having a lunch break. He walked towards the room they had set aside for breaks. It had a coffee machine, a microwave, a few chairs, a table, and a small TV. Two of the office staff were already in there talking. They were watching a news broadcast on the TV. One of the staff, Jane, was halfway through talking as William entered the room. '... sooner. That dock admin ain't tough enough,' she said.

Her fellow worker, Sarah, shook her head and said, 'my sister-in-law told me it's unscrupulous boat owners. They moor up, pretend to be fishing boats. Moment the officials turn their back, up go signs, advertising cruises.'

'Guess so,' said Jane.

'Them boats are old wrecks,' said Sarah.

William was looking over their shoulder at the news item that had started this conversation. The camera operator was zooming in on a rescue boat. It was picking up people from the lake. He shook his head.

'I should say, you get what you pay for...' said Jane, smiling.

William saw a close-up of the boat as it raced to shore. For a moment he just stared, then his eyes went wide. Given the attitude of his staff, it was just as well Louise had not visited the Chicago Office of TSU. Sitting, looking cold and white, in the front of the rescue boat, was his wife.

'Look at that woman,' said Sarah. She pointed at the TV. 'She won't save the pennies anymore,' she cackled.

Jane laughed and agreed and said, 'prob'ly got a tight husband.' Then they both noticed William, standing in the doorway staring, red faced, at the TV. He glanced at them, apologised for interrupting their lunch, and left.

William headed out of the office and down to the docks. It was not a surprise that he discouraged Louise from visiting the Chicago Office after that. Having seen the New York Office, she had no plans anyway. But William increased her entertainment budget considerably; much to her surprise and joy.

Jane's Home, Chicago, USA

People have many hidden secrets. That evening Jane got home from TSU to find her husband sitting watching football on TV. He heard her come in and said, 'Len's boats a gonna.'

'Was that his on the news? I didn't recognise it,' said Jane. She walked in, shaking her head.

'Yeah, he's in the county jail. He won't get away with this 'un,' said her husband.

'Has he got no sense? Can't you speak to him?' said Jane. If she had a high horse, she would climb on it.

'He's your brother,' said her husband. He looked up briefly, then back at the sport.

'Don't remind me,' said Jane. She walked through to the kitchen to make a start on their evening meal.

***

Jake felt as if his luck had changed. As he sped along the highway, his mobile tracker beeped repeatedly, and the RV he was following came into sight. He slowed and kept about fifty yards behind it.

A sign for Minneapolis came up. That was a place he knew well and had several motels he enjoyed staying in. Then things improved further. The RV with his quarry inside turned in to a campsite just a hundred yards away from his favourite motel. He could walk from there. He followed them into the campsite and checked where they set up camp. Then went and booked into the motel. He celebrated with a three-course meal. He had survived on snacks and take out since the chase began. At last, he had them cornered. He would wait for nightfall.

Chapter Twelve

July 1997

A campsite near Minneapolis, Minnesota, USA

Unaware of the danger nearby, Pearl and Hilda were settled for the night in their RV. Pearl was desperate to share her news with Hilda after her failed attempt a few nights earlier. So, that evening, as they both sat playing cards, Pearl finally had her opportunity. There was a haunted look behind her eyes, and she half-whispered, 'there is more than just me.'

Hilda checked around the RV and said, 'have you invited guests dear?'

'No, that came out wrong. I mean, I'm not alone,' said Pearl.

'I know you have a cat called Merlin,' said Hilda.

'Not Merlin,' said Pearl.

'I see, you mean visitors from other planets.' Hilda pointed through the skylight, towards the stars.

Pearl looked at the night sky for a moment, then said, 'I mean, I was adopted as a child.'

'You never were. You'd have told me.' Hilda looked indignant.

'I'm telling you now,' said Pearl.

'But I've known you since we were children.'

'I realise that. It's something I only found out recently.'

Hilda peered at Pearl accusingly and asked, 'how recently?'

'Just before we came to America.'

'Well... I suppose that's all right then. I am your best friend. You don't keep secrets from best friends,' said Hilda.

'There's something else,' said Pearl.

'You have royal blood?'

'Of course not.'

'Pity, I always wanted a princess as a best friend,' said Hilda.

'I have a twin sister.'

Hilda stared at her with a gaping mouth, 'a twin sister?' She gazed out of the window. The sun was just setting over the distant hills. Young people in the RV next door were sitting outside drinking cans of beer. They were a large group and quite rowdy. Hilda glanced out at them, shook her head. Then back at Pearl and asked, 'where is she? I need more information.'

Pearl was quiet for a while. She stood up and went over to the sideboard. Then turned towards Hilda. 'You knew my parents. Well, as I now know, adoptive parents, and what lovely people they were. I couldn't face looking through their things. Finally, I did it last month. When I was clearing through their boxes, I found a few bits. They had a photo of me and my twin sister when we were first born. They also had a special box.' Hilda looked up knowingly and Pearl nodded. 'It contained letters from the family who adopted my twin sister.'

'That special box. You got out the other day. That lady rummaged through,' said Hilda.

'Yes,' said Pearl.

'I wonder why your parents didn't show you the box when you were younger?' Hilda asked.

'I'll never be able to ask them,' said Pearl.

The young people outside started shouting. There was banging and crashing. Hilda and Pearl both stared out of the window. People were running around; car headlights and torches were shining. They both stepped outside and asked one of the nearest young people what was going on. A man had been spotted with a gun prowling about the site. The young folk had all chased him off, throwing things at him. Then the campsite owner had fetched a pump-action shotgun. The last they saw of the man he was haring down the road as if he was being chased by the devil himself. They had called the police.

After all the excitement calmed down, Hilda and Pearl headed back into their RV and Hilda said, 'now, where were we?'

'I was showing you this box,' said Pearl.

'Oh yes. Just think. If we had known of this box when we were children. We could've had a secret club, all about you and your twin sister. I've just thought, where does she live? Is she in Kilburn too? Have you contacted her yet?' Hilda had so many questions.

'She lives in America. The family who adopted her lived in Marlan, Ohio. At least they did years ago when the letters were written. The last letter I found was dated 1937. And no, I haven't made contact.'

Hilda mumbled on about secret clubs and twins, then sat up straight and asked, 'is that the real reason you wanted to come?'

'Yes, I'm sorry. I was hoping we could have a look at the town. See where she grew up. Try to find her,' said Pearl.

Hilda stood and walked over to Pearl. She wanted to make her point strongly. 'You are my best friend, Pearl. Of course, we can go there. I would have wanted to do the same if I were you. Besides, it'll be fun, an adventure. We can have our secret girls' club to search for your sister. It's just we're older now,' said Hilda.

Pearl smiled. 'Thank you, you're a great friend. That means such a lot.'

'What's her name? Do you know if they changed it?'

Pearl gulped and wiped the corner of her left eye. 'It's Ruby. That's the name they used in the letters. Ruby Davies, if she isn't married.'

'It's a treasure hunt, for a ruby. You're both named after gemstones,' said Hilda. 'Can I see the box now?'

'Hang on a second,' said Pearl. She went and fetched the box of letters.

Hilda clapped her hands when the box arrived and said, 'oh goody, we even have clues and a treasure chest.' She looked through a few of the letters, then said, 'It's a very fancy box. What are these letters on the lid? Is that the maker?'

'The VW?' said Pearl. 'I'm not sure.'

'Volkswagen, do you think?' said Hilda.

'It'll be someone's initials, I guess, Hilda. Not a car.'

'Of course, I knew that.'

'I guess Victoria or Victor, there aren't many names beginning with V. Because it's a pretty box, I suppose I assume it's a woman's so Victoria. Maybe our mother's name. It would make sense if it was her box. The W must be her surname,' said Pearl.

Hilda picked up the photo of Pearl and her twin sister as babies. She turned it over and noticed an indentation in the back. As if something had been written on a sheet above it.

Pearl hadn't noticed that in her dark bedroom in England. Here, as the evening sunlight streamed in through the RV window, the indents showed up clearly. Hilda handed it to Pearl; she got out a pencil and lightly rubbed the side of it over the marks. A signature appeared. They both studied it for some time.

'Victoria Worth, VW, your mother, perhaps?' said Hilda. 'Another clue?'

'I wonder how we can find out?' Pearl spoke wistfully. 'Victoria Worth. But how did I end up in England and my sister in America?'

'First things first. Let's find your sister,' said Hilda. She got out a map and studied it for a while. 'Looks like we could go to Marlan, Ohio, this way.' She pointed out a route. It completely missed the meeting with William and Louise in Chicago. Hilda had forgotten all about it.

The Nearby Motel

Jake lay on his bed, shaking. Maybe his luck had not changed after all. What was it with these old women? Did they have their own private army? He would need to wait until his hit man arrived.

August 1927

St Mark's Parish Church, Kensal Green, London, UK

The woman who walked up the aisle at St Mark's parish church was unrecognisable. Anyone who had seen her struggle off the ship at Southampton seven years earlier would deny their own eyes.

It is a pity that Pearl had no way of looking back seventy years at this event. It would have interested her. Victoria Worth was indeed the mother of Pearl and Ruby. Having been forced to give them up for adoption seven years earlier, her life had changed. But not all for the better. Ironically, at the time of this wedding, Pearl and Hilda were at Miss Wentworth's Academy, a school in Kilburn, not two miles from the church. Yet Pearl and Victoria were each was unaware of the other. So close and yet so far away.

Soon after leaving the maternity home, where Pearl and Ruby were born and forcibly adopted. Victoria had spent a few days on the streets, hungry and desperate. One day, Lucian Kendal passed her by. He had recognised that she was no ordinary beggar, but from a wealthy background. The dirt and rags did nothing to hide her beauty inside or out. He had acted in an honourable and caring way, providing shelter at a local boarding house for free. A true Samaritan, of Biblical quality, so it seemed. He expected nothing in return. At least at first, Lucian's plans were more long term. Lucian's outer smooth and loving demeanour hid a hard and brutal nature. It was a side of his life never shown to Vicky; his pet name for her. She fell in love with this knight in tarnished armour. Hence, seven years later, he was waiting for her at the altar, not two miles from one daughter she had been forced to abandon. The other was far away in America.

Vicky and Lucian were being married in a very low-key way; it suited them both to keep things secretive. Lucian, because of his dislike of publicity, Vicky had no wish for news of her marriage to reach her estranged family. Lucian headed up an international crime family, but one that had a respectable front. To his future wife, he was a legitimate entrepreneur, a lie he was keen to uphold. He moved in exalted circles, which comprised bribed judges, politicians, and senior police officers. He counted landed gentry among his friends. Vicky saw all the people visiting their home as a confirmation that her husband was honest; she did not know of the bribery and corruption. He kept that side of his 'businesses' from her. If anyone had suggested her husband had people hurt and killed, she would have laughed. Not her Lucian. Yes, he could be rough around the edges, but he had a heart of gold. Sometimes you see only as much as you choose to see.

To Lucian, Vicky became his well-bred wife from New England, a trophy for his arm. But also, an expert in saying the right thing and hosting dinner parties in style. She brought a quality that lifted him into a new level of society and acceptance. She taught him a better way to speak and act. Even more doors opened to him. Politicians and celebrities saw the couple as 'one of them.' They were an accepted part of the establishment. Unbeknown to Vicky, she was his way into more of 'polite society.' Once accepted, he blackmailed and bribed those who were foolish enough to draw close to him. Lucian had seen Vicky's potential as a key to doors, previously locked to him. That was why he spent seven years wooing and deceiving her into marriage. It was a lie that could not last. After a few years, she was the only one blind to his true nature. The parties continued. But the smiles and small talk were forced. No one dared cross Lucian.

July 1997

Minneapolis, Minnesota to Marlan, Ohio, USA

Hilda & Pearl blew right past Chicago, that windy city. They got caught up in their search for Ruby and forgot they were meeting William and Louise. They just carried on to Marlan Ohio. Pearl would have normally been the one to realise such a massive oversight. But now that she had told Hilda about Ruby, all she could think about was finding her sister. She really hoped that Ruby was still living in the same place mentioned in the letters. It was a long shot, but all she had to go on. Or that there would be an obvious way to find her once they arrived in Marlan. The anticipation of meeting her sister was building and she could not bear to think about failure. After that she was determined to find out who Victoria Worth was. It must be their mother, surely; whatever happened to her? Why had she given them up for adoption?

***

As they set off on their search, every move was being tracked. Jake watched them on his satellite tracker as they headed towards the small town of Marlan, Ohio. He shook his head. He was glad to be at a distance after the debacle of the other night. It still made him shiver. The hit man he planned to hire was not yet in place, so he just monitored their route, waiting.

Marlan, Ohio, USA

Hilda and Pearl finally arrived in Marlan, Ohio and pulled up near the outskirts. Pearl needed to gather herself before they headed to the address she had from the letters. Her anticipation had been building, so much was riding on that place. As they sat by the side of the road, Hilda grew bored. She spotted a house with a giant kennel in its backyard. The kennel was painted red, with a white Snoopy shape cut-out on top. She wanted to look closer.

Pearl was distracted by her thoughts. When Hilda got out, Pearl asked, 'where are you going?'

'Just off to have a closer look at that kennel,' said Hilda.

'You can't go wandering up people's drives. They have guns in places like this and shoot trespasser,' said Pearl.

'Don't worry, back soon.' Hilda strolled up the driveway towards the amazing structure. She arrived at the shed and stood staring up at the white Snoopy cut-out.

Inside the house, Annie was passing the rear window when she spotted the intruder. 'Peter,' she said, 'there's a stranger in the yard.' Her husband, Peter, came across. 'Looks a harmless old lady.'

Annie peered out of the window. 'Can't be sure. Look how she's dressed.'

'How did Kanga get out?' said Peter. He watched their dog head towards Hilda.

'You'd better get out there,' said Annie.

Peter walked out the back door and Annie followed a few steps behind. As they rounded the side of the house, they saw Kanga nuzzling into Hilda's hand.

'You're a lovely dog, aren't you?' said Hilda. She glanced up at the approaching couple. 'Hello, is this your delightful dog? I love her scarf.'

Annie had been about to challenge the interloper. The unexpected compliment caught her off guard and she said, 'yes, she is. Her name's Kanga. I made the bandana.'

'Ah, Kanga, as in Ru's mother in Winnie the Pooh?' said Hilda.

'We love Winnie the Pooh,' said Annie. She overtook Peter and came up to Kanga. She tickled her belly as she rolled on her back. Annie stared at the strangely dressed lady who had invaded her yard uninvited. Hilda's wrinkled smile looked down at Annie. Peter had caught up and was standing next to her.

'I love the kennel,' said Hilda. 'Who painted it?'

'Joint effort, mainly Annie,' said Peter. He smiled at his wife.

'Annie?' said Hilda. 'Lovely name, and you are?'

'Peter,' he held out a hand. 'Fancy a drink? Hot one today. Come sit on the porch.'

Hilda followed Annie and Peter to the porch. Annie asked, 'ice tea?'

'Ooo!' Hilda clapped her hands in delight. 'They have that in the movies. Yes, please.'

Annie headed inside to make it, and Peter indicated a rocking chair on the porch. Hilda checked the chair, then through the window into the house. Her eyes caught sight of all the wonderful pictures on the walls and, with a squeal of delight, she rushed inside. Peter was left standing by the rocking chair. Hilda stopped in the entrance hall of the house. She stared at the walls overflowing with gorgeous photos and paintings.

One caught her attention, a ballet dancer. Hilda did an approximation of a ballet dance over to the picture and stood before it. Her eyes caught the cosy chairs by a brick fireplace. She pirouetted and danced over to one of the chairs and said, 'a real fire.'

Peter had regained his ability to move and caught her up. He said, 'it doesn't work, maybe you'd prefer outside?'

Hilda was already sitting in the chair by the fire, the rug on her knees. 'I could get very at home here.'

Peter looked at Hilda, fear in his eyes. Annie walked in with the drinks. She nearly dropped the tray when she saw Hilda sitting by the fire. Annie had a Nerf water gun under the stairs. She glanced at it for a moment. But then she glanced back at Hilda and said, 'oh, I see you've found a comfy chair,' her eyes gazed pleadingly at Peter, '*inside*!?'

Annie handed Hilda the ice tea and put a plate of cookies on a small table in front of her. She kept looking at Peter and the door. He just shrugged.

Hilda took a sip of the tea and said, 'it's cold!'

'It's ice tea,' said Annie. She glanced at the cup and back at Hilda.

'I didn't know that meant it was cold,' said Hilda. She put the cup down in disgust. She stared at the plate of cookies. 'No chocolate ones? But they look delicious.'

As they chatted to Hilda, they realised she was not a threat, but a very delightful lady. From where Peter was sitting, he could see the RV parked out the front.

He asked if that was how she had travelled and found out that Pearl was still in it. They invited Pearl in as well. She was reluctant to come inside. Her mind was on Ruby's house, but with a little persuasion, she entered.

Time flew by, full of laughter and fun. Peter even had an impromptu dance with Hilda. Brought about by a discussion of the difference between English and American dance styles.

Pearl told the young couple all about their reason for being in Town. Peter and Annie stared at each other oddly. Then they asked Pearl a few more questions about her twin sister.

Annie recounted a tale about a local 'haunted house.' It wasn't really haunted, just deserted. Had been since the mid 1930's. They were too young to know the full story of what had happened there. There were whispered accounts the children shared when they were growing up about it. No one went near the house, except on a dare. It's a ruin now. Peter told them it was called Big D's Farm, on Mill Lane. Pearl had turned white. She excused herself and went to sit in the van.

Hilda stayed longer and left them her address and saying they should visit if they ever made it to England. Afterwards, they kept in contact. When she returned to the RV, Pearl was looking stressed. She told Hilda that ever since Peter gave the address; it had filled her with dread. That was the address on the letters. It must be her lost sister's house. Her focus had been on Ruby and whether she was still alive. They headed off to find the farmhouse. It was at this point that they met Orville at Big D's Farm. Whilst it was a scary meeting, he gave them important information. Both about the murders of Ruby's parents, Ed and Ginny Davies and Ruby's escape to New York.

Chapter Thirteen

1928 – 1938

Lucian Kendal's home, Kensal Green, London, UK

Nine months after the marriage of the crime baron, Lucian Kendal to Victoria Worth, they had a daughter, Penelope. That name may ring a bell. At boarding school, her friends had a sweeter name for her, Bonbon. Her best friend at school was Jayne, later the Duchess of Somershire.

Lucian had hoped for a son, but no more children followed. He decided his daughter would head up his business after his death. Once she reached aged ten, he felt that a suitable age to begin her initiation into every part of his growing empire. Who wouldn't think aged ten old enough to start a life of crime? Didn't Fagin have a similar idea in Oliver Twist? Of course, that was fiction, whereas this was real life. Lucian had started far younger. Perhaps he also had Oliver Twist as a role model.

If Penelope had a good and loving nature inherited from her mother, Lucian soon quashed it. He filled her mind with ways to profit from crime and elude the law. He rigorously drummed the three Rs into her. Though perhaps a different version to the ones taught at school. Penelope learnt how to 'rob' people, 'rub them out,' and yet appear 'righteous.'

As young Penelope grew up, she gained a particular fondness for diamonds. Her dad kept an extensive collection of them in his safe. Adding to them regularly from safes belonging to others. He taught his daughter that diamonds were a solid investment, better than cash. Not only a girl's best friend. She took all these lessons into adulthood.

Once Lucian taught his daughter all the workings of his business, it was only a matter of time before Vicky discovered the truth. Penelope would chat about her newfound knowledge over breakfast. She kept forgetting to keep it secret. Stuff just slipped out, like the time she was eating a boiled egg with her mom. As she cracked the shell, it reminded her of the lesson her dad had given her the day before. She said to her mom, 'dad said skulls crack as easy as this shell. But only if guys deserve it. Dad was clear on that. No one crosses a Kendal.'

The double shock of hearing her husband's true nature and that being from her ten-year-old daughter was devastating. She confronted Lucian about it, telling him she would go to the police if he didn't stop. His reaction was unexpected; he just laughed. Then he told her to go to the police, reminding her that the police commissioner was a close friend and how often he dined with them. When she then suggested going to the newspapers, he asked if that would be one run by Lord Harling or Billy Wallace: both good friends and regular visitors. Vicky was more afraid than she had ever been in her life.

***

That night, Vicky crept into their daughter's room. She had packed a small bag with clothes, money, and passports. It took a while to wake Penelope. After waking Penelope said, 'what is it mom?'

'We have to leave; things are not right.' Vicky tried to be as quiet as possible.

'What do you mean?' asked her daughter.

'Your father's doing bad things and we are in danger.'

Penelope stared at her mother as if she was mad and said, 'daddy told me you might say strange things. He explained you're not well and I should call him.'

Vicky felt a rising sense of panic. She pulled at her daughter's arm saying, 'get up. We need to leave now.'

Penelope shrank back in the bed, pulling away from her mom, and said, 'no, go away, I'll call daddy.'

'The things your father is teaching you are wrong. We must escape.' Vicky tried to reach across the bed.

'Daddy says family is the most important thing. Family and love. Anything else is lying and I must ignore it.' Penelope clambered out of the opposite side of her bed and stood as far from her mom as possible.

'I know you've spent a lot of time with your daddy. That hasn't been my choice. But you must listen. Remember that stealing and cheating and murder are wrong,' said Vicky.

'Daddy says that sometimes we must do things to protect our family. Love is strong, not weak. The Kendal family is a powerful family. Other people are weak, and they might try to harm us.'

Time was going by, and Vicky was worried Lucian would hear. Penelope was speaking loudly. Vicky made one last desperate plea. 'We must leave now. I can explain more later. I'm your mother; children listen to their mothers.'

Penelope gazed at her mother for a minute, then shouted, 'daddy, daddy!'

Vicky rushed out of the room, bag in hand. As she left through the front door, she heard her husband calling her name. Running down the street with just a bag containing all her worldly possessions, she had a sense of déjà vu.

July 1997

Chicago, USA

William and Louise were awaiting Hilda and Pearl in Chicago. They had decided not to talk about the sinking cruise ship. Louise out of embarrassment over a poor decision and William because he felt guilty his wife had felt the need to skimp.

Having yet to speak to Hilda and Pearl, they were unaware of the overshoot. Chicago was living up to its reputation. It was so windy that William was struggling to stand up straight as he walked down the street. He was being a gentleman and helping Louise as she walked beside him. She was pleased to have chosen trousers that day. Especially as she noticed a couple of ladies pass her struggling to maintain their decency while walking normally. A Scotsman passed, and they gained the answer to a long-held question, 'what do Scotsmen wear under their kilts?' William suggested he may not be a typical Scot.

At the hotel, William and Louise found a message awaiting them: 'Sorry we forgot about meeting you in Chicago. See you in New York.'

'But we just came from there,' said William. His voice went up a pitch. 'I have an office to set up in Maryland. I will call them back and say we'll meet them there.'

A campsite on the outskirts of New York, USA

Hilda and Pearl had arrived on the outskirts of New York and found a suitable campsite. They were on the trail of Pearl's sister, Ruby. Sixty years earlier, in 1937, she had headed there after her parents' murder. She could be anywhere now. It seemed an impossible task. But Pearl had a feeling that she would find her sister. They were twins, and that gave them a special link. She had always felt a sense that she was missing something. Now she knew what.

After the long drive from Marlan, Ohio, they needed to rest before heading into the New York City.

'I need to rest my little pink cells,' said Hilda. 'Before we go sleuthing.

'Your what?' Pearl stared at her.

'You know, Hurtles Porridge says it in Agatha Christie.'

'Do you mean Hercule Poirot?'

'Him too.'

Pearl shook her head and then started to make a cup of tea.

That first night, they were sitting in their RV looking out at the heavy rain; the windows were misted up. They couldn't see beyond a few yards. Hilda shivered and said, 'reminds me of all those school sports we did in the rain.'

'Too true,' said Pearl. 'I nearly caught my death of cold sometimes.'

As they sat and chatted, they relived past events, travelling back to the 1930's. Pearl and Hilda had lived and been at school so close to Kensal Green where Pearl's half-sister, Penelope, had grown up. What a different life they have had if they all known each other. Not a better one, but different. Lucian and Vicky had considered Miss Wentworth's Academy for Penelope, a few years later. But in the end sent her to a fancy boarding school. That was how she met the future Duchess of Somershire. Penelope was eight years younger than Pearl and Ruby. But Hilda and Pearl knew none of this at that time. Their minds were on a wet day at school.

June 1934

Miss Wentworth's Academy, Kilburn, London, UK

Rain was hammering down, forming rivers down the middle of the road. Paths were more like streams. Hilda and Pearl had their rain macs on, but they served little purpose. Hilda felt like she ought to be swimming rather than walking along the road. Drenched to the skin, she trudged onwards, imagining herself as a fisherman on a high sea's trawler. Even though Pearl was walking alongside, she might as well have been on a different street. Their hoods and the heavy rain made conversation impossible. As they trudged along the street, getting more and more wet. A car passed them in which two dry occupants were on their way to the train station. Those lucky passengers were none other than Victoria née Worth and her six-year-old daughter Penelope. The train would whisk them off to the seaside. Where Lucian had a hotel. He hoped to join them later.

Unaware of this chance passing, Hilda and Pearl trudged onwards. Once they arrived at school, there was a general instruction to congregate in the changing rooms. When all had gathered, they were told to change into their sports clothes and hang up any wet clothing to dry.

Hilda and Pearl took the longest to get ready. Too much talking. They had their hockey outfits on and were giggling and joking as they walked into the maths lesson.

'Jolly hockey sticks,' said Hilda. A final gale of laughter filled them both.

Unfortunately, being the last in the class, everyone else was quiet. The entire class, and the maths teacher, stared at them.

'Are you two quite finished?' said the teacher.

'Sorry Miss, yes Miss,' said Hilda and Pearl in unison. Then they sat down. They stole a quick glance at each other and stifled a giggle.

'We are going to study equations,' said the teacher.

Hilda stared at Pearl, who was miming a yawn. She spluttered a restrained laugh.

'Who was that?' asked the teacher, looking around. Everyone was silent.

'Very well, but any more disturbances and I will take it very seriously.'

Hilda settled down for her usual Maths lesson daydream. Not a subject she enjoyed. After all, why did she need to learn her times tables? She usually travelled to imaginary places in her mind. Today she planned to visit a castle, as a princess, of course. Knights would joust and try to win her favour. A perfect line of soldier's rode up to her. They bowed before their princess; Hilda acknowledged them. There were three lines of seven. Hilda wondered how many in total that came to. What a pity she had no easy way of knowing. Would the dragon visit today? Whenever it did, such havoc and noise ensued. Those flames always caused such damage. Before Hilda knew it, the lesson was over, and she had not even finished her imaginary adventures. Oh well, geography next, more exploits in that class.

Walking between lessons and looking out of the windows, the rain was still hammering down. There were deep puddles everywhere. No outside play today. The playground was just visible through the half misted and rain-soaked windows. It looked like a lake. 'There's one good thing,' thought Hilda, 'no hockey today.'

For the last lesson, all the girls gathered in the sports hall. Time to hear from the sports mistress that hockey had been rained off. Hilda stood next to Pearl at the back. As usual, she was not listening. The room went silent. Hilda was speaking to Pearl, she was partway through saying, '... well, I wasn't going to let her get away with that.' Hilda stopped and looked around at the staring faces. The sports mistress said from the front, 'ah, I see you've joined us at last, Miss Shilton. As you are already in your hockey kit, you can all head straight out onto the pitch.'

'What? But it's raining, Miss,' said Hilda.

'Don't hang about. You'll need to keep moving to keep warm,' said the sports teacher.

***

Hilda stood shivering in the rain. Such cruelty having them play hockey in torrential rain. No doubt the sports mistress would have liked to see Hilda do a bit of actual playing and less standing around grumbling. Just at that moment, the hockey ball was hurtling towards Hilda. An opposition team member had propelled it. Hilda's team was shouting to her, something about defending. By the time Hilda had understood what was required of her, she was watching the opposing team member send the ball into her goal. This would not add to her popularity in team games, as they already chose her last. Still, she reasoned, they cannot choose you less than last.

After the game, only Pearl walked back with Hilda. The goal Hilda had let in lost them the game; her teammates were not pleased. The girls filed into the changing room, dripping with water. Hilda suggested they did not need a shower as they were already so wet.

'You don't need one, anyway. I never saw you move, Silly Shilly,' said one of the other girls. She was using Hilda's nickname, based on her surname, Shilton. All the girls joined in,

'Silly Shilly, silly, Shilly, silly, Shilly, silly Shilly.' They stopped when the sports mistress walked in. The sports mistress said, 'come on girls, don't stand around, you'll catch a chill.'

Sport was always last thing Friday. Hilda and Pearl showered and changed into their now dry clothes from the morning. They were soon wondering why they had bothered. As Hilda and Pearl walked home in torrential rain, their macs did little to keep them dry. A sou'wester would have done little. The rain had become even heavier, and the wind blew horizontally. The paths were now rivers. Hilda and Pearl wished they had wellingtons on.

July 1997

A campsite on the outskirts of New York, USA

Hilda and Pearl sat in the RV in almost identical weather to those school days. The difference being that they were inside, and no cruel schoolteacher was forcing them to play hockey. Hilda looked at Pearl and said, 'you know, one thing I miss about those days.'

'What's that?' said Pearl.

'The lack of aches and pains,' said Hilda. They both nodded and laughed.

Having received the message from William, they mentally noted that they needed to head to Maryland after New York. Many things were going to happen before they reached that state.

New York City, USA

They decided they didn't want to drive a large vehicle into the city. So, they used public transport. Their first port of call was the central library. That always seemed such a reliable source of reference in the movies. If Ruby made it as a cook, there might be an article on her to be found there.

Once they had travelled in by train, they walked the last part to the library. They were typical tourists, staring up at the towering buildings and overwhelmed by the volume of people. As they were walking through a concrete canyon, Hilda stopped and looked up. Pearl noticed and turned around to join her. She tried to see what Hilda was looking at. Hilda was pointing high up, above one of the tall glass and metal buildings. Pearl was one of those people who is ever prepared. She rummaged in her bag and produced a small pair of binoculars.

Two people standing looking up at a building is already a curiosity for other passers-by. If one has a pair of binoculars, that interest is redoubled. A few people stopped and stared, trying to see what Hilda and Pearl were captivated by. Pearl was having difficulty. Even with the use of magnification, it was not clear what Hilda had spotted.

'What is it you've seen?' asked Pearl.

'Remember that film, the one with aliens?' said Hilda.

Unfortunately, the road they were standing on was quite noisy and the only part of the sentence that Pearl heard was aliens. So, she said, 'which film with aliens?'

Some people near the two of them heard the word, aliens. A crowd gathered about five deep. Those further back were asking those in front about what was happening. Various interpretations were given. They ranged from an alien invasion to a film about aliens being made. Some even claimed that a rapper called 'Alliene' was about to turn up in a helicopter.

A passing police patrol car saw the rapidly increasing crowd. They pulled over to check if their help was needed. The person they spoke to told them that a PC gamer had decided to jump off a building after losing a game called, 'Attack of the Aliens.' The officers called for backup to contain the crowd and the fire service arrived to put out a net to break his fall. Then one officer headed into the building to talk down the non-existent gamer. Over the next half an hour, barriers went up, fire trucks arrived, the police chief and mayor heard of the incident. Helicopters and vans from the local and national news arrived. It was quite a story. If only an actual story existed.

Meanwhile, the cause of all the fuss was standing looking up at the building, shaking her head. She turned to Pearl and said, 'no, I don't think they filmed it there. The building shape is wrong.' Then, noticing the crowds, she said, 'Oh my goodness. I think we had better go. It's getting terribly busy here.' Hilda and Pearl pushed and weaved their way through the crowds. As they arrived at the outside edge, a barrier was just being put up by a newly arrived police patrol car. The officer assembling it let them through. It surprised him they were trying to leave, and he said, 'most people are trying to get closer.'

'Closer to what?' said Hilda.

'I'm not sure,' said the young officer, 'a rapper or an alien. All a bit mixed up.'

'An alien?' said Hilda. 'I was right, "An Alien in New York" was shot there.'

'There's a wounded alien?' said the young officer. He grabbed for his radio, but when he turned to ask Hilda more questions, she had gone. He carried on with his update to HQ. Saying into his radio, 'an alien may have been shot, over.'

Pearl had pulled Hilda away from the growing crowd. Having heard Hilda's comment, she did not want her adding confusion to a serious police issue. The entire event turned into a major incident, but that was not a dreadful thing. The police chief and mayor had been planning an exercise in disaster readiness. Once the facts were all in, that it was just a false alarm and they realised there was no emergency. They treated it as an exercise. They told the press they had planned it as a secret exercise all along. It was a face-saving measure, but it worked. The regular news bulletins showing people lying on stretchers having fainted from shock or heat exhaustion in the crowds were then part of the plan. The hundreds of officers milling around, setting up roadblocks and disrupting that part of the city, became part of the plan too. News reporters talked of a well-coordinated effort rather than a folly. One could almost feel that Hilda should have been given a medal for starting this brilliant plan, if they had known it was she who had done so. Seeing the mayor, sitting at his desk in private, checking the costs, head in hands, perhaps it was as well they did not. The police chief was also less bright and magnanimous about the whole affair when sitting looking at his mounting costs.

New York Central Library, USA

After leaving the police cordon around the 'so called' alien invasion, Hilda and Pearl continued towards the library. The streets on their route were much quieter than expected. Everyone was caught up in 'the alien invasion that wasn't.' In 1997, they still housed the main New York Central Library in a copy of a Grecian Temple on Fifth Avenue. That is where Hilda and Pearl arrived after their peaceful walk through the concrete canyons. On arriving at the temple to reading, they asked at reception for the reference library. They were in luck. Normally you needed to book ahead for a microfiche machine, but someone phoned to cancel while they were standing waiting. They had been caught up in a problem downtown, something to do with an alien abduction. Hilda and Pearl were directed to the Bill Blass Public Catalogue Room. They had timed it right as the following week the library was closing for major restorations. In the catalogue room they were set up with a microfiche. As Hilda sat at her station, she felt that all she was lacking was a magnifying glass and a deerstalker hat. Her woolly bonnet didn't seem quite right. 'Daydreaming will not get the job done,' she told herself. So, she set to work.

The two ladies checked the indexes for old newspaper records. They scanned through The New York Times and The New York Post first, each of them taking a paper to search. They searched from 1937 up to the present. If Ruby had come to New York and made it as a cook. The only way to track her would be if she had won a prize or been mentioned in a review. So, they just checked the culinary reviews and awards. That was still a massive amount to check through.

After many hours of searching, they found an article about Ruby Davies from Marlan, Ohio. She had received a promotion at The Walberg Asteridge Hotel to head chef. The existing head chef had retired and passed the baton to her. There were first-hand accounts of her culinary genius. They planned to visit the Walberg the next day. While they were at the library, they checked the name Victoria Worth. Nothing came up. If they had thought about it longer, they would have realised they needed to check back to the 1920's and 1930's. Some mysteries take longer to uncover; besides, Victoria had travelled to the UK in 1920 and married Lucian Kendall in 1927 in London.

Walberg Asteridge Hotel, New York, USA

Next day, Hilda and Pearl, decide to arrive at the Walberg Asteridge Hotel, in style. So, they got a taxi to drop them at the entrance rather than just walk up. A doorman, decked out in uniform, opened the door, and welcomed them to the hotel. The doorman knew all the current guests and seemed surprised when the taxi drove off, leaving no luggage for these new guests. He turned and opened the entrance door, his hand in a casual position, ready to accept any gratuity. Hilda saw his hand and, thinking she understood something of American culture, gave him a low five hand slap. The doorman checked his hand, expecting money to have been transferred; but it was empty.

Hilda strode up to the reception desk with Pearl a little behind. There were no other guests waiting, but the receptionist was on the phone. She was handling yet another cancellation. Ever since the alien shenanigans of the day before, regulars had been cancelling. Unbeknown to her, the cause of her troubles stood before her. Hilda saw a bell and hit it firmly. The receptionist glanced up and frowned. She finished her call and said, 'welcome to The Walberg Asteridge. May I take your name, please?' Any surprise at their mode of attire had long been overcome by the variety of rock, pop and film stars that frequently stood before her.

'It's not my name that is important, dear,' said Hilda.

'I beg your pardon?' said the receptionist.

'Ruby Davies is the important one,' said Hilda.

The receptionist looked beyond Hilda at Pearl, standing expectantly behind. She was used to PA's and managers sorting things out for millionaires and stars of various sorts. 'I see, Ruby Davies,' said the receptionist. She looked through the bookings list. 'No, I can't find her.'

'Well, you wouldn't, would you? Not in that book,' said Hilda.

'Does she not have a reservation? I am sure we can sort something out for our more important clients,' said the receptionist. There were plenty of rooms available.

'I'm sure she has a lot of reservations,' said Hilda, looking behind her at Pearl and shrugging. 'But the important thing now is to look in the kitchen.'

'Our kitchens are of the utmost quality. The standard is unparalleled anywhere,' said the receptionist.

Hilda smiled and said, 'yes, we know, she is an excellent chef. A culinary genius.'

The receptionist nodded in understanding, a false understanding. She must have assumed that Pearl was a celebrity chef. 'I can, of course, arrange for you to be shown the kitchens as a professional courtesy. If you would like that?'

Pearl came forward and said, 'yes please.'

The receptionist obviously felt that Pearl was important enough to warrant a manager as an escort. She called the duty manager through to take them on a guided tour of the kitchen. He'd been having his break and came in, still smoking a cigar. He asked the ladies if they minded him finishing it, as it was a nice one; not to be wasted. They both enjoyed the smell of a quality cigar and were happy to let him continue.

As they all entered the extensive kitchens, Pearl was excited. She was ready to meet her twin sister for the first time. The kitchen was a busy and noisy place, sou chefs and chef de parti preparing lunch. Kitchen porters bustling around; the washing up pile was already high with all the preparatory utensils. It sounded like they had entered a multi-cultural bar, all the languages being shouted and spoken around them. The head chef was standing over in one corner, her back to them all. Pearl could hardly contain her excitement. Could this be her long-lost twin sister?

The head chef of The Walberg Asteridge, Jen Li, had a brilliant sense of smell. She needed it, along with a great palette. The duty manager may enjoy a nice cigar, but Jen did not allow them in her kitchen. Turning around, she shouted, 'get out of my kitchen, no smoking allowed!'

The manager apologised and left smartly. Pearl stopped mid-stride and stared at the stranger before her. They had a short and awkward conversation; Jen knew nothing of the chefs before her time. Then Pearl and Hilda joined the manager in the corridor. It confused him who they were and why they were visiting. After a fraught conversation he returned to his interrupted break time, leaving Hilda and Pearl with the receptionist. She was now far less helpful. When they tried to gain information on Ruby, they were told; it was confidential.

They left the hotel feeling sad and with no other avenues to pursue. Pearl was feeling very low after the temporary high of thinking they were near.

Chapter Fourteen

July 1997

A campsite on the outskirts of New York, USA

When Hilda and Pearl returned to their RV from the Walberg Hotel, there was a general mood of despondency. They sat down for an evening meal in an unusual silence. Pearl was exhausted and downhearted. She said, 'we'll never find my sister, nor who murdered her parents.'

'Nonsense dear, with me on the case, we will have this case solved in no time.' Hilda sounded more confident than she felt.

Hilda tried to cheer Pearl up, but none of her usual methods worked and they went to sleep that night, both feeling quite low. Next morning, Hilda got up and went for a walk around the campsite. She met a man from Somerset, Kentucky. When he told Hilda all about his Somerset, she was astonished. They compared notes. Somerset, England, was a place Hilda had visited many times as a child, especially Weston-Super-Mare and Clevedon. They quickly realised that the two places could not be more different if they tried. Somerset, Kentucky, was hot and humid. Somerset, England, was wet and often cool. When they compared recollections of the two Somerset's, they laughed at the differences.

Pearl came looking for Hilda to say that breakfast was ready, and the man from Somerset, Kentucky, said his wife would be looking for him. As they parted ways, the man asked if they had been to see any Broadway shows yet. Pearl said that she didn't want to go to one. But Hilda liked the sound of it and after pleading with Pearl all day, she finally relented. She agreed that they both needed a break, and maybe it would give them fresh eyes for their detection.

When they tried phoning the box offices at a few theatres, all the shows were fully booked for many weeks ahead. But before hanging up on one theatre, the person on the phone suggested a place they could try for re-sales. They found a show that they both fancied seeing and they bought the tickets for the following night. Not great tickets. They were way up in 'the gods,' the upper circle. So, they got hold of some binoculars for Hilda. Pearl already had some which had been useful in the alien hunt.

Hotel Room, the Bronx, New York, USA

At a small run-down hotel in the Bronx Jake was going over the details of his plan with a professional hit man. Jake had hired him to help regain the stolen diamonds from Hilda. Not that he particularly wanted to kill Hilda, although if that happened, he would not be unhappy. The other night at the campsite, he had only planned to frighten them with his gun. It was only a replica, anyway. After the fight he received he had changed his approach. He needed someone who would stop at nothing to get the jewels back. If that meant killing one or both troublesome old women, so be it. He was running out of time and patience. The last thing he wanted was for B to order a hit on him for failing in the job she had given him.

Jake had the right man for the job, highly recommended. He could not afford to fail. With his professional back up, he would succeed. Everything should be perfect. Since when do things go perfectly?

It was a sweltering day, and the hotel room had no air conditioning. They were both wearing suits, highly incongruous in the setting and unsuitable to the conditions. The hired hit man shook his head and said, 'all of this for some old bird?'

Jake stared at him and said, 'she's slipped through my fingers several times.'

The hit man shrugged. 'It's your money.' He removed his gun from a metal case, expertly took it apart, cleaned it and reassembled it, then put it in his holster.

Jake watched him and nodded. Jake was smiling. Far too prematurely.

New York City, USA

Next afternoon, Hilda and Pearl travelled by train into the city. Jake and his hired help had used the bug planted in Hilda's RV to track them to their current campsite. They had arrived earlier and were now shadowing them the whole way. Jake wanted to find a quiet place to jump Hilda. The campsite was not it. Besides campsites now haunted Jake. He preferred anywhere but a campsite. By the time Hilda and Pearl arrived in New York City, they were tired and hungry. So, they searched for a restaurant - it was still a couple of hours until the show.

The restaurant they choose was a family run Italian called Papa De Luca's. The restaurant, tucked down a quiet side road, had been styled to appear just like a small Italian Town, rather than the centre of New York. Papa, De Luca's grandson Roberto and his wife Sophia now ran it. Inside, the effect was even more strikingly Italian. Another thing added authenticity to the New York Italian feel. Two heavies waiting outside, intent on doing the ladies harm - it felt like a mafia movie. Jake's hit man was getting impatient. He wanted to just go into the restaurant and snatch the bag there. Jake told him to wait until they were somewhere quieter. There were too many people about. Instead, they also went inside the restaurant for a meal and watched the two ladies.

As it was early evening, the restaurant was only half full when Hilda and Pearl arrived. A few regulars were scattered around the cosy interior. Italian music was playing softly in the background. Roberto and Sophia turned out to be a lovely couple. They not only cooked tasty food but gave guests a warm welcome. The moment they realised it was Hilda and Pearl's first trip to New York and to their restaurant, they treated them like royalty. Nothing was too much trouble. Roberto and Sophia explained the menu and chatted about the local New York, Italian culture. After the meal, Hilda asked them to come and sit at their table. They all shared family stories. Hilda was interested in the music they were playing and what kinds of dancing they did. Before she could drag Roberto up for a dance, Pearl told them of her hunt for her twin sister. She explained the blank they had drawn trying to find her in New York. It disappointed Hilda that her opportunity for a dance went by, but happy to let Pearl talk about her twin sister.

Sophia told them she had heard the name Ruby Davie's as a famous cook. But couldn't remember when or in what context, but it was recently. No matter how much she tried to remember, she couldn't. When they left, Hilda gave them William's office details. That way, if she remembered, she could contact him. He could then pass on the information to Hilda and Pearl at their next phone call.

Hilda and Pearl so enjoyed their time with Roberto and Sophia that time slipped by. Pearl saw it was getting late and told Sophia they would miss their Broadway show. Fortunately, Roberto could fetch them a cab fast. Sophia's brother, Ricardo, was a taxi driver. Jake overheard and requested their bill; he sent his hit man out to call them a cab while he paid.

***

In Ricardo's taxi, Hilda and Pearl found he was a driver who had no concern for safety or the rules of the road. Ricardo sped through New York, honking his horn, and shouting out of his open window. Acting like everyone else was in his way, but they arrived fast. Jake and his accomplice had paid for a cab to follow. It had a hard job keeping up. But the extra cash Jake offered meant that he just about managed.

Broadway, New York, USA

On arrival at the theatre, the front was so busy that Ricardo suggested dropping them on a side street. Hilda and Pearl were just keen to disembark. As they got out, Pearl said she would join the queue, then give Hilda her share of the taxi money later. Hilda paid the taxi and followed Pearl.

Jake's taxi pulled up behind Ricardo a minute later. This was their moment, a quiet side alley, Hilda on her own just leaving the taxi and heading up the side street. It was perfect; Jake paid for the taxi while the hit man leapt out. Jake made sure that the driver was looking at him rather than the street. That way, he would not see the attack.

By the time Jake's hit man leapt from the taxi, Hilda had disappeared. Moments earlier, after paying Ricardo, she had been heading past the stage door towards the front of the theatre. The door opened, and a young man spotted Hilda. He said, 'at last, come on, this way.' Then grabbed Hilda and pulled her into the door, closing it after him. Jake's hit man stared up the empty street, puzzled.

Hilda's normal clothing was an exact match for the costume of lead in the show. If it surprised the stagehand that the principal actor was already in full costume out in the street, he didn't show it. All he showed was relief. He had been checking out of the door every two minutes. The actual star of the show was extremely late. So, the stagehand rushed Hilda in through the stage door, expressing gratitude the whole time that she'd finally arrived. The stagehands' thanks and praise, along with an entry through the stage door, prevented Hilda from complaining. She loved to be treated as special. It didn't occur to her that Pearl might wonder where she was.

The hit man turned to Jake, who had just finished paying for the taxi and was now on the street and said, 'she's gone.'

'What do ya mean, gone?' asked Jake. He glanced up and down the street.

He had expected to see his accomplice holding the bag and Hilda on the floor dead or at least injured. Instead, he saw an empty street. In the distance, Pearl was rounding the corner to the front. She was also looking round, wondering where

Hilda had gone. Not seeing her, she carried on to the queue, obviously thinking Hilda could catch up. The hit man stared at Jake and shrugged. Jake walked over to the wall and kicked it. His foot hurt, and he leapt up and down.

On Pearl's arrival at the box office, Hilda had still not caught up. So, Pearl left Hilda's theatre ticket there, with her name and description, then headed inside and climbed all the stairs to take her seat in the upper circle.

After kicking the wall Jake hobbled over to his accomplice. He told him to stay outside and watch for Hilda in case she reappeared, then limped painfully towards the theatre. He had seen Pearl at the corner and was going to follow her. There were ticket touts hanging around and he bought an expensive ticket. Inside, he wandered down to the front of the theatre and looked back towards the audience. He spotted Pearl high in the circle and headed upward.

Meanwhile, Hilda had arrived at makeup. The costume designer stared at what Hilda was wearing and then at the costume on his hanger. He huffed and walked off. The makeup artist shook her head and told Hilda that the costume designer could be a drama queen. Having been prepared backstage, they then took Hilda to the wings, ready to enter on cue. Being dark in the wings, her fellow actors could only see the costume and assumed it was the correct actress.

The real actress arrived late and started banging on the stage door. Her taxi had broken down, and she had to walk the last block. Jake's hit man checked his photo of Hilda against the woman banging at the stage door – nothing like her. This was not the week for this famous actress. The other day she had been caught up in a false alarm over a suspected alien takeover of New York. No one answered her banging on the stage door. They had everyone they expected, and drunks sometimes banged on the door.

***

Hilda stepped out on stage; this was where she was meant to be. It was a musical comedy, and she knew the song and started singing at the top of her voice. The opening number was a complex song and dance. Hilda loved dancing; such a grand passion for her. But she was not Broadway standard. She had a good go at copying her fellow dancers. Not that the lead actress was meant to just copy the chorus. The lead actress had special moves, ones that Hilda knew nothing about. Moves that the choreographer, watching, horrified in the wings, had planned, and sweated over for months.

Various chorus line dancers waved and signalled, indicated, and gesticulated to Hilda. Trying to get her to go to her line or position. They even tried to show a few of her moves. The total effect to the audience was increasingly funny, which, for a musical comedy, worked brilliantly. Unfortunately for the director and stage managers, it was less convincing; they stared in shock from the wings. The other dancers and actors made the best of things. They tried to fill in missing moves, take hold of Hilda and fire fight the mistakes. They deserved a medal, or at least a pay rise, none of which they received.

The opening number was building to its crescendo, where Hilda was meant to mount a circular rising platform in the middle of the stage. There was a semi-circle of fireworks that would go off behind her. Whilst on the platform, they clipped her on a wire. She already had the harness on. They fitted it when she was offstage. Then, during the fireworks, she would rise into the air on the last notes of the song, while the chorus line all turned towards her and waved flags. The overall spectacle would be awesome.

Several of the other actors had realised Hilda was not the right actress and this finale could go very wrong. Having subtly checked she had the harness on, they then started corralling her towards the platform that would rise. The director threw his script on the floor as he watched three people mount the central platform. The crew who operated it checked the weight limit and decided it should hold. Just as well, dancers weigh only a little. Once Hilda was dancing around in the centre of the rising section, the two dancers on either side of her clipped the wire into her harness. They then stepped off just in time as it rose. The fireworks went off, and they joined the chorus line of flags.

Three lots of fireworks went off simultaneously. To understand all three, we need to step back a few minutes. One stagehand fancied a quick cigarette and on opening the stage door, in burst the actual star of the show. She pushed past him and ran to the side of the stage, arriving just as they connected Hilda to the wire. She was too professional to burst on stage. Instead, she grabbed the director and exploded, metaphorically, like a firework in his face.

The second lot of fireworks came because Jake had reached Pearl and was demanding to know where her friend was. Just as he asked that question, Pearl lifted a wavering hand to the stage. Jake turned, saw Hilda and shouted some expletives. Pearl stood and told him to wash his mouth out with soap. The surrounding audience shouted shhh! Then an usher tried to escort Jake from the building. He was punched on the nose for his trouble and Jake left anyway, at speed. Jake was on route to the backstage area to find Hilda. Pearl was also finding herself motivated to get backstage.

The real fireworks were, of course, on stage. Having been hooked onto a wire, Hilda found her range of movement limited. As the music built to a crescendo, she wanted to do something dramatic, so she spun. That was all she found she was free to do. The wire then lifted her, and the spin speed increased. A selection of multi-coloured flashing lights shone up towards her spinning form, then the fireworks went off. They were noise, mixed with a shower of sparks and tinsel. Banners dropped from the rear of the set and the chorus line all formed a semi-circle in front, waving their flags. The total effect was quite spectacular. The audience went wild, standing, cheering, whistling, shouting encore.

So that she could take a bow, Hilda was lowered, and two actors came to unhook her. She was feeling dizzy after spinning and staggered a bit, but her fans needed a bow. They got a wobbly one, which they assumed was acting. The real actress was seething in the wings. The curtain came down, but before Hilda could be removed, the sheer level of applause, and shouts of encore, forced another curtain call.

Once the final curtain came down, the director questioned Hilda. He realised it was not her fault, so she was just asked to leave. But as she was leaving, a throng of press arrived to praise the amazing new lead actress. The director changed his mind and asked if she could do any more shows, much to the horror of the real actress. Hilda looked at the press, the horrified actress, and the director. Then said, 'I have had a wonderful time, thank you dear, but my friend Pearl and I are on holiday.'

'You're a tourist?' said the director, open-mouthed.

'Of course,' said Hilda.

The real actress was aghast. She said, 'she shouldn't have gone on, anyway. I bet she's not even a member of Equity?'

'Equity, what that?' asked Hilda. Then she walked off to find Pearl. Who was standing at the stage door banging and being refused entry.

The director turned to the real actress, and the assembled press, biting his lip, and wringing his hands.

Jake had paid the stagehand to let him in along with his hit man. However, they had been directed to the wrong person and had grabbed the actual star of the show, putting a bag over her head from behind. They only realised outside when they took the bag off. This gave Hilda a chance to escape unnoticed. Hilda and Pearl headed back to their campsite by train. Hilda was full of the excitement of being in a Broadway show.

Jake and his accomplice headed off downhearted. The hit man kept saying that Jake should have listened to him. That resulted in him being paid off and sent packing. Jake thought that Hilda and Pearl were much more clever adversaries than he had first assumed. If only he knew the truth, they were just lucky.

***

The next day, William phoned his mother to check she was all right. She just talked about the Broadway musical. It has sometimes been suggested that as you get older, your memory gets poorer, but Hilda's memory had never been wonderful. So, it is not a surprise that after all the excitement of her accidental starring role in the musical. Hilda totally forgot to tell

William to expect a phone call. The restaurant owner Sophia might phone with information about Ruby.

TSU Corp Office, Chicago, USA

It is the nature of business that they get phone calls from many people that are of absolutely no interest to them. They give these calls many names, cold calls, time wasters, sales calls, but whatever you call them, you just don't want them. The Chicago office was based in a building with a shared reception. A call came through from the reception. Sophia De Luca was phoning from an Italian Restaurant in New York for William. He told the receptionist it must be a call about audits and to refer her to the New York office. The receptionist was overly diligent in her duty. Even when Sophia explained she needed to talk to William on a private matter, she would not put her through. She decided Sophia must be trying to sell something.

The real reason Sophia was phoning was because she had remembered something. The day after Hilda and Pearl left her restaurant, she remembered where she had seen Pearl's sister, Ruby Davies' name, mentioned. Sophia had been reading one of the food magazines, and an article in it had been about Ruby. The article was all about her rags to riches, rise to fame. It described how this small-town girl found fame and fortune in New York in the 1930's. How she had a natural talent which was discovered by a Michelin star chef, who took her on as an assistant. It then told the story of how some years later this chef had retired, then recommended Ruby's takeover from him. He was the head chef at the Walberg Asteridge hotel. Ruby's innovative and creative cooking had drawn people to the hotel restaurant from all over the country. One person who particularly loved to eat there was the current first lady, Evelyn. She first went there with her father when she was a child. He owned the hotel chain. In later years, she went with her fiancé, Doug Meyer. He was a politician, who after they were married ran for president and won.

When Evelyn's husband became President Meyer, The First Lady had been keen to employ Ruby as the White House chef. It had taken some convincing, but in the end, Ruby had agreed. Seeing it as a once in a lifetime opportunity. Evelyn's father was the most disappointed to lose such an amazing chef. But his daughter's wishes always came first, so he made no objection. He would have opportunities to dine at The White House residence with his daughter.

None of this amazing story made its way to William at first. But Italian women are not so easily fobbed off. She called her brother, Ricardo, the speed demon taxi driver, and told him to drop everything. She had a vital mission. The business executive he was transporting did not understand why he was unceremoniously dropped off. But, if Sophia called, then Ricardo answered - immediately. It had always been so since they were little. Despite the urgent response, Sophia was still tapping her toes when Ricardo arrived.

Ricardo looked apologetic as he pulled up. Sophia jumped into the taxi. She had no time for excuses and said, 'just go, fast.' She passed him the address.

TSU Corp Office, New York, USA

We should note that Sophia was a beautiful young lady. She had also dressed ready for a meal out with her husband later, as it was their regular date night. The TSU office in New York was the nearest office address that Sophia had. She had phoned the Chicago office, where William was currently based. But would not travel that far, just to pass on some information. She reasoned that if she turned up at one of William's offices and explained the personal and urgent nature of her business, he would speak to her. It was not the best course of action for William's moral reputation.

Sophia arrived at the small TSU New York Office. She could easily gain entry at the building's main reception. Her looks distracted the young guy manning the main reception. He just let her through with a nod. She ascended the elevator. The TSU office lacked its own reception desk. Sophia walked straight into Karen's personal office, being nearest to the elevator. Karen looked up at the uninvited interloper and asked, 'can I help you?'

'I have urgent and personal business with William,' said Sophia. She had a breathless, husky quality to her voice. Karen was unimpressed and impatient at being interrupted by an uninvited visitor.

'He's in the Chicago Office,' said Karen.

'I know. He will not take my call,' said Sophia.

'I see,' said Karen. But what she saw was probably not what Sophia meant. She stared at the vision of Italian loveliness before her.

'Can you phone him and tell him to take my call?' asked Sophia. Her eyes widened, but Karen just snorted.

Tom knocked on the door and said, 'Karen, have you...' he paused, gazing at Sophia, who turned to look at him. He said to Sophia, 'hi, I'm Tom.'

'I need to speak to William,' said Sophia. She tipped her head slightly. She was wearing a beautiful sapphire necklace, set in an intricate gold filigree clasp, it hung some way below her neckline. The sapphire fascinated Tom. He was admiring the workmanship of the clasp, or the way the sapphire caught the light.

'Tom, did you need something?' asked Karen.

'Did I?' said Tom. He looked dazed. 'I've forgotten.'

'I must sort this out now. Can you come back?' said Karen.

'How about I help this young lady,' said Tom. Walking up to Sophia, 'and you get on with your important work?'

'Oh, can you help… Tom, is it?' said Sophia, with what seemed like a genuine girlish glee.

'You just come with me,' said Tom, leading Sophia out of Karen's office before she could object. Sophia allowed herself to be led by the hand. She explained she needed to urgently call William on a private matter, Tom's eyebrows raised.

Ray was next to the coffee machine, and he noticed Sophia being led out of Karen's office by Tom. He went over to see if he could assist. He appeared equally surprised at William's 'friend.' Although he also seemed quite interested in the ground around her as she walked. Sophia was used to being a distraction to men and had occasionally used it to her advantage. Most of the time, she found it insulting and demeaning, as she often told her closest friends. Her husband, Roberto, was a man who saw her as a complete person, the beauty outside and within. Sophia stood watching Tom and Ray fluster and fuss around her. She seemed faintly amused, but also expectant of help.

Tom phoned the Chicago office. Ray stood nearby, looking like an eager puppy. They told Tom that William was not in. So, Tom explained to the Chicago office why he was calling. He said, 'there's a young lady here.' Tom nodded at Sophia. 'An incredibly beautiful young lady.' Sophia smiled wearily. 'She needs to speak to William urgently on a very private matter.'

After being asked for Sophia's phone number, he requested it, and she wrote it on a piece of paper and passed it to him. He gave the number to the Chicago office, then hung up. He also popped the paper with her number in his pocket.

Chapter Fifteen

July 1997

Leithly Hall Somershire, UK

Back in the UK, a break in the case against Jake Vort, AKA, The Ghost, had occurred. Jayne, the Duchess of Somershire, returned from her holiday in the USA. She had been staying with her friend Penelope Kendal, whom she called Bonbon. She was unaware that Penelope headed an international criminal organisation. To Jayne, Bonbon was just her old school friend. Whenever Penelope had Jayne visit, she made sure all evidence of her true occupation had been hidden. Is it called an occupation when you pedal in murder, extortion, blackmail and selling drugs?

Jayne had used her husband's safe to store important documents and her own jewellery. So, on her return to the UK, she placed her passport and travel jewellery back in it. Whilst she had the safe open, she decided, on a whim, to enjoy her recently inherited diamonds. Holding them up to the window light, she noticed a difference in their glow. Whilst she was no diamond expert, the eyes of Hora diamonds had a special something about them. She suspected they were not genuine. Later she had experts confirm it.

Jayne was not only wealthy, but wise. She had fitted additional hidden security systems to her house. Having bought them on a whim and fitted them herself, only she knew of their existence. A purchase she made in Japan on holiday, they sold everything electronic there. The man selling it had explained that even a child could set it up. An insult perhaps, but her technical skills were not great. It was a pin-hole camera that filmed in infra-red, ultra-violet and ordinary light all at once. The Ghost had become overconfident in his abilities to wipe all evidence of his burglaries. When he took the diamonds from the safe, he took off his mask whilst admiring them. Now Interpol had their first photographs of The Ghost and they found he was traceable. Jake Vort was not a ghost, after all. He had a UK driving licence and passport; they set about tracking him down and finding out all about him. He had relied on not being seen, rather than an alias.

A hotel, New York City, USA

Ignorant that his identity was now known. Jake was in a New York hotel planning his next move. Having got rid of his hit man, he now needed a team of even better-quality professionals, people he could trust, people as efficient and effective as himself. They say that people are blind to their own faults. But perhaps he just needed more feet on the ground.

TSU Corp Office, Chicago, USA

People can be quick to judge and take extraordinarily little information to create entire stories about others. The Chicago office of TSU only had four staff, but they were chatty. Or is that gossipy? Jane had taken the phone call from Tom in their New York office about Sophia that was meant for William. She called her colleague Sarah over. This was valuable information that needed sharing. Jane had already added to the phone call she received, as she said to Sarah, 'that British guy, you know, the one who's over here to interfere.'

'William Shilton,' said Sarah.

'That's the one, well he has a mistress here, an Italian one,' said Jane.

'What! But I thought his wife was with him.'

'So, he says, but have you met her?' Jane pursed her lips.

'The dark horse,' said Sarah.

'Not only does he have a mistress, but she's coming here. I have a phone number for him to arrange the details.'

'It makes me sick the way men carry on.' Sarah shook her head.

***

A bit later, Sarah was at the coffee machine with other staff members, Dean and Simon, the office manager. Sarah said, 'William isn't the clean-living guy we all thought.'

'Less gossip, more work,' said Simon. He walked off.

Sarah pretended she was speaking to Dean and said, 'his mistress is on her way here, a drop-dead gorgeous Italian. Young enough to be his daughter.'

Simon stopped and turned around. He asked, 'what?'

'The New York office phoned to confirm it all. I guess they wanted to warn us, what kind of guy he is. Not clean-living Bible Believers like us,' said Sarah. She sipped her coffee. This was an odd comment from her, as the only use she had for a Bible was levelling up an old table.

Dean shook his head in disgust. He slept with a different girl most weekends. If he were not so busy at work, it would be every night. But morals are something we hold up to judge others by; not ourselves. Jesus said something about a speck of dust in our brother's eye and a plank in our own, warning us not to judge others. The Chicago office staff of TSU had either not read that part in The Bible or felt it didn't apply to them. Maybe they hadn't read the Bible at all. By the time William came back into the office from an important business meeting, one that would secure all their jobs for many years to come. The Chicago staff were all ready to judge him as an adulterer, a cheat, and a philanderer. Some of them were half watching the door, expecting a young Italian girl to burst in. William asked Jane if there were any messages. She slammed a note on the desk with Sophia's number on it. He glanced at it, screwed up his face and asked, 'who's this?'

Jane snorted and said, 'I'm sure I don't know.'

William stuck the paper in his pocket. After he had been sitting in his office for a few minutes, Simon knocked and came in.

Simon started carefully by saying, 'business in America is very ethical.' He stared at William in what he hoped was a meaningful way. 'We believe in a high moral standard.'

'Same in the UK.' William glanced up at Simon, his brow furrowed.

'It's important that staff are not seen as doing anything…' Simon stopped, gazed out the window for a moment. 'Unsavoury.'

William nodded and said, 'absolutely, I would hope that you would come down hard on anyone doing anything like that.'

'Well, here's the thing, I don't have the authority in every case,' said Simon. He shuffled uncomfortably.

William sat up straight. 'I grant you the authority.' William thought the matter resolved. He picked up some paperwork and read the columns of numbers.

'Oh!' said Simon. He stared at William for a moment and then blinked hard. 'Ah, well, umm. I think it's important to be above reproach. Don't you agree?'

William distractedly said, 'yes quite.'

'Married men should not be seen to stray,' said Simon.

'Absolutely,' said William. He started jotting notes next to the columns of numbers.

Simon became bolder. William agreed, rather than getting cross. He said, 'in no circumstances should they have mistresses.'

'Yes, yes,' said William. He ticked the column with satisfaction, then he looked up with a smile. 'Was there anything else?'

'No, I think that covers it,' said Simon. He walked out with a half-smile. He told the staff that he had dealt with the situation.

***

At the next pre-arranged phone call between William and Hilda. They had a general chat and planned on where to meet in Maryland. It was not until William was saying goodbye that Pearl mentioned Sophia. She asked if he had heard from her. He had almost forgotten about the attempted call and the message in his pocket. Taking it out, he promised to ring after they hung up. When William rang Papa De Luca's restaurant, Sophia was busy, but called him back after ten minutes. She was cross. It had taken so long to get hold of him but told him about the newspaper article. William called back Hilda and Pearl; they had been waiting in a café. At last, they found out that Ruby had a job at The White House.

But that left Pearl with a problem. How could she get in to see her sister at The White House? Was there a public phone number? Could you ring the switchboard and ask for the kitchen? They headed back to their RV to think it through and chat to some locals. It felt as if they had found her, but in the most inaccessible place.

Hilda was overjoyed that they had found Ruby. But it still left a mystery to solve. Who killed Ruby's parents? How could they solve that?

A hotel room, Bethesda, Maryland, USA

William's last TSU Corp office to set up was in Maryland, close to Washington, DC. He and Louise moved on from Chicago to a hotel nearby. This was the office William had told Louise he had least looked forward to. Larry Campbell lived in the area. He was Harold's university friend and the future CEO of TSU Corp once it was all up and running. Larry had already been in touch a few times with William, and they had booked to meet in Maryland.

Louise asked William why he was looking so distracted during their evening meal. Which was when it all came out about his anxieties. William said to Louise, 'Larry's such a successful entrepreneur. I feel intimidated. I don't enjoy his sense of humour.' Louise glanced away, a smile playing on her lips. Then, having straightened her face, she looked back and said, 'it'll be fine.'

When William met with Larry the next day, it was an anti-climax. No teasing, no jokes, just business. Larry did not make him feel small or inadequate. The meeting was helpful. Things were organised and set in motion. However, there was one amazing revelation. Larry told William that his daughter was The First Lady, married to the President of the United States. It took a while before the meaning of that sunk in. William was glad Larry had left that information until the end. He felt off balance after hearing it.

Bethesda, Maryland, USA

After returning from his lunchtime meeting with Larry, William had the afternoon free. He spent it with Louise. They were staying at a hotel in Bethesda. It was a beautiful sunny afternoon, and they set off to walk into the town centre.

There was some sort of event on. Stalls were laid out on either side of one street selling craft and paintings. Louise enjoyed herself, stopping at every stall. It was busy, but there was plenty of space to get around. William was not really that interested in art, so he held back from the stalls. Every so often he would be called over to appreciate a piece Louise was viewing until he saw the price. At which point, he then pointed out its failings.

They found a coffee shop with tables outside; it had a Parisian feel about it. They sat soaking up the sunshine and drinking the coffee. Louise looked happy with her newly purchased art. William appeared content to have stopped shopping. They were the picture of a holidaying couple.

'No work this afternoon?' asked Larry. He seemed to appear from nowhere. William jumped. He had been half asleep in the sunshine.

'Oh! Hello, umm, well, yes, no,' said William, stammering.

'We are having a break, Larry,' said Louise. She smiled up at him.

'OK for some,' said Larry, a twinkle in his eyes.

'Do you live near here?' asked Louise.

'Just up the road, would you like to visit?' said Larry. 'You're obviously not busy.'

'Ah, now I have work to do. This was just...,' said William.

Larry cut him off and said, 'relax, I'm just joshing, come over to mine.' He led them to his car, parked nearby, and drove them out of town to a hilly wooded area. They drove up a long driveway and then came to a high metal gate. He pressed a button in the car, and it opened. The driveway inside was long and winding. They passed tennis courts on one side and a swimming pool on the other. The house seemed raised as they approached it. There were three other cars parked out front. William thought Larry had guests but found out later that they were all Larry's.

The front doors were huge double doors. A lady in a grey uniform greeted them. Larry asked her to fetch drinks for them by the pool, and they headed to the swimming pool. The pool was part shaded by a wooden structure. They sat beneath it on wonderfully comfortable chairs. It was not long before the drinks arrived, shortly followed by a tall, beautiful woman. She was introduced as Larry's wife, Helen.

Larry used the opportunity to chat to William about business strategies. Helen complained that he never stopped working and sent the two of them off into Larry's study. She and Louise enjoyed the peace by the pool. It was such a warm day that she suggested a swim and found a spare costume for Louise. When William and Larry finally joined them again, Helen and Louise were floating in the pool, drinks in hand. Helen suggested they stay for an evening meal, on the proviso that Larry refrained from work talk at the table.

Before the meal Larry was keen to show them around his extensive grounds. At the back he had a small helicopter on its own landing pad. He told William that he could get to Dulles Airport in minutes, where he had a private jet. William commented on how brilliant that must be. He often had to sit in traffic to get to work by car and he only lived ten minutes from the office. Larry suggested William could become rich and have his own helicopter and private jet if he applied himself. William just shook his head.

The White House living quarters, Washington DC, USA

Most people assumed that being The First Lady meant that Evelyn Meyer lead a charmed life. Somehow avoiding all the normal things which ordinary people go through. Anyone thinking that, would be shocked by reality. It was the school holidays, so the Meyer's children were home and still asleep in bed. Doug Jnr. aged eleven and Amber aged nine and ¾. Those

¾ were important and should not be forgotten, on pain of death. Evelyn had kissed her husband goodbye that morning. Doug Meyer, or 'The Leader of The Free World,' as he liked to remind her, when he was losing an argument, was off running the country. She really wanted to get on with all the charitable causes she valued. But she objected to leaving the care of her children to others, unless essential. These were critical and formative times with her children, as she kept telling her husband, her friends, and her staff. It was 9 am, and she repeated her call to her children, room by room, 'Time to get up!'

Doug Jnr. was still under his duvet and no sound came back to her. Amber half opened sleepy eyes and turned over. The third time must have been some inbuilt limit for Evelyn. She pulled back Doug's covers and shouted, 'now buddy, move it!'

He jolted and sat up saying, 'what gives mom?'

She repeated the like to Amber, who stared at her shocked and said, 'mom!'

A few minutes later, two dishevelled figures, vaguely resembling the Meyer children, were sitting in the kitchen. Even The First Family had breakfast watching TV. Evelyn was cooking waffles. Not a usual occurrence, judging by the stares from her children and the comment from Amber, 'I want Angel Krispies, like always.'

The phone rang and Evelyn grabbed it, as if it was a lifeline, 'yes?... Oh dad.'

'Hi sweetheart, you sound stressed. You, OK?' asked Larry Meyer.

'Fine,' said Evelyn sharply.

Larry knew when to pursue a subject, and when to leave it, so he said, 'fancy lunch?'

'What! You coming here?' asked Evelyn. She knew her dad preferred Ruby's cooking to anywhere else, except... 'or Big Joe's Burgers?'

'You mind reader,' said Larry.

Evelyn turned to the kids and said, 'gramps wants to take us to Big Joes.'

Larry felt he could hear the cheering, not just down the phone, but across the miles. Evelyn only allowed her kids to go there on rare occasions. Larry said, 'see you there, at one.'

'Dad?'

Larry had the phone part way down. He put it to his ear again. 'What is it, sweetheart?'

Evelyn walked a bit of a way from the kids and said quietly, 'was it hard?'

Larry was silent for a moment, looking at the books on his study wall, then said, 'you mean the kids? Was it hard bringing you and your brother up?'

'Guess so.' Evelyn changed from one foot to the other and bit her lip.

Larry sighed. 'But you know what? I wouldn't change it for the world.'

She hung up and walked back to the kitchen. The waffles were burning, and Doug Jnr. was just asking if he could play with his Nintendo. Evelyn looked longingly at the door.

Big Joes Burgers, Washington DC, USA

The manager of the local Big Joes Burgers had a love hate relationship with a visit from The First Family. It was fantastic advertising. People wanted to go where they had been.

But when they visited, the security teams descended first and cleared out a large section. He lost most of his seating area.

Evelyn always used a trip to Big Joes as an excuse to forget any diets. That applied to the whole family. It was an occasional treat. Seated in a large booth, the four of them had their meals laid out on trays. Evelyn had a Big Joe Double with fries and a diet coke. Her dad had a Big Joe Triple Stack, his fries and coke were extra-large, Doug Jnr copied his gramps. Amber was currently off beef and had Big Joe Chicklets with a salad and Big Joe Strawberry Shake. A few of the security guys inside the restaurant had Big Joe Burgers they were surreptitiously munching.

As they ate, Larry shared the reason he wanted to get together. It would have been easier to share that information with just the two of them. Instead, they had two already lively kids, pumped up by junk food. As Larry started his explanation, Amber was looking around for the mayo. A security agent fetched some, and it arrived just as Larry got to the end of his first sentence. Evelyn was just raising a few questions when Doug Jnr finished his burger and fries, he was ready for a Joe's Mom's Apple Pie. Larry had barely explained all the ins and outs when Amber was ready for her dessert. She had a Big Joe Choc Deluxe, Evelyn joined her.

The White House living quarters, Washington DC, USA

Back at The White House that night, in The First Bed, which presumably is much more comfortable than any other bed in America. Evelyn was telling Doug Senior, The President, all about her day. Normally, he used that time to catch up mentally on his day. Nodding and making appropriate noises as she spoke. After recounting the difficulties of the children at breakfast, Evelyn mentioned their trip to Big Joes. Doug sat up and took notice. He said, 'you could have rung my secretary; I may have been free.'

'Big Joes' burgers is not the important bit. My dad said that a British company he's involved with, are setting up here in the US,' said Evelyn.

'What kind of company?' asked Doug, or rather the President.

'An accountancy firm. He's an investor and gonna be CEO,' said Evelyn.

'I see,' said Doug. Although it was uncertain that President Meyer would have seen. He had been a soldier prior to being elected. His family had enough money to fund his election campaign. He had plenty of experts to help him with any financial questions, but he was no expert on economic matters. Which may have been an issue had that been highlighted to the voters. His campaign had run on the slogan: 'Put the economy into safe hands.'

Evelyn was staring at her husband; he was daydreaming about burgers. She gave him a nudge and asked, 'what do you think?'

'About what?' asked Doug.

'Inviting the English guy who's setting up the company to The White House?' said Evelyn.

'I've missed a step.' Doug frowned.

Evelyn explained her dad wanted to foster strong ties between the administration and this new company. She told him of her dad's links with one of its directors. How he had met the guy they had sent out to set things up. Her dad had asked if they could invite him along, put him in touch with the right people. Plus, of course, her own dad's interest.

'So long as it doesn't smell of corruption, using our links to give your dad's company a leg up,' said the president, presidentially.

'Isn't it just capitalism, communication, connections, networking?' asked Evelyn.

'I guess we could invite this guy, William, is it? To a dinner with other industry leaders. That would be fair,' said Doug. He had taken off his presidential hat.

'I'll get planning. Now, about the rest of my day...,' said Evelyn.

'OK, let's hear it,' said Doug. He laid back and continued to listen, while thinking about the political situation in East Asia.

A campsite on the outskirts of New York, USA

While William and Louise were in Bethesda, hobnobbing with the rich and famous. Hilda and Pearl were sitting on makeshift chairs in a campsite on the outskirts of New York. No doubt Doug Meyer would have an appropriately rousing and inspiring speech for them, not that Hilda ever lacked inspiration. What she needed was calming down a bit.

As they sat down for their last meal at the campsite outside New York, Hilda was fidgeting. She jiggled her legs and clapped her hands, then said, 'how about a last trip into New York City tonight?'

'What!?' said Pearl in shock.

'It'll be fun, a girl's night on the town,' said Hilda. She seemed ready to spring off her seat.

The sun was just disappearing below the horizon and Pearl had been gathering things together into the RV, ready for their ongoing journey the next day. She did not look ready for a night out 'on the town.'

'I can't imagine a worse idea. We need to pack, ready to leave first thing,' said Pearl.

Hilda was crestfallen. Her legs stopped jiggling, and she stared at the ground. Pearl seemed to hesitate, then she carried on packing. After a few minutes Hilda asked, 'what about going after you've packed?'

'No!' came the cry from inside the RV.

Hilda opened her mouth to reply and then thought, I will try again in a few minutes, give her a chance to calm down. Pearl never changed her mind, and they did not go on a girl's late-night trip into New York that night. They were unaware that a late-night trip into New York would have been a lot safer than their plans for the next day.

Chapter Sixteen

July 1997

A campsite on the outskirts of New York, USA

Just as Pearl was about to drive off from the campsite, Hilda had an announcement, 'I've just remembered, I have a cousin in Philadelphia. Is that a big diversion on our way to Maryland?'

Pearl slammed on the brakes and looked long and hard at Hilda. She was remembering how much Hilda had already gone out of her way hunting for Ruby. She took a deep breath and said, 'alright, let's look at the map.' They checked out a route to Philadelphia, the city of brotherly love. It surprised them how close it was to New York, just a couple of hours, even for their slow-moving RV.

A campsite near Philadelphia, Pennsylvania, USA

After finding a campsite on the outskirts of Philadelphia, Hilda and Pearl checked the transport options available. The train looked best, so they headed into the city to meet Hilda's cousin. On route, Hilda rummaged in her bag for her address book and found the entry for Winnie. Pearl stared at her and said, 'you haven't checked where we're going yet?'

'I know roughly, just getting the exact place,' said Hilda. She didn't look convincing as she searched through her address book. She found the entry for Winnie with a sigh of relief.

The address in Hilda's book was of Winnie's deceased parents. A house that had long since been sold. Winnie, Hilda's cousin, was the daughter of Ruth and Elmer Wright. Ruth was Hilda's aunt on her mother's side. Winnie had written at the time to invite Hilda to the funeral. She didn't turn up.

Hilda had sent Christmas and birthday cards to her aunt and had letters telling her how well Winnie was doing. The letters were typical Christmas 'Round Robins.' Hilda heard how Winnie had won awards, scored the highest in exams, gone to the best university, got the best job ever. Hilda almost expected to hear that Winnie had been canonised by papal decree or married a prince. Once Winnie's parents died, she had moved into her own place. But not sent her cousin Hilda the address.

Winnie had met Hilda once, as a child, at a family wedding in England. Hilda had insisted on 'showing her how to boogie.' When Winnie had complained to her mom, Ruth just laughed and told other stories of Hilda's antics. Whilst Ruth had meant them as an example of how embarrassing Hilda was. Winnie had seen how similar Hilda was to her mom.

Hilda and Pearl arrived at the address of Winnie's late parents. Some people claim that life is devoid of coincidences, but as we have already seen, life is full of them. The original purchasers of the house had sold it after just nine months. The new owner was a Ms Wilma Theresa Peterson. On her doorbell was the abbreviation WTP. Let no one blame Hilda for her assumptions about what that stood for. She arrived expecting Winnie to be living at that house and to have married. Who can blame Hilda's conclusion about her new surname? Some may say it unreasonable to think she would have married a person named after a famous teddy bear. But teddy bears were on her mind a lot in America. So, is it really that unreasonable? Stranger things have happened. There must be people with the surname Pooh.

Hilda arrived, ready for a friendly family repartee with her cousin Winnie. So, when Ms Peterson answered the door, Hilda laughed and said, 'Winnie the Pooh, I assume.'

Did such a friendly remark deserve threats of the police, and shouts to leave her premises? Did it really warrant such abusive language and anger from Ms Peterson?

Hilda explaining who she was didn't seem to help. It just caused more problems. When Hilda said, 'think of us as Piglet and Tigger.' Ms Peterson replied in a most impolite manner.

As they left, Hilda said to Pearl, 'I can see why it is called the city of brotherly and not sisterly love.'

They returned by train to the campsite, in need of a night's rest before a day exploring the city. That meeting had taken the wind out of their sails.

A low-cost hotel, Philadelphia, Pennsylvania, USA

The vehicle tracker Jake had planted on Hilda and Pearl's RV was proving helpful. He tracked them to the outskirts of Philadelphia. Then his tracker packed up. He had seen the site they were on. But wasn't keen to venture onto it and fit a new one. He paid someone to do it on his behalf. He moved into low-cost a hotel nearby while he awaited the availability of his specialist ops team. They were on another job and not available until the next day.

Even though he was expecting a big pay-out on the diamonds, his expenses were mounting up. Two lots of tracking devices. The specialist to fit the second. A hit man. The special ops team. Many nights in hotels and motels.

In between jobs, he lived a lavish lifestyle in the Caribbean. He owned a large estate with an extensive staff, his wife had extravagant tastes. He budgeted for each job based on its complexity and length. This one had far exceeded both. Unfortunately, it was time to update his buyer, B, on the lack of progress via her contact.

***

Sometime later, Jake hung up the phone. B's contact, a lawyer, had repeated the earlier veiled threats. This time, they were far less veiled. B was angry to have heard that Jake had cancelled each of their previous handover meetings. Jake told the contact to reassure B that his new team would succeed. Now Jake was feeling anxious. The lawyer had made some very un-lawyer like remarks at the end of the call.

Jake had a sense of panic about the latest time and place for the diamonds to be delivered in Los Angeles, California. Delivery was in just three weeks' time. It would take him time to get there, even by plane. First, he had to get the diamonds. He wished he felt as confident as he had sounded on the phone.

New Scotland Yard, London, UK

While Jake was hoping to close in on Hilda, the UK Police were finally gaining more information on him. Having discovered his name, they had been tracing details on his life. One of the junior staff had just brought news through to his chief at New Scotland Yard. Jake had a house, well, more of an estate, on a British Protectorate Island in the Caribbean. Jake returned to the UK often enough to keep his UK tax status. The junior staff member had also discovered that Jake was married with two children, a boy and a girl. They passed this information on to other international crime agencies.

New Scotland Yard had yet to receive back all their enquiries from passport control. For the time being, they were unaware that Jake was in the USA, but they had instructed a team to call at his home. It would take a while to set up. There was a lot of administration involved.

Philadelphia, Pennsylvania, USA

Hilda and Pearl headed back into Philly the next day. This time, they tried a combination of the bus and underground trains. Hilda was always up for adventure and exploration. Hilda and Pearl had an enjoyable time walking around the back streets. The one thing they found odd was the way old and new buildings ran together. In England, often entire streets or areas are from one era. So that you will walk down a street of 18th century houses. Or visit a village full of 17th century cottages. In Philly they found an old house next to a brand-new office building, then a less modern one, then an old one – a curious mix. There were streets with higher proportions of older buildings, but not in the way they were used to. Pearl pointed out that it was the difference between walking through a city and hearing about it or seeing it in a movie. They found that about their trip, being in America differed from seeing it on the screen.

***

Jake's special ops team finally turned up. He felt brave, so they stormed off to Hilda and Pearl's campsite – he was going to catch them unaware. But they had left even earlier. Jake was determined not to let this get him down. He sent his five men around the site, questioning everyone. They needed to find out exactly where his quarry had gone. He couldn't just wait for her at the campsite. Time was not on his side. His team all had false Security Service ID's. After half an hour, they found someone who had chatted with Hilda. She had told them about wanting to visit The Liberty Bell. Jake and his team headed into Philly.

By the time Jake and his team were heading into the city, Hilda and Pearl had already explored the old town area. They were now feeling hungry. Hilda suggested they must try a Philly Cheesecake. That was a famous local delicacy. So, they found a small low-cost eatery and ordered a piece each. The server asked, 'fried onions?'

Hilda frowned at him. 'I want a cheesecake dear; you do know how to make them?'

Pearl apologised for her friend and told him. 'Hold the onions.'

When the cheesecakes arrived, Hilda stared at her beef filled Italian bread, with a cheese topping. Then said, 'I don't remember ordering a sandwich. But that's a tasty idea to have this before our pudding.'

'That is the cheesecake,' said Pearl.

'Don't be silly dear, this is a beef sandwich,' said Hilda.

'They call this a Philadelphia cheesecake.'

'I knew they had a problem understanding the difference between chips and crisps. Even gas and petrol, but this is just ridiculous.' Hilda clicked her fingers to call the server over. Pearl tried to stop him, but he was there straight away.

'Can I help?' asked the server.

'You seem to have a problem understanding how to make a cheesecake,' said Hilda, holding up her plate.

The server looked at the perfectly made cheesecake and then at Hilda and asked, 'what's the problem?'

'It has beef and bread in it, young man. Have you got a pen and paper?' asked Hilda. The server nodded, getting out paper and pen. Hilda said to him, 'right, you need to crush up some biscuits, preferably digestives. Mix them with melted butter. Press that into a dish.'

Pearl intervened and said, 'hold on Hilda, you are telling them how to make a British cheesecake.'

'A proper cheesecake,' said Hilda.

'No, it's different,' said Pearl. She smiled at the server. 'It's all right, you can go.'

It took a lot of argument before Hilda accepted that the food before her had the right to be called a cheesecake. On finally tasting it, she found it delicious and even wanted a second helping.

Their next port of call was to be The Liberty Bell. Jake and his special ops team had arrived there some time earlier and were questioning visitors. They were wondering if they had missed Hilda. But at that moment Hilda and Pearl were walking up The Independence Mall, they were not rushing. A group of people had gathered in The Independence Square, which looks more like a park, with trees and walkways through it. Hilda had an insatiable curiosity and had to know what they were doing. Pearl followed; half interested herself. They discovered the group were pensioners from Florida. On a guided tour around Philadelphia. When the group heard Hilda and Pearl speaking, they were keen to welcome a couple of Australians. After Hilda corrected them, they were even happier to welcome a couple of British pensioners into their group. The two became the physical and conversational centre of the group.

The newly enlarged group progressed onwards to The Liberty Bell. On seeing the important historic monument, Hilda told them it did not impress her, either with its setting, or the bell itself and said, 'look at that, it's cracked. I could recommend a bell maker in England to fix it.'

At first the group was shocked, then they laughed at her English eccentricity, assuming she was just joking. Pearl grimaced at each of Hilda's comments. Pearl said to Hilda, 'it's part of its heritage, knocks and bumps are part of life.'

Hilda gazed through the glass at the insurance building behind and said, 'not an impressive setting, is it? Look at that, you can see a building behind it.' There were nods of agreement from the group. One of them informed Hilda about plans to move it.

Jake's team were milling all around the group, looking between people. But somehow, every time they looked towards Hilda, she was blocked or turned the other way. Perhaps some higher force was protecting her. All Jake's team had guns and would not have hesitated to use them, even in a public place.

Before the group of sightseers left the bell, Hilda sighed and said, 'I wish I could ring it.' Everyone stared at the protective glass surrounding the bell. There was a shared sense of relief.

Hilda's cousin, Winnie, walked past them, unseen, heading back to work after lunch. She worked at the very insurance offices Hilda had commented on a little earlier. No doubt we often pass someone to whom we are related unaware.

The group, with Hilda and Pearl included, headed off down the street a short way from the Liberty Bell, next stop, the old town. Hilda and Pearl felt they had already seen enough of that part of Philly, so they parted ways. But not until they exchanged addresses. Jake and his group did not see Hilda and Pearl head off to the train station and back to their campsite. At the campsite, it surprised Hilda and Pearl to hear of security personnel looking for them. As the other campers and staff were treating them strangely, they moved on to a different site.

Back in the centre of Philly, by The Liberty Bell, Jake was looking around desperately. His special ops team grew impatient. They had another job that night. After three more hours, he called off the search, paid the team off and sent them away. They were an enormous expense. Heading back to his hotel, he was sluggish. Once he arrived, it surprised him to find that Hilda's tracker showed they had moved on from Philly. He sat on the bed and sank his head in his hands. What was he going to do? This job was costing him a fortune, and he had made no money on it yet. How could two old ladies be defeating him? He was a master criminal, he never failed. These two women were outsmarting him. Maybe they were super clever. Pretending to be simple old women. Perhaps they worked for one of his competitors? Anxiety makes us imagine many strange things.

TSU Corp Office, Maryland, USA

Having made plans with her husband to invite William and his wife to The White House. Evelyn, the First Lady, wanted to see the new company he was setting up local to her. So, she got her assistant to contact TSU and ask if she could visit the office. Her assistant was busy and delegated the job to a junior who had not been there long. The junior spoke to one of the staff at TSU, Maryland. She did not fully explain who she was phoning on behalf of, Nor the purpose of the visit. William received a muddled message to say that the CEO of a charity called The First Ladies wanted to visit. He assumed there had been a mix-up and ignored it.

This meant that when Evelyn arrived with a full entourage of security, staff, and press, confusion reigned. William stood open-mouthed. He had no clue who this lady with the enormous staff was. The rest of the TSU staff recognised her immediately and welcomed her as The First Lady. This gave William a chance to catch up and respond appropriately. The TSU offices were not big enough for everyone. It was only meant as a starting office, while they established the company in the USA. Some of the press and extra staff had to wait outside.

The TSU staff looked at William in a different light after the prestigious visitor. Anyone who received visits from The First Lady had powerful connections. Although they whispered between themselves about whether The First Lady was aware of his immoral behaviour. William was glad to meet Larry's daughter. Evelyn said it would be wonderful to meet his wife.

Having spoken to Pearl about her sister a day or two before, William saw an opportunity open to him. He chatted to Evelyn about her chef, Ruby. Before William had fully explained about Pearl, Evelyn said, 'I would like to invite you and your wife to The White House for business lunch on Wednesday. That way I get to meet your wife, and you will both meet our chef and taste her wonderful food.' William could not have planned it better. Maybe that's because he had not.

A hotel, Maryland, USA

Later, when William told Louise, she was both delighted and horrified at the idea. 'What do I wear at The White House?' she said.

William was feeling overwhelmed by the opportunity and said, 'Just this once, you can go to a top dress shop and get whatever they recommend.' His face regretted the words as soon as he spoke them.

He was even more dismayed when Louise suggested that his suit also needed replacing; he argued it had done him for years. But Louise explained that a ten-year-old suit from Marks and Spenser's, would not do for a visit to The White House.

Louise enjoyed the next day of shopping. Buying her dress and helping William choose an appropriate suit was much more fun for her than for him. He spent that evening pouring over his personal account spreadsheet. He was not looking his usual self as he added up and balanced the figures. There were too many items on the expenditure side. His boss, Harold, had forgotten to tell him that there would be extra expenses available for certain contingencies. Whilst their clothing would not be covered, there were many things on his list that would be. He had that happy revelation to look forward to on their return home.

How they organised their household budget was typically well planned. But unfortunate for a big trip like this. Louise's salary from teaching, paid for utilities, weekly food, and regular housekeeping. William's salary paid the mortgage, car, insurance, and extra items, like holidays and unforeseen expenses. The American holiday was all coming from his salary.

***

Louise was a transformed woman when they were getting ready for their visit to The White House. Dressed as she had never been before. William had to look twice and gave her an admiring smile. His own suit made him feel smarter and somehow better; Louise smiled at him.

They did not know what to expect as they got in a taxi and headed for The White House. At the front gate they were checked for weapons and then taken through to the private quarters of The President, and First Lady.

Evelyn introduced them to her children, Doug Jnr, and Amber, who then disappeared immediately to find some fun. The tour was amazing, not only of the private quarters but also the rest of The White house. No standing at the back of a large crowd, trying to hear a tour guide. They got to spend longer, go to places the public could not visit and hear stories not told on any public tour. Evelyn had overseen the complete interior re-design of the private quarters; it was her interest and hobby. She had trained as an interior designer but gave it up once she became First Lady. Now she spent her time championing worthy causes, which were close to her heart. She headed up many charities and was on the board of many others. She also liked to spend as much time as possible with her children.

For luncheon, the meal was every bit as delicious as they expected. It was only a basic meal. There would be a five-course formal meal later. But not basic by Louise's standards, she looked at the tasty morsels open mouthed and then tucked in.

Evelyn brought Ruby out to meet Louise and William. Louise told Ruby about Pearl and her search, which caused Ruby to get tearful. She had not even realised she had a sister or the adoption; it made her intrigued and eager to meet her and find out more.

To make sure that TSU was not seen as being treated more favourably than other companies. Evelyn had separated out the private tour and luncheon from a formal evening meal, which included lots of other business leaders. She made sure that William was photographed and interviewed at that event rather than the private one.

The formal dinner was amazing and helped explain why Ruby was such a celebrated cook and had been sought after by Evelyn. At her age, Ruby should have retired. But she acted like the captain of a ship, planning and directing its culinary direction. The sou chefs under her often went on to became famous.

Evelyn had said she would try to organise a get together for Ruby and Pearl. But the pressures of her life meant that it slipped her mind after William and Louise left.

Chapter Seventeen

July 1997

A campsite on the outskirts of Philadelphia, USA

Hilda and Pearl had yet to hear from William and Louise about meeting Ruby at The White House. Nor had they heard of Evelyn's promise for them to visit. So, when they returned to their RV campsite, they went in search of advice on how they could contact The White House. Wandering around the site, they asked folk they met how to phone The White House. Most were suspicious of two foreigners asking that question, the ones who knew: feigned ignorance. One lady they met suggested they look in the phone directory. Surprisingly, it was listed. Pearl was nervous about phoning such a prestigious place, so Hilda said she would do it. They found a pay phone and made the call. After they answered the phone Hilda said to the operator, 'this is Hilda Shilton. I'd like to speak with your kitchens please.'

'Is it a business or a private matter?' said the operator.

'Oh, I'm not sure. Neither of those sound right. I'm a person,' said Hilda. She looked at Pearl, who was watching her anxiously.

'Let me clarify. Are you phoning on your own behalf or as a representative?' said the operator.

'Ah,' said Hilda, glancing at Pearl and smiling. 'I am representing someone.'

'Who are you representing?' said the Operator. She looked at the other operators sitting next to her and shrugged, seeming to say. 'I have a slow one here.'

'Pearl,' said Hilda. She felt confident of that answer.

The operator checked her list of approved companies and said, 'I don't have a Pearl on my list. How are you spelling that?'

Hilda said to Pearl, 'how do you spell your name dear?'

The operator interrupted, saying, 'wait a minute, did you just ask a person next to you how to spell their name?'

'Yes, I was never particularly good at spelling. Whenever I had a spelling test, my pops used to say, "doing your best means stop trying." I live by that. That's why I can't spell,' said Hilda.

Pearl whispered to Hilda, 'the saying is, doing your best means never stop trying.'

'Oh dear, no wonder pops was so disappointed with my results,' said Hilda.

'What's all this got to do with anything?' said the operator. The supervisor had come over to see what was happening.

'You asked me to spell Pearl's name. Have you got memory problems? I get those sometimes. It's my age. Is that your problem?' asked Hilda.

'No, it isn't,' said the operator. 'My memory is fine.'

'What's the problem?' asked Pearl.

'This lady doesn't know what she wants,' said Hilda.

'I heard that. I *do* know what I want. I was asking the name of your company,' said the operator. 'But you were giving me the name of your friend.'

'My company, what company? You really are most confusing. Are you sure that you are quite with it? It is not your fault, you know, dear. Many of my best friends have gone a bit strange in their old age,' said Hilda, using her best gentle voice.

'I am not strange, not strange at all,' said the operator. Her supervisor patted her back sympathetically and mimed an action that meant, 'shall I take over?' The operator shook her head firmly.

'Why do you want to speak to someone in the kitchen?' said the operator sharply. The supervisor showed she should be gentler.

'I told you, dear, it's about Pearl. Have you forgotten already? It's those memory problems. Have you seen a doctor?' asked Hilda.

'There is *nothing* wrong with *me*!' shouted the operator. The supervisor gently took hold of her and took the headset. Then instructed another staff member to take her away. By the time the supervisor had put on the headset, Hilda was saying, 'hello, hello, are you still there?'

'This is the supervisor. The lady you were speaking to was taken ill.'

'She did seem to have problems, dear,' said Hilda.

'How can I help you?' asked the supervisor.

'Put me through to the kitchen, please,' said Hilda.

'Who is calling and what is it in connection with?' asked the supervisor.

'I've already told the other lady all that,' said Hilda.

'I am sorry if you could just tell me,' said the supervisor, in her professional, gentle voice, the one she used in training.

'Private Pearl,' said Hilda, she tried out a short form. She was bored repeating herself.

'Ah, you're a soldier,' the supervisor saw the light, maybe not the true light. 'Is this about the VA dinner that's coming up?'

'Yes,' said Hilda, wanting to get through as quickly as possible.

'I know who you need to speak with, connecting you now.' There was one ring, then a voice said, 'Sergeant Barnes.'

'No, no, no, I need Ruby,' said Hilda.

'Who is this?' said Sergeant Barnes.

'Hilda, and I need to speak to Ruby.'

'You have the wrong extension. Ring the switchboard again,' said Sergeant Barnes, then he hung up.

Hilda rang again. Depending on your viewpoint, a rather unfortunate or fortunate thing happened next. Some workers were carrying out repairs on the road nearby and they cut through the telephone cable. These workers did not just cut through the phone line to the phone box, but for the entire block. They also cut off the electrical power for that block.

Hilda carried on talking for a few minutes before she realised that the line was dead. She assumed the operator had cut her off. Hilda and Pearl returned to the campsite feeling frustrated. If only they had known that plans were already underway for Pearl to meet Ruby.

On arrival at their RV, Hilda put on the radio to cheer them up. A local radio station, WGXRS, was playing, and the presenter was mid-flow: '... Cooee I certainly never expected that, did you Sammie? No siree. Did you hear about the blackout downtown? Utility One Z went and cut the power and phones. Bet they were in a whole heap of trouble. Time for more tunes here on WGXRS, to tap your toes and get ya movin.'

Hilda did tap her toes; she liked this radio station; it played old tunes she enjoyed. Music and dancing always helped her concentrate. Although the chatter and adverts were inane. Hilda found that as she danced around, her thoughts came into focus. She had a nagging thought in the back of her mind about how to find out about Victoria Worth. She must be Pearl and Ruby's, but what happened to her?

Philadelphia, Pennsylvania, USA

Next day, Hilda and Pearl were at a Waffle and Pancake House for their arranged phone call. There was a public phone near the back and Hilda was holding it in such a way that Pearl could hear as well. Louise said to them, 'we got invited to the White House and met Ruby...' That is as far as she got; Pearl squealed with delight. She was so excited that she skipped around the Waffle House, shouting, 'they met her, they met her.' She danced in between the tables and in front of the counter. The patrons look up and wondered at the sight of the old lady dancing down the aisles. Meanwhile, Hilda heard more about the trip to The White House and felt like she was missing out on two fronts. She wanted to join Pearl leaping around The Waffle and Pancake House, and she was hearing of a missed trip to The White House. Louise told her that The First Lady was trying to arrange for Pearl to meet Ruby.

After the phone call, Hilda joined Pearl for a bit of dancing and then suggested they have a plate of waffles to celebrate. She had never had a plate of waffles before. But they always seemed tasty in the movies. They also ordered a large milkshake each.

When their food and drink arrived, Hilda stared at it with a smile and wide eyes. They tucked into the mountain of waffles. They had each ordered a sharing plate of waffles, designed for eight people. The server assumed that more guests would join them, or they would take some home. Pearl just ate a couple. She was too excited thinking about finally meeting her long-lost twin sister. Hilda struggled to manage them but had a good go. The milk shakes were also huge and had whipped cream on top. Hilda felt like a child again and kicked her legs as she started on her milkshake.

All that was lacking was another dance. Hilda glanced around for a jukebox. Fortunately, there was one over on the back wall. She pranced over to it and chose a rock and roll tune. An older man had just finished his breakfast at the table next to the jukebox. He chose the moment the music started to stand up. As he turned towards the door, that was also towards Hilda. She took that as an invitation to dance. Grabbing his hands, she jived.

The man Hilda had grabbed was known as a good sport and a decent dancer. He had retired ten years earlier and had nowhere else he urgently needed to be. Hilda and the man jived to 'Run-around Sue.' They did not do a full jive with lifts and throws. It was a toned-down version, with kicks, twirling, and hands, but they had fun. At the end Hilda's impromptu partner joined Hilda and Pearl for a chat. He told them he was a widower and had three grown up kids. They told him about their adventures, their spirit, and life. When he left, he thanked Hilda for brightening his morning. When Hilda and Pearl left, quite a few people at The Waffle and Pancake House felt the same way. They had brought a bit of brightness to an otherwise ordinary day. Pearl had an extra spring in her step.

TSU Corp Office, Maryland, USA

It is a little-known fact about small satellite offices of a corporation that the staff often call each other up to share information. Not just important business reports, but also gossip. It is not official and certainly would not be sanctioned. The phone calls are part of the day to day running of the company. The calls kept the data flowing about shared corporate clients. Made sure that network updates were working on the clunky and outdated computer system they used. But once you get people talking on the phone about work, they will inevitably talk about people. Especially when there is juicy gossip to share. William was the subject of such delicious chatter. Specifically, the visit of a pretty, young Italian girl some days earlier. She became younger and prettier at every re-telling. Everyone in The Maryland Office of TSU knew all about William before he had ever arrived. He never understood the women's offhand attitude towards him, nor the men's winks. William's increase in standing that came after the visit of The First Lady was waning.

The scene had been set for a major misunderstanding. One which was about to get a lot worse. Have you noticed how problems seem to mount up? So, it was with William. Unfortunately, the First Lady's personal assistant was an Italian lady called Sophia. The same name and nationality as the restaurant owner in New York. The same Sophia that the TSU staff thought William was committing adultery with. Just when things were already confused. This second Sophia, the First Lady's PA, phoned William at work with information about Hilda and Pearl's visit to The White House. Clara, one of TSU

Maryland's staff, answered the phone with her usual question, 'who's calling?'

'Sophia Milan.'

'Who would you like to speak with?' asked Clara.

'Mr Shilton,' said Sophia.

Clara tried his line. It was engaged, so she said, 'I'm sorry, he's busy. Can I take a message?'

'No, it's a private matter. Can I please wait?' said Sophia.

Having heard the stories about William's Italian dalliance, Clara said, 'a private matter?'

'Yes, it is,' said Sophia.

'I'll put you on hold,' said Clara. She waved to another staff member, Kelly, to come over. 'It's that Italian bit.'

'No!' said Kelly 'I thought Simon in Chicago, put paid to all that.'

'Obviously not, and him having links with our President,' said Clara. The two ladies started to stand at the mention of their President, then thought better of it.

William's line became free. Clara re-connected to Sophia and said, 'sorry for the delay, putting you through now.'

'Thank you,' said Sophia. She had been humming to herself when Clara re-connected her.

Clara rang William's office. He answered, and she said tersely, 'a... woman for you.'

'Who?' said William.

'Sophia Milan, on a... *private* matter. Are you in to take her call?' said Clara.

'Oh, umm, yes,' said William.

Clara put the call through, but 'accidentally' left the call connected to her speakerphone. Clara and Kelly nonchalantly stood near the phone, listening.

'Hello, Sophia,' said William.

'Ah, Mr Shilton. I have information for you,' said Sophia.

'More information?' asked William.

'Yes, it relates to the twins,' said Sophia.

Kelly and Clara drew nearer to the phone. Twin babies. This was more salacious than they expected.

'Twins? Oh, you mean Ruby and Pearl,' said William.

Kelly called another staff member, John, over. She said to him quietly, 'they've named the kids already?' He shook his head in mock disgust.

Sophia said to William, 'Evelyn wondered about the meeting with Ruby.' Sophia had an interesting voice on the phone. Her Italian accent just kept enough lilt to make it sound attractive.

John strained to hear the conversation. Kelly shook her head and said, 'Evelyn, another woman! And he's not even met both his own illegitimate kids yet.'

William got out a notepad. He wanted to make sure he remembered and said, 'I'll talk to Hilda tonight.'

Clara stared at Kelly in horror and said, 'he's got another one on the go.' John gave William a mental pat on the back. He whistled. 'What stamina, four of them.' Clara and Kelly shook their heads.

Sophia said to William, 'when you talk to your mother and her friend Pearl. Can you ask them if they would like to visit The White House? The President and First Lady would like to invite them for a personal tour. Much like the one that you and Louise enjoyed. That way Pearl can meet her twin sister, Ruby.'

'Just Hilda and Pearl?' said William.

'That's what I was told to convey. I must go. Goodbye,' said Sophia. She hung up.

William hung up and stared at the phone. He was disappointed.

But the scene in the other room was far more extreme. Clara was staring at Kelly in disbelief. John looked at Clara and said, 'I thought you said Sophia was his bit on the side.'

The recriminations continued for quite some time. Their response to William changed markedly. He became an object of respect and high regard. It is far too easy to make judgements based on little or no information and get things completely wrong. The next phone call to the Chicago Office was far frostier.

***

Back at their hotel, William told Louise about the trip and that they were not included. Her response was to tell him not to be greedy. They had enjoyed a wonderful tour. Now it was Hilda and Pearl's turn. If she knew of the extra twist in store for Hilda and Pearl, maybe she would not have been so gracious. Although, knowing Louise, her big heart and generous nature, she would still have been happy.

The White House, Washington DC, USA

Sophia Milan, Evelyn's PA, heard from William the next day. Hilda and Pearl would love to visit, so she arranged everything. Unknown to The First Lady, The President had been making his own plans for the date she had organised. Finding a gap in his busy schedule, he had booked a weekend away at Camp David as a surprise for his family.

When President Meyer told Evelyn about his plans, she said that she could not cancel such an emotional re-union for Ruby and Pearl. So, she convinced her husband that Ruby, Pearl, and Hilda should join the trip to Camp David. As he is only The President of the United States, his plans were obviously subject to his wife's approval - at least the family ones. He agreed 'on the firm and unequivocal understanding that they could still have time together as a family.' He announced this in a commanding and authoritative way, reminding his wife, 'I am in charge, my decision is final.'

Evelyn said, 'of course,' as she carried on with the arrangements for Pearl and Hilda's visit. Even Presidential plans can go wrong when Hilda is involved.

Cheap motel near Washington DC, USA

In a very dingy and tatty motel on the outskirts of Washington, Jake was on the phone to his wife, Laura. He said to her, 'I'm about ready to give up.'

'You can't.' said Laura. She was lying on a sunbed, by their pool in the Caribbean.

'This old lady's beaten me,' said Jake.

'Pull yourself together, Jake. You've never been beaten in twenty-two years. Besides, you know what B will do. She'll hire a hit man and she won't just kill you. Think of me and the kids,' said Laura. She took a sip of her cocktail, then waved to one of her maids that she needed more shade.

'I suppose. But you don't understand, I've tried everything. I don't know what else to do,' said Jake. He was lying on a bed, its sheets stained and tatty. There was a rusty old fan by his bed. It clicked annoyingly.

'What's that racket?' asked Laura.

'It's the fan.'

'Turn it off. I can hardly hear you.'

'It's all that's keeping me cool.' Jake looked longingly at the fan. He was only wearing his shorts.

'Open a window.' Laura finished her drink and held it up for her maid to fetch and refill.

Jake stared out of the open window at the searing sun outside. 'Yes, love.' He clicked off the fan.

After finishing on the phone, he got up, got dressed, and headed out of the door. He reluctantly drove to the campsite where Hilda and Pearl were staying. He must be brave for his family's sake. Hilda and Pearl were not there. He found a camper van for hire near to them and settled down to await their return. Feeling exhausted, he fell into a restless sleep.

Jake's home, the Caribbean

In Jake's Caribbean home Laura hung up the phone and shook her head saying, 'Wimp.'

One of her maids walked over and said to Laura, 'there are two police officers at the door.'

'What?' said Laura. She sat up straight.

'They want to speak with you.'

'Did you say I was in?' Laura stood.

'No, miss.'

'Good, go back and say that I'm not here. Ask them to come back tomorrow.'

The maid headed back to the front door to lie to the police. Meanwhile, Laura dialled her husband; the hotel reception told her he had just left. She ran upstairs and packed, calling to the children to do the same. Jake had planned for this possibility, and Laura grabbed a bag of cash and false passports.

CHAPTER EIGHTEEN

August 1997

The White House, Washington DC, USA

Pearl and Hilda arrived on the outskirts of Washington, DC, to prepare for their visit to The White House. The campsite they found was ideal, a short walk to a Greenbelt Metro Station. They could then get a train in and walk the last bit. Their first day at the site, they headed in to explore the route.

It was during that day Jake tracked them and found they were not in their RV and so hired a camper van on their site. On their return that first night Jake had fallen into such a deep sleep that he did not wake until they were leaving for The White House. Hearing movement, he leapt up and followed, but only saw them at a distance until they were on the crowded train.

The day of Hilda and Pearl's visit was humid, not unusual for summer in Washington, DC. They arrived at the main gate feeling sweaty and ready for a drink and a sit down. Jake stayed back because of the crowds. He had no gung-ho assistants with him this time. Jake watched as the two old women, who were giving him such trouble, entered one of the most secure locations on the planet. He shook his head; then walked away, smiling. Perhaps the heat and frustrations were getting to him.

Hilda and Pearl were fully expectant that a drink and a sit down lay ahead. Marching up to the guard on duty, Hilda announced their names and who they were there to see. The young man looked the two old ladies up and down suspiciously. Then at his list, then back at them. He went over to the control booth and chatted to the person inside. Their brief conversation involved much gesticulation and glancing at Pearl and Hilda. The woman in the booth made a phone call, after which both she and the soldier outside checked Hilda and Pearl for weapons. A thorough and to Hilda unnecessary precaution. The guard took them through the gate to a holding area, where they were ignored. When they asked what was happening, they were told to wait. Hedges surrounded the holding area. CCTV cameras pointed at them from every conceivable angle. There were a couple of benches around the inside of the enclosed grass area, which measured about thirty feet each way. Hilda felt thirsty, so she walked over to the Marine who stood at the only entrance. Whilst he had appeared to be ignoring them, the moment she moved towards him, he challenged her, saying, 'please remain where you are, ma'am'.

'I'm thirsty. Can I have a drink please, dear?' said Hilda. She licked her dry lips.

'It won't be long,' he said.

'But it's already been ages, just a glass of water,' said Hilda.

The marine looked at the old lady before him. She reminded him of his gammy. He said over his shoulder, 'got any cans in there, Kat?'

'Why?' asked Kat from the control booth.

'Ladies thirsty,' said the marine.

'We ain't meant to engage,' said Kat.

'Come on, just a coke,' said the marine.

Kat brought a can of coke out and handed it to the marine, saying, 'on your head Bingo.'

Bingo handed the can to Hilda. She said, 'thank you.' Then took a sip. 'Ooo, this is fizzy.' Hilda passed the can to Pearl. Hilda turned back to the marine and asked, 'is Bingo your name?'

'Nickname, just silly.'

'You like Bingo?' asked Hilda.

'Zero kills,' said Bingo, shrugging.

'Oh,' said Hilda. 'I'm glad to hear it.'

'Enjoy your drink,' said Bingo. He returned to his station by the entrance.

After about five minutes a small squad of marines turned up, armed with what seemed to Hilda, like sub-machine guns. They surrounded the two of ladies and pointed directions. Hilda kept saying that they were just there to see the First Lady and not criminals, but the soldiers kept quiet. As they passed Bingo, he whispered, 'it's OK, don't worry.'

After being frog marched across the lawn, between some flower beds and through a hedgerow, they came to a wide grass area. A large helicopter sat on a landing pad; its blades were turning slowly. Marines were guarding the surrounding area, along with men in black suits and sunglasses. They held the two ladies in place to one side. No one spoke to them.

Hilda thought they were going to be taken off to prison for an unknown crime. She wished she could go back and see Bingo. He had seemed unlikely to make her his first kill. Maybe it was an offence in America, to visit the First Lady in a purple track suit. Pearl had asked her to dress smartly; now she wished she had listened. While they were waiting, some TV and press crews arrived. They set up near the helicopter. Two cameras pointed at Hilda and Pearl. They waved half-heartedly. Perhaps the event was going to serve as a warning. 'British visitors should dress more formally at The White House,' thought Hilda. She considered making a plea on the TV for William to come and save her.

Then a door at the back of The White House opened. Some people in black appeared, they were checking the area. President Meyer and The First Lady followed along with their children. One of the secret service men led the family's dog, Hunter. The entire group headed to the helicopter. The First Lady stopped by Hilda and Pearl. She apologised and explained that a last-minute change of plan meant they were going to Camp David. Then she was escorted onboard the helicopter, followed by a bemused Hilda and Pearl.

***

On the Marine One helicopter, Evelyn joined Pearl and Hilda at the rear and gave a fuller explanation. When she had booked for them to visit, she didn't know her husband had already planned a weekend away at Camp David, so Hilda and Pearl were included. They would meet Ruby there, who had gone ahead to prepare the menus. Now they were speeding towards Camp David on Marine One. Evelyn returned to her family and left Hilda and Pearl to enjoy the flight. They couldn't believe the size of the helicopter and that it had a bathroom. Although they barely had time to use it before they were landing, they didn't even get time to request a drink. Just as well, they had shared a can of coke. So far, their trip to The White House was a lot more stressful than they had expected.

Camp David, Maryland, USA

As the helicopter flew in over Camp David, Hilda looked out of the window and thought that it must be the wrong place. All she could see were trees and hills. It got lower and lower, and the trees got closer. Then, with little warning, they were in a small clearing, surrounded by marines and people in black suits. Everyone was armed and looking around, ready for a bad guy to jump out at any moment. Hilda wondered if they were worried about an attack of wild deer. Or maybe she would see more teddy bears. Hilda peered out of the window hopefully, but no bears of any type appeared.

Secret service agents escorted President Meyer and his family from the helicopter first. Then Hilda and Pearl joined his general entourage in a long line heading for a single level wood building. It looked to Hilda like a hunting lodge out of an old Western. As they entered the main hall, that impression was confirmed. The walls were lined with half logs and there were animal trophies on some walls. Through one of the wide doorways, there was a room with a large open fireplace crackling away in its centre.

A familiar-looking lady was standing by a doorway to the right. Whilst not identical, this was obviously Pearl's sister, Ruby. On seeing Pearl, she ran towards her. Grabbing her hands, then just stared into her eyes searching for something, neither spoke for a while. Time passed, emotion welled up, then Hilda said, 'Ruby?'

Ruby glanced at Hilda, as if seeing her for the first time, and said, 'yes.'

Pearl had tears in her eyes and just said to Ruby, 'I can't believe I finally meet you.'

'That's what I was going to say, dear,' said Hilda.

The sisters stared at each other, tears running down their cheeks. 'All these years, the pain you've suffered after your parents - murdered,' said Pearl. She gulped.

'Where's my room?' said Hilda. 'I am ready to freshen up, as you say, over here. Really, I want to use the toilet. Oh sorry, I mean the little girl's room, or is it the powder room?'

Pearl frowned at Hilda, then shook her head and said, 'only you.'

'What?' said Hilda.

'I apologise for my friend. She has a heart of gold, but no sense of timing,' said Pearl.

Hilda looked between Pearl and Ruby and said, 'it's my bladder, not me, also I could really do with a cup of tea.'

Ruby smiled at Pearl and Hilda and said, 'we can catch up later. I'll show you your room Hilda and sort out some tea and cookies.'

'You're a wonder,' said Hilda. She gave Ruby a hug.

After Hilda was safely ensconced in her room. Ruby and Pearl found a quiet corner to sit and chat about all the missed years. Some of them, at least. They had many to catch up on.

***

That night Hilda just couldn't sleep, being in a strange room and bed. She got up and put on a dressing gown. A great blessing to all the staff she met, as her nightie had a few too many holes. Louise kept telling her to replace it, but Hilda insisted, saying, 'it's got years left yet, waste not want not.'

Hilda headed out of her room and found herself face to stomach with Chad, a very tall Secret Service Agent. He asked what she was doing, and she explained she couldn't sleep. She told him that normally when she had these problems; she made herself a cup of tea and had a biscuit. He took her to the kitchen; it was deserted late at night.

When there, Chad boiled the kettle and poured water into a cup. He then looked around for a tea bag. He was about to dunk that into the cup when Hilda stopped him.

'What are you doing, dear?' asked Hilda.

'Making you a cup of tea,' said Chad.

'That's not how you do it. No, no, no, let me show you,' said Hilda. She put a tea bag at the bottom of a fresh cup. Re boiled the kettle and immediately poured it onto the tea bag.

'What's the difference?' asked Chad, looking puzzled.

'Tea must brew in boiling water, it's not like coffee. It needs the boiling water to release the flavour,' said Hilda.

'Every day's a school day,' said Chad. He fetched himself a coffee, and they both sat at a table. A tin of cookies sat in the middle.

'Oh, these are nice,' said Hilda, eating one. 'I saw in a movie that you secret agents...'

'Secret Service ma'am,' said Chad.

'None of this ma'am, call me Hilda,' she said. Then picked up a cookie and ate it.

'OK Hilda.'

'These biscuits are nice.' Hilda munched her biscuit.

'We call them cookies.' Chad took one himself.

'Like the monster?'

'I guess so.' Chad smiled.

'You Secret Service men...'

'And women.'

'Really? Whatever next?' Hilda shook her head.

'Equality, you know.' Chad got up to stretch.

'But are they as big and strong as you?' Hilda was looking at Chad's muscles.

'You'd better believe it,' said Chad.

'Well, I heard you would take a bullet in the place of The President. Is that true?'

'Only as a last resort, but yes,' said Chad.

'Whatever would your mother say, dear?' asked Hilda.

'You know, lots of folk have asked me the first question. No one has ever asked what my mom would say. I don't rightly know.' Chad scratched his head. 'I guess she would be proud.'

Hilda glanced up at him, then shook her head. 'If you were my son, I would be prouder if you stayed alive. You're a fine young man.'

Chad stared at the cookie jar and frowned. Perhaps he was thinking his mom would prefer him to stay alive. Or he remembered the wonderful cookies she baked. Hilda felt tired and got up to head back to her room. She noticed a big red button on the wall that matched the one next to her bed. She asked Chad what it did. He explained they were panic buttons; they were everywhere in the residential quarters. If you saw any threat, an intruder, or any danger, you just pressed it. The marines would muster into the building within minutes. Hilda frowned and said, 'it's just as well I pressed the right one when I woke up. The red button is awfully close to my light switch.' She bid Chad goodnight and said, 'I hope I don't accidentally press it when I turn off my light.'

As Chad followed her back to her room, he looked a little anxious. Maybe the thought of The President being woken by a false alarm in the middle of the night was not an appealing idea. As they reached Hilda's room, Chad said, 'I think I should come in and make sure you press the right button once you're in bed.'

Hilda drew herself to her full five feet three inches and spoke sternly to him, 'you most certainly will not young man. My pop warned me about people like you. Trying to get into my bedroom on any excuse. A sheep in wolfs clothing he called men like you.' She left a very confused-looking Chad standing, staring at her closed door. He paced for the next half an hour. No alarm bells rang. The marines stayed in their barracks; he breathed a deep sigh.

***

Chad was on duty the next afternoon when Hilda was wandering around bored, Pearl and Ruby were out for a walk, catching up on years of lost time. Ruby had left her sou chefs in charge of preparations for the next meal; having first planned it. The President and First Lady were out boating with their children and a small contingent of security. Hunter, the dog, was having a walk with his keeper. There were those who suggested they only had a dog for publicity reasons. The household staff saw none of the family play with or walk with Hunter. They may have done so when no one was looking. The American public loved Hunter and the family photos of the black Labrador sitting proudly in the family group. They particularly enjoyed the Meyer family Christmas photo.

Hunter was always in the centre, sitting proudly. Doug Jnr. normally had an arm around his neck. Amber would be snuggled up on the other side. President Meyer and Evelyn standing tall behind their family. A twinkling Christmas tree to one side, the pile of unopened, pretend presents underneath. The entire room decorated to perfection by Evelyn, her eye for interior decoration widely admired. The moment the camera had snapped the last photo, Doug Jnr. and Amber would spring up and run from the room to play with their toys, given as a bribe. His keeper would then take Hunter away.

Cheap Motel, outskirts of Washington DC, USA

Jake returned from The White House to his motel not long after Hilda, Pearl, and the First Family took off in Marine One. He heard his wife had tried to call him. But he could not get hold of her when he rang back. He would wait until she rang again.

His wife, Laura, had her own problems to focus on. She would not be calling Jake for some time. Having grabbed her escape bag, she had to get away safely before thinking of anyone other than herself... oh yes, and the children, of course.

The reason Jake had not been phased by Hilda and Pearl heading into The White House soon became apparent. He had contacts, ones who would gain him access. He had not become an international jewel thief overnight. Nor did that position come without ways into high places. He knew many of the right people in the right places. One person had been particularly useful over the years. She was not someone Jake told his wife about. He tried to convince himself that their relationship was all business; but that was far from true. Colonel Sasha

Kiens was a marine working for The President. She headed up an elite team that guarded The White House and Camp David. Depending on where The President was in residence.

She was a brilliant and well-respected soldier. Who also happened to be a rather attractive young lady from a wealthy family. They only tolerated her career once she started working for The President. Jake met her at an exclusive party. He was there scouting out a family jewel. Her father introduced Sasha to Jake. He was an attractive man, and his cover was as a rich, single entrepreneur. They seemed to hit it off from their first meeting. Jake decided not to rob her family. Instead, he developed his relationship with Sasha. She was a wealth of information and had loads of fantastic connections. Some were political movers and shakers. That was ten years earlier, and he saw her as often as he could.

Jake may have told himself that his relationship with Sasha was purely information gathering. But did that really involve a week alone in a luxury hotel in the South of France? She may have mentioned a name or two in the throes of passion. Who can discern such things? He certainly got much information from her contacts over the years. Jake was careful to only steal from one or two of her extensive group. He didn't want a pattern to become visible in his thefts. Neither Sasha nor any of her friends had any inkling that Jake was The Ghost.

Until Scotland Yard had received the photo from the duchess, no one had ever connected Jake Vort and The Ghost. His only criminal record was for speeding in England, which meant that even the most thorough background checks came back clean. He was unaware that things had changed. The UK police had only just heard from immigration and passport control Jake was in the USA. That information was just about to be passed to the FBI.

Unaware of all this, Jake contacted Sasha and told her he was in the States. He was not disappointed to find she was working. She was at Camp David. Which must mean that was where his target had gone. He needed to gain access. After a bit of persuading, he gained an invitation as her guest at the marine quarters attached to Camp David. They would only give him access to the barracks and the surrounding grounds. He would need to face the problem of reaching Hilda once there. Jake arrived at the barracks about the same time as information about his real identity reached FBI headquarters. Luckily for him, the file was handed to a very busy man. He threw it on his desk, unread, and carried on with another file he was reading.

Camp David, Maryland, USA

Hilda was not the sort of person who enjoyed doing nothing. As she wandered around, followed at a distance by Chad, her security shadow, she was deep in thought. Thinking on its own was not something Hilda normally practiced, it had to lead on to action. She noticed in her trip around the residence that there were many small tables and chairs that were placed in unusable locations. Under stairs, in small corners, along corridors. Hilda felt their locations were odd, too drafty, inconvenient, or just plain silly. What Hilda did not consider, nor would she understand, was the idea of 'dressing' a room. Putting items of furniture in place purely for a visual effect. To give a room a pleasant ambience. Such a notion would be laughable to her.

Hilda moved the tables and chairs around to 'more sensible' positions. Places they would be practical. Chairs around tables ready to use, seats in cosy corners. Chad was chatting with another agent when she started. He did not spot her do this. A harmless old lady could be given leeway to do as she pleased. No doubt a decision he would come to regret. After a long and interesting chat with his colleague, Chad turned around. Hilda was just moving the last table and chair in the main living area. She surveyed her work with satisfaction. He gazed at it in horror. Everyone was due back in the next half an hour.

Interior design was no more Chad's skill than Hilda's. He stared at the jumble of chairs and tables. Or, as Hilda saw it, the comfortable groupings of tables and chairs. They were now laid out for cosy meetings of six to eight people at various points around the room. Chad called for help. Several agents ran in, guns drawn ready. They looked very impressive, like a scene from an action movie. Then quickly realised it was not that kind of help Chad needed and holstered their weapons. They all looked disappointed. A lot of head scratching ensued until one bright spark fetched some magazine photos of the room. They were pre-release photos sent for approval by the editor.

No one told them that the magazine photographer, Josh Shilton, had done a bit of his own furniture moving before the shoot. He had looked at the room and had a similar thought to his gran; the room did not look quite right. So, he had moved things around a bit to make it more photogenic. Still, there was time for all that to be discovered. Hilda objected to all her hard work being undone and tried to stop them, but to no avail. They placed everything in the same positions as the magazine article, not as original. We should note that the only person in residence who noticed, or cared, about the proper arrangement was Evelyn. As she had been instrumental in the re-decoration and dressing of Camp David. She had enjoyed re-designing Camp David as much as re-designing The

White House private quarters. Interior design was both her past career and her current passion.

As President Meyer and family walked in, complete with security entourage. Hilda sat on a chair and watched them arrive on their way to prepare for the evening meal. Evelyn stopped part way across the room and looked around. She had not liked the way the magazine photographer had made free with her design. It had taken her ages to put things back after he left. She walked over to a small chair and table that was placed next to a tall plant and stood looking at it. Then she said, 'this is simply not right.'

Hilda leapt to her feet and joined her and said, 'I'm glad you agree. I tried to put everything in more sensible places. But this lot,' she pointed accusingly at the security staff, 'stopped me.'

Evelyn looked at Hilda, then around the room and said, 'you moved everything from how it was this morning?'

Hilda nodded proudly and said, 'yes, I thought you'd approve.'

Evelyn shook her head and walked off. Maybe she did not trust herself to be civil. Hilda looked at the security staff in triumph. But they had more fully understood The First Lady's response. They refused to move anymore furniture without her approval. No matter how much Hilda tried to convince them otherwise. They had to corral her out of the room.

There was still an hour until the evening meal. Having been shooed from the living area, Hilda headed to her room. She sat in front of her dressing table and looked at herself, saying, 'well I can't improve on perfection.' Then it occurred to her that her skin looked a little dry. She rummaged in her bag for the tube of cream that she knew was there. To her surprise, she found a jar of expensive face cream. Thinking that it must be Pearl's, she borrowed a bit before returning it. The cream felt very luxurious, and she applied a good amount. Her fingers hit something hard. 'Whatever is that?' she thought. Feeling around in the jar, she removed two large glass looking objects covered in cream. She went to the tap and washed them off. Once she had dried them thoroughly. She stared deeply into them, one in each hand. There seemed to be such a depth and beauty to them, they glowed blue.

'Well, I never,' she said aloud. She decided they must be crystals Pearl had hidden in the cream, as a surprise. Hilda loved crystals. Maybe Pearl had bought them as a present for her. Although how the jar ended up in her bag, she could not imagine. Still, she must return it to Pearl. First, she put them back in the jar of cream. It's just as well that Hilda had never claimed a gifting in finding lost jewels. To her an uncut diamond was just a crystal.

She went to Pearl's room, knocked, no answer, and entered. Pearl was in the shower. Hilda put the jar in Pearl's suitcase. 'There,' she thought, 'now she can surprise me, or whoever, with them later. I really hope it's me.'

Hilda walked out of the room smiling and rubbing her hands in expectation. She headed out of the residence carrying her handbag. A lady always needs her bag. She had every essential in hers. Chad watched her go and checked his watch; thirty minutes until the evening meal.

Stepping out of the residence, Hilda glanced left and right. She went right. That is always the right way to go. She came across the Marine barracks after a short walk.

Jake was just walking out of the barracks door considering how to reach Hilda and he bumped into her. At last, his luck had turned. He just needed it to hold.

When Jake apologised to Hilda, she heard his British accent and felt safe. She vaguely recognised him but couldn't think where from. Maybe he was a security agent. Jake stared at Hilda's handbag quickly, thinking about how to achieve his aim. He suggested she accompany him. Assuming that he must be a security agent, Hilda agreed. They walked away from the building towards a wooded walkway. It was an exercise area for the marines. Jake checked around. There were no people or cameras. His luck was holding. Things couldn't be any better than this. He grabbed Hilda's bag and ran into the woods, laughing. She shouted after him.

Realising he was too fast to catch, Hilda headed back to the principal residence and told Chad what had happened. Chad didn't immediately take Hilda seriously. He thought she was being overdramatic. Her earlier antics had made him cautious. Hilda thought about the incident and began to realise where she had seen Jake before; at the airport. But still couldn't understand why he'd taken her handbag.

***

Meanwhile, Jake was emptying the bag in desperation. He had the right bag this time, but there was no jar. He headed back to the marine barracks to make excuses and fled. His mind raced as he made his escape. What to do? First thing was to convince B's contact that all was going according to plan. Arrange the handover. The last thing he wanted was a hit put out on him. Next, he had to contact his wife, make sure she was safe. Then he needed a plan. A last and desperate plan.

***

By the time Chad realised Hilda was telling the truth and spread the word about an Englishman accosting her. Jake had already gone. Colonel Sasha Kiens stared at the soldier, giving her that information in shock. It was a double shock for her. The FBI officer with Jake's file had finally read it. He sent out a flash message to all government agencies. Sasha was still holding the message that had a scan of Jake's passport photo when the soldier arrived with information on the attack. Jake, the man she cared about, the man she trusted. Perhaps even loved? The man *she* had let into Camp David was an international jewel thief! But *more importantly,* he was *married*! How dare he!

***

Hilda was upset about losing her handbag. But as Pearl explained, they could replace it. Hilda was not convinced and felt more relieved when the patrolling guards found her bag. The president's security was increased until they had made sure that Jake had left the area. Everything was double checked to make sure he had poisoned nothing or placed any bombs. Hilda complained at the close body search. It became obvious he had only targeted her. They were unsure why.

After the extra checks, the evening meal went ahead. Ruby was a brilliant chef and had won many awards. When she worked for Evelyn's father, Larry, at The Walberg Asteridge, he had always praised her cooking. Since her arrival as head chef, meals at The White House and Camp David had become talked of and highly prized. Journalists who dined there often wrote more about the food than the politics. An oversight that was corrected by the editors before publication. As the guests gathered for dinner that evening at Camp David, and the first course was served, it was obvious why Ruby's culinary genius was so well regarded.

Hilda sat next to a military aide, General Ned Lundy. The President had brought him along for a debrief on the situation in the Middle East. The General found the lady seated on his left an unusual addition to the Camp David crowd. She kept asking him about the various medals he wore and why his uniform had four stars on it. Many times, he tried to fob her off with a quick answer. Then turn to his right to speak to the White House Chief of Staff. Hilda just tugged at his arm and asked another question. He became frustrated with the constant interruptions. On one of her interruptions, he turned and said, 'will you please...' Then he noticed Hilda was standing and pointing to the head of the table. He turned slowly and saw that everyone was staring at him. President Meyer was standing with a glass in his hand. Ned scrambled to his feet, apologising, and joined the toast.

On sitting again afterwards, Ned made sure he responded promptly to Hilda's sleeve pulls, just in case. In the end, he found it simpler to stay facing her. Finding that she had his undivided attention, Hilda asked a question that had been nagging at her, saying, 'Are you the person who presses the second button?'

'What second button?' asked Ned.

Hilda looked at Ned and shook her head. She said, 'you know dear, in all the movies, they have two buttons. One that the president presses and one that a big wig General presses. Are you the big wig?'

A light seemed to come on in Ned's eyes and he said, 'you mean the nuclear trigger?'

'No, the one that sets off the bombs to destroy the world,' said Hilda.

'You do mean the nuclear trigger,' said Ned.

'It's not a gun. In the movies it is in a big black case and has lots of flashing lights,' said Hilda.

'Hollywood makes things look overly dramatic.'

'You mean it's not like that?' Hilda picked up the cup of tea she had especially requested. She took a sip, grimaced, and replaced it.

'I can't discuss operational details with you,' said Ned.

'I wasn't talking about hospitals. I was asking about atomic bombs,' said Hilda. Some people nearby stared at them.

'Operational means the way things work. It's not an appropriate topic.'

'I see, hush, hush, eh? I understand. My pops was in the,' Hilda changed to a stage whisper, 'secret service. A bit like James Bond.'

'Pops?' said Ned.

'Yes, my pops,' said Hilda.

Pearl, who was seated on Hilda's left, had been listening to the last few sentences, said, 'she means her father.'

'That's what I said, but I can't talk about what he did. Really, I don't know what he did,' said Hilda.

Pearl then distracted Hilda long enough for Ned to escape. Those who had overheard the exchange were looking relieved that they had not been seated next to Hilda. Still, there were a few meals left that weekend and the seating arrangement was fluid. Ted made sure of that. A few of them had the delight of sitting next to Hilda ahead of them.

Penelope Kendal's seafront condo, Los Angeles, USA

Penelope Kendall, AKA, B, had just hung up the phone on her lawyer. She paced around her spacious lounge and then strode onto the terrace and stood looking out to sea. Her face set. She called over one of her serving staff, 'a G&T.' They nodded and rushed off to make it. She had gained the habit of that drink from her time in England.

B walked back inside, taking the drink from her staff. She made a phone call and a few minutes later, a man appeared. He seemed the sort of man you wouldn't want to meet on a dark night... or ever. B scowled at him and said, 'get ready for the handover next week. Jake has messed me around too many times over these diamonds. He doesn't leave afterwards, right?' The man nodded and left.

Chapter Nineteen

August 1997

Camp David, Maryland, USA

It has often been noted that joy and sorrow go hand in hand. Some have even observed that light is shown up by its contrast to the darkness. Yet few would choose to suffer and those that do are seen as abnormal. Suffering and pain come into our lives whether or not we choose them. It's how we cope with them that is the real difference between people.

Ruby and Pearl found time to sit and chat uninterrupted at several points during the weekend at Camp David. They explored both of their lives, laughing, crying, and sometimes just sitting in companionable silence. Ruby had not realised her parents' sent letters to England and was delighted to read them. One thing they both shared was how wonderful their adopted parents had been. Much as they wanted to know what happened to their biological mother. It wasn't because of any lack of love from their adoptive parents. Both now knew that they were chosen. They always knew that they were loved. They could no longer ask why their parents had not mentioned the adoption.

Sadness had come early for Ruby with the shocking murder of her parents. The more recent death of Pearl's parents was still fresh and hard for her to process. For both, finding out they had a twin felt both half expected and yet amazing. They had always known there was a missing part of themselves.

Ruby and Pearl shared photographs each of them had of themselves as babies. But Ruby's lacked indented writing on the back. So, she was excited to hear about the name Victoria Worth. Ruby had a battered old case, which she had always assumed belonged to an old aunt. But as it held the same monogram VW as Pearl's fancy box, they realised it must be Victoria Worth's case. Ruby fetched the case, and they scrutinised it. The only information inside was a maker's mark, K. Giles and Sons, Connecticut. They asked Evelyn if she knew anything of a Victoria Worth of Connecticut. She promised she would ask around. There was so much they needed to find out. They didn't know where to start. The sisters had a shared interest in each other. As they talked, parts of a jigsaw were being discovered and put into place, missing parts of themselves.

After the twins had shared time together, Hilda had a few questions to ask Ruby about her parents and the time in Marlan. Ruby found it hard thinking back that far but did her best. When Pearl and Hilda described Orville, the neighbour, they met in Mill Lane, this led to Ruby telling a story from her youth.

1930's

Marlan, Ohio, USA

Ruby told her sister about living in Marlan in the thirties. A small and close-knit community. Everyone attended one of the five churches in town. Hardly anyone had travelled beyond the town limits.

Every Saturday night, they held a 'Big Band' dance in the town hall. Life had a rhythm. Monday to Friday, she worked at the diner. Friday night they all went to The Picture House, Saturday the 'Big Band' dance, Sunday morning Church. Then it all started again the next week.

Time felt unreal, like they were living in a dream. They didn't deserve it. Looking back, Ruby described it as feeling like borrowed time. Perhaps she read that back into it. Life was good, people were friendly. Everyone knew everyone else, although that couldn't have been the case. Maybe it just felt that way.

Then there was one guy, Orville Stanley. He was an outcast even at school. Strange child, no one liked him. Ruby thought back, remembering. He lived next door to them, but that was still a distance. She could only remember bits about his family, snatches of stories, whispered by adults. Did they mistreat him? Something made her say that as she recounted the tale. She seemed to remember a twin brother who drowned when they were younger. Orville's house had always seemed so dark, unwelcoming. His pa collected junk in the yard. At night, so little light came from the dirty windows of their worn-out property. Ruby only saw his mom once; she fetched Orville from school when he got beat up - tatty dress, scraggly hair.

She had an odour, like dead meat and stewed cabbage. That couldn't be right, could it?

Looking back, Ruby felt guilty at her thoughts about Orville and his family. He had a limp. No, not just that. He acted strangely. Then she recanted. How could she be so negative about a disabled child? He had a gentle smile; his eyes were kind. Back then, in the thirties, things were different. Besides, she was a kid. No, she shouldn't give herself an excuse.

August 1997

Camp David, Maryland, USA

As they sat in a room in Camp David, Hilda stared at her and said, 'kind, gentle, eyes and a limp?'

Ruby nodded and said, 'yes.'

'He didn't seem that way to us when we met him. His eyes were dead, like pools of inky blackness,' said Hilda. 'He wasn't limping. He strode off down the road.'

'Odd, maybe...' started Ruby.

'Then there were the things he told us.'

While Hilda spoke, Pearl took her sister's hands.

Hilda continued, 'how he described your mother: "Her apron was dirty, a smudge of soot on her face." How did he know? He spoke in such a way. As if he was remembering.'

Ruby turned white and said, 'yes, how could he know that? That's what she looked like when I found her. But it wasn't mentioned in the papers.'

'So how did he know? Was Orville a suspect?' asked Hilda.

'I doubt they even questioned him. The sheriff was useless. He said there was no solid evidence,' said Ruby.

'Isn't this evidence? Saying what she looked like when she died? Plus, there are forensics now. Then there was another memory: "Ed shouldn't have come out." What did he mean by that?' said Hilda.

'I always thought they should have searched harder. It was odd about Orville,' said Ruby. She stared at the ceiling.

'I found his dead eyes scary,' said Hilda. Pearl nodded in agreement.

'Those dead eyes again,' said Ruby. She looked at her sister and Hilda, questioningly.

'Yes, the grey, dark eyes. They were so frightening.'

'But he had a warmth in his eyes. Almost a twinkle. He was an odd child, that much is true, and I was scared of him. But when you looked in his eyes... they weren't dead,' said Ruby.

Hilda looked hard at Ruby and said, 'and what about the limp? Or lack of it.'

'No limp at all?' asked Ruby. 'It was a serious problem for him as a child.'

'Maybe he's had surgery.' Suggested Hilda.

Ruby sweated, and her skin lost all its colour. She stared unseeing into Hilda's eyes and said, 'I've just remembered something else. When I was about eleven. It's something I've blocked out.'

'You don't need to talk about it,' said Pearl, putting her arm around her sister.

'I must, it's important,' said Ruby. She stared off into the distant past, remembering, 'I think he murdered Ellie. She was only ten years old, such a lovely girl. Hurt no one....' Ruby's voice choked up with tears. Pearl held her tighter. After a few minutes, Ruby said, 'he may have drowned her in a well. I saw him coming back from the well. His clothes were torn, bloodied, covered in mud. At least I thought it was him, but without the limp, maybe I got it wrong.'

'What happened at the time?' asked Hilda.

'I was young. My memories are mixed up. But I think his ma said he was with her. Everyone thought I imagined it, made it up,' said Ruby.

'His mother was covering for him, by the sound of it. I have an idea what happened. But I think we need some legal advice,' said Hilda. 'It's odd he wasn't limping then either.'

***

If you are seeking legal advice, then a gathering of politicians and legal advisors is a good place to start. Ruby wanted justice for her parents and now she had a start point. Hilda, Pearl and Ruby had an initial chat with Evelyn, who was more than Ruby's employer and The First Lady. She had become a friend over the years. Things started moving fast. They passed information to the local police in Ohio. Questioning of Orville began, and a re-examination of the facts. The physical evidence, which had been kept in storage, was re-examined, and Orville's DNA could matched with modern technology. He had been in contact with the bodies. There was enough for a court case. That would happen many months in the future. It involved a trip back to the USA for Hilda and Pearl; they were witnesses to things he said, things only a witness of the murder would know. But Hilda also felt there was more to it. Something not quite right.

On remand in prison, Orville claimed he was innocent. All the other physical evidence pointed to his guilt. What other explanation could there be? Hilda needed to think and for her that involved more dancing.

Orville had an answer. One that made no sense. His twin brother, Wilbur, had committed the murders. But the authorities had a death certificate for his brother. He drowned, age ten - an impossibility.

***

On the last evening of the weekend at Camp David. Many of the guests were sitting around in a large room with the central fireplace. Those that had not gone out for a walk or retired early. The fire was more for show than warmth, as the evening was not cold. Secret service guards were patrolling inside and out. One of them was following her usual pre-set course within the room when she tripped over a chair leg. A chair that was not usually sticking out so far. The replacing of the furniture after Hilda's rearrangement had not been perfect. Evelyn kept noticing the discordant placement of furniture. Not pleasing to her designer's eye. She had plans to re-organise everything on her next visit.

Music was playing in the background. The President's kids soon got bored and headed off to a games room out back. Hilda stood and started swaying and dancing around to a tune that was playing. President Meyer smiled as he watched her. He had always loved music and dance. He asked Hilda. 'Do you know the tune?'

'It reminds me of dances at the Pally,' said Hilda.

Evelyn asked about the Pally. Hilda explained it was a dance hall in London, a place she had first danced with her husband. Hilda danced nearer to the President and immediately, three guards surrounded him - hands on their guns. He waved them away, laughing.

'I can show you the dance,' said Hilda.

The President got up and took her hand. The guards looked on in surprise. After a few turns around the floor, he was really enjoying himself. He even had the volume increased. Then, letting go of Hilda, he turned to his wife and took her hand for a dance. Other people in the room joined in the fun. One of The President's aides danced with Hilda. He was exceptionally light on his feet. They made a wonderful dance pairing. Pearl and Ruby glanced up from their chat. Ruby stared in amazement. She had never seen such a display at Camp David before. Pearl said to her that this was 'the Hilda effect.' After which they both laughed, then got back to catching up. Doug Jnr and Amber came through to ask if they could stay up later than usual. Seeing their parents preoccupied, they left quickly, before being seen. They had a late night that evening.

At the end of the night, once he and Evelyn sat. President Meyer said to Hilda, 'you're an extraordinary woman Hilda.'

'Thank you dear,' said Hilda. She didn't seem to be at all out of breath.

'You won't be surprised, given my position, that my staff has checked you out,' said The President.

'Really? What a boring job for them,' said Hilda. She raised an eyebrow.

'On the contrary, you have done some incredible things. I gather you even appeared on stage in a Broadway show. Although that was an accident, so I won't be telling immigration.' The President laughed. 'I gather that you've solved a few mysteries over the years as well.'

'One or two, it was fun though,' said Hilda.

Evelyn looked at Hilda with a big beam on her face and said, 'you have a similar idea of fun to Dougy.'

'Dougy?' said Hilda.

'Sorry, pet name for my husband,' said Evelyn.

Dougy smiled and said, 'you're a woman after my own heart. I love your passion for life. Everything my people found out shows it.'

'Well, as I always say, I'm gonna live until I die,' said Hilda.

'That's a good adage to live by,' said the President.

'I never was much good at adding and subtracting,' said Hilda.

'Not that kind of adding.' Laughed The President.

'Oh, I see.' Hilda looked at him blankly.

Evelyn said, 'what I heard about you, from your son, you're a dynamo. Whereas he's more reserved.'

'Stick in mud, our William. I like to live life to the full,' said Hilda. She kicked a leg in the air.

The President and First lady were in full agreement with that sentiment. They got up, arm in arm, to leave. Pearl came over to Hilda and they chatted for a while. Pearl was keen to tell Hilda all about the person they met at Marlan, Ohio, and that there would now be an investigation. But she also wanted to check that Hilda on her memory about him not limping. Hilda agreed that he had walked fine. Pearl passed that information back to Ruby later.

The two friends sat for a while looking around at the exalted location in which they found themselves. Not something they would have imagined when they first planned their trip. Hilda had certainly not sold the trip short, it was 'the trip of a lifetime.'

The White House, Washington DC, USA

At the end of a wonderful weekend at Camp David, Hilda and Pearl were on the flight back to The White House on Marine One. Flying over Washington in The Presidential Helicopter was an experience few enjoyed. Not something you could buy as an excursion. Hilda waved royally, even though no one could see her.

As Hilda and Pearl got off the helicopter and they were saying goodbye, Evelyn realised she had not shown her guests inside the White House. After a hurried discussion with her husband and some aides, she invited them in. She showed them all around the private quarters while her husband headed to the Oval Office to get on with running the country. It had either been on hold while he was at Camp David, or he had run it from there – probably the latter.

After their tour of the private quarters, Evelyn, Pearl, Hilda, and Ruby had morning coffee together. Evelyn told them, 'I checked on the name Victoria Worth of Connecticut with my dad. He's a font of historical knowledge and tells me the Worth's used to be a wealthy family in Connecticut.'

'Did he know anything about Victoria?' asked Pearl.

'No, he only knew that the family fell on hard times in the Wall Street crash,' said Evelyn.

'I guess that's why the case I have is so battered and worn,' said Ruby.

'I wonder if there's a way to find out more,' said Pearl.

Evelyn spoke in an encouraging tone and said, 'I have a friend who researches in 20th century history. I'll ask her what she knows.'

Pearl and Ruby thanked Evelyn. Everyone tucked into a delicious selection of cookies and aromatic coffee. Evelyn then asked Chad if he would show Hilda and Pearl the more official parts of The White House. She asked that he include The Oval Office, if possible. But just before they left, Evelyn took Hilda to one side and had a serious word, saying, 'please don't rearrange any of the furniture. It has been put where it is for a reason.'

'Of course, dear, I wouldn't dream of it,' said Hilda. Evelyn didn't look totally convinced.

Evelyn asked, 'isn't your surname Shilton?'

'Yes dear,' said Hilda.

'It's an odd coincidence. The photographer who moved all the furniture for the photos was called Josh Shilton,' said Evelyn.

'Really, small world. Thanks for a lovely weekend,' said Hilda. She waved a cheery goodbye and headed off on the tour.

They had the most incredible tour ever. By the time they arrived at the Oval Office, President Meyer had left for a meeting at The House. Hilda and Pearl were about to be shown the Oval Office. But Chad received a phone call and asked them to take a seat. As they waited, Ruby came by and started chatting with Pearl. Hilda was bored, her feet were just off the floor, the chair she was sitting on was quite high, and her legs were short. So, she swung her legs in different ways. She looked around for something of interest and noticed that she was sitting next to a door to the Oval Office. One assistant headed in to drop some papers on the President's desk. She returned to her desk in the antechamber. In the time they were in there, Hilda had a tantalising glimpse into the inner sanctum of power.

Checking to see that no one was watching, Hilda got up and opened the padded door. No obvious alarms went off, and no one shouted. She walked in and stood in the centre of the room. It was indeed oval, but not as big as she had imagined. She considered sitting on one of the two sofas. They were arranged around a monogrammed carpet in the centre of the room, but then she noticed the desk. A large wooden desk with a leather chair behind it. A powerful symbol for an important man. The desk was mostly empty. 'Where were all the papers needed to run a country?' Hilda wondered. On the desk sat a couple of phones, a light, a blotting pad, a pen set and an empty filing tray.

She walked over to the desk. No security people ran in, and no bells started ringing. For a moment, the rose bushes outside the window distracted her. Then she sat in the President's chair and span it around a few times. Stopping it to face the desktop, she felt immensely powerful. She glanced around the room; the furniture looked badly placed, but she remembered her promise to Evelyn and left it alone.

Leaning back in the large comfortable chair, she pointed an arm in the air. Then said, 'I appoint Hilda Shilton, Ambassador of Fun.' She giggled like a schoolgirl. A note lay on the desk in front of her. She read it and smiled. Then she noticed a red phone. She reached towards it and thought, 'no, that would be wrong,' Then she glanced around. All was quiet. She kicked her legs and checked the phone again. 'Perhaps just to pick it up,' she thought. She reached forward and grabbed the phone, putting it to her ear. The operator said, 'hello sir.'

'Hello dear,' she said.

She heard some mumbling in the background. Then the operator said, 'is this a drill sir?' Hilda did not sound like the President and no doubt confused the operator. The operator then said, 'please identify yourself.'

'Hilda.' She smiled; this was more fun than she expected.

Unfortunately, the emergency codeword for that day was HILDA. The president had been asked for a new code word just after he heard about Pearl and Hilda visiting. He had found her name unusual and chosen it as the code word. One of those unconscious and unfortunate decisions.

'Confirmed, HILDA. What is your request, sir?' said the operator.

'All information on Area 51 urgently,' said Hilda. She was not keen to be called Sir, but the person on the phone was obedient.

'Understood.' Using the word "urgent" gave Hilda's request a coded meaning. The operator responded accordingly. 'Is there an imminent threat? Do you want to increase status to level RED?' asked the operator. Hilda frowned, thinking red was a colour she liked.

Fortunately, for many people and perhaps the world, at that moment Chad walked in and grabbed the phone from Hilda. He spoke a few words, explained the mix up. Then stood down the military response status from RED to GREEN. He had a few stern words to say to Hilda, about going places she should not, and doing things she should not. But he could have joined a queue for that, with her son at the front.

Hilda and Pearl had a brief look around the rest of The White House. A tearful farewell between Pearl and Ruby, promises of future meetings. Then they left The White House.

After Hilda had left, Chad spoke to the CCTV operative for The Oval Office. Her only excuse for not responding immediately to a stranger entering the Oval Office was surprise and shock. She could not believe her eyes. Who would expect a lady dressed in purple track suit bottoms, with bright red hair and a blue bonnet, to walk boldly into the Oval Office? Then sit in the Presidents' chair. She assumed she was imagining it, or that it was a test. After all, they gave the correct password. They gave the operator a less taxing job after the incident.

***

When President Meyer returned to his office, a highly top-secret file awaited him. It had its own security guard accompanying it. He had to sign for its release and then looking at the cover page it read, 'open when alone.' He sent everyone out and requested all recording equipment turned off. Opening the outer cover, the title page read, 'Area 51.' His eyes went wide. Why had he been sent this? Surely this place was apocryphal, a place of science fiction. He opened the file and his eyes opened even wider.

CHAPTER TWENTY

August 1997

A campsite on the outskirts of Washington DC, USA

The FBI had been waiting to talk to Hilda since they received the information on Jake Vort, AKA The Ghost, being in the USA. Not wanting to cause problems with the Secret Service, they waited until she returned from The White House to her campsite. Almost the moment Hilda and Pearl closed the door to the RV, a nondescript black car pulled up outside. They had been watching and waiting. Two people in black suits got out, one was wearing sunglasses, he knocked on the RV door. Hilda answered it saying, 'no thank you, we don't want any today.'

He was not that easily fobbed off and said, 'FBI ma'am.'

'I told you dear, I don't want any FB anything's,' said Hilda.

'No, we're the FBI,' said the agent.

'That's very nice for you, I'm sure. Goodbye,' said Hilda, closing the door.

The FBI agent looked round at his colleague. She indicated he should knock again; he did. Hilda answered again, and shook her head and said, 'you again.'

'We need to speak to you, ma'am,' said the agent.

'Don't call me ma'am. You all have a nasty habit of doing that,' said Hilda.

The other FBI officer took over and said, 'it's about Jake Vort.'

'You're a woman,' said Hilda.

'Yes, ma... madame,' said the female FBI officer.

'I don't like madame either,' said Hilda.

'What can we call you?' said the female officer.

'Hilda is fine.'

'We need to ask you about Mr Vort.'

'Mr who?'

'Mr Jake Vort,' said the female officer.

'I don't know anyone by that name.' Hilda called inside to Pearl. 'Do we know a Jake Vort, dear?' After hearing a negative from inside, Hilda was about to close the door again.

'Can we come in and explain?' asked the female officer.

'Well, I suppose if you must,' said Hilda, she let them enter the RV.

Pearl asked if she was needed and, having found that they only wanted to talk to Hilda, she went off for a walk. The officers questioned Hilda to find out why Jake wanted her bag. They got nowhere on that; she had no idea. If they had concentrated on anything she had found out of the ordinary on her travels, they may have got further. Hilda still thought the diamonds she found were just crystals. Less shiny than she was used to, but they did have a nice blue glow. Ones Pearl had bought for a friend, hopefully her. Hilda did like crystal things. She had a collection of crystals on her sideboard; they were lit up by an overhead light. There were crystal hearts and cubes, roses, and houses. It made a beautiful display. Of course, two multi-million-pound diamonds would make a splendid addition. It would also have helped if Pearl had stayed. Because then she could have dismissed the idea of having bought the crystals.

The FBI was aware that Jake had stolen the diamonds. They just hadn't figured out where Hilda fitted in. Jake must have used her as an unwitting courier, but why was he chasing her? Usually, if a smuggler used an unwitting courier, they would regain the smuggled item as soon as possible. New Scotland Yard had a team going through footage of CCTV at the airport on the day Jake flew out. They had yet to find the bit that confirmed their suspicions of Hilda being used as a courier. Even then, they would need the corresponding footage at Portland Airport to realise he had failed to get the diamonds back. Before they left, the FBI agents told Hilda that Jake's name and photograph had been circulated to all law enforcement agencies. He would be very unlikely to trouble her again. What optimists they were.

***

Next morning, Hilda was rummaging through her bag looking for a pack of sweets when she found her art pad. She had not done any sketching or painting since Colorado.

That also made her realise she had not asked President Meyer about Area 51. She must remember next time. Before packing her art stuff away, she needed to use it again.

Hilda set up outside the RV and started drawing a steady stream of volunteers. People at the campsite had seen Hilda on TV with their President and wanted an original Hilda Shilton, signed by the artist. They assumed it was because of her art that they invited her to The White House. Her pictures looked childlike and simplistic. But many people struggle to understand how a series of boxes could be art, or an unmade bed, or splattered paint. At least they could see that the stick drawings were a crude representation of them. When they heard she had also drawn nudes, a few people started to undress. But Pearl stepped in briskly and kept order.

***

Sometimes small things have big repercussions. This was the case with something Hilda saw at Annie & Peter's house in Marlan, Ohio. Annie did not know that something she showed Hilda would put such a childish idea in Hilda's head. Who could have guessed? As Hilda had left their house a few weeks earlier, she spotted something that she wanted to know all about. Annie was happy to oblige. She even demonstrated it. Ever since she saw and heard about it, Hilda had to have one. All she needed was the opportunity. When she was out shopping at a large Tallmart store, she spotted exactly what she wanted. Pearl was busy stocking up on essentials for their last few days. So, she missed Hilda go to the till, buy it, and hide it in the RV.

On their next phone call to William and Louise, they agreed that Hilda and Pearl would meet up for a trip around Washington, DC, itself. In some ways, having already met The President and toured The White House, it seemed an anti-climax. But there were still things to see, and the four of them had not yet done anything together in America. They had not even met up since being in the USA.

Lincoln Memorial, Washington DC

The four of them got together at The Lincoln Memorial. The plan was to walk from there up to the Washington Monument and then on to the Smithsonian. They would see how tired they were after that. No one could understand why Hilda needed such a big rucksack. It was new; she had bought it on her last shop. Perhaps that was what she had hidden, or was it the contents? Louise said that they would have lunch out, William's treat, which caused him to nearly choke on the sweet he was sucking. Hilda just told them they would see what surprise she had later.

They all posed for photos at the Lincoln Memorial and started walking along the pavement by The Lincoln Memorial Reflecting Pool. They had a look at the World War II Memorial and then walked on to the base of the Washington Monument; it was huge. They sat on benches set in a semi-circle around a circular paved area at the base. It surprised them when only William and Pearl fancied going up in the elevator to the viewing platform. Normally Hilda was up for any fun. She had spotted a bag search and did not want to leave her rucksack with anyone, all very curious.

Hilda checked her watch and said it was time to go. Everyone found that strange, but they followed. As they arrived at The Smithsonian, a barricade was hurriedly put up and police appeared from nowhere. Hilda put her rucksack at her feet. Then a motorcade appeared with The President and First Lady in it. They were on a last minute arranged visit, opening an exhibit at The Smithsonian. Hilda had seen a note about it on President Meyers' desk the other day when she was in the Oval Office. She remembered from Camp David how The President loved surprises and his sense of fun. She was about to give him just that. The Secret Service was not as keen on surprises, especially ones like Hilda planned.

She pulled out a large bright yellow Nerf Super Soaker from her rucksack and pointed it at President Meyer as he got out of the limousine. Even a super soaker has a limited range. He was far too far away for her to reach him with the water, much to her disappointment. The sight of a weapon appearing from a bag caused an immediate response from the Secret Service.

'Gun, gun, gun!' came the cry over their intercoms.

President Meyer was being bundled back into the limousine, surrounded by guards. But not before he had glanced up and seen Hilda. As did Chad, his lead bodyguard. Having seen Hilda with a water pistol, Chad immediately gave the 'all clear.' Too late to prevent Hilda being wrestled to the ground and handcuffed. But in time to prevent President Meyer from being whisked off to an underground bunker.

Once everyone had recovered, and they had released Hilda. President Meyer smiled a little about it. He had Hilda brought over and warned her not to do such a silly thing again. While Hilda had a moment alone with President Meyer, she said, 'I wanted to talk to you about the real Area 51 in Colorado.'

If it is possible to freeze. Not breathe or move even a millimetre, the President achieved that. Then he burst back into life and shouted, 'what! Where did you hear that?'

'I met one of the aliens in Colorado,' said Hilda.

The President bundled Hilda into his limousine and pressed a button. They sat alone in the car; the windows turned black, and everything went quiet. The President got out a strange-looking device from his inner pocket and spoke into it, 'investigate loose delegate, A51 compromised. Standby.'

He stared at Hilda, and asked, 'how did you know of the real location of Area 51?'

Hilda felt important, and she smiled broadly. Then said, 'it was obvious, especially after I met one of the aliens.' She was completely clueless about what President Meyer was really talking about.

'Listen carefully,' said President Meyer. 'You have somehow stumbled on a very, very secret bit of information. You cannot tell anyone. Not family or friends.'

'Not even William?' said Hilda.

'No one!' said The President.

'Oh, all right dear. Not even Pearl?' asked Hilda.

'No one!' said The President. In a very firm and presidential way.

Hilda looked crestfallen. But when she got out of the limousine, she appeared strangely angelic. As if they had given her a holy missive. Chad had been looking for her. He hadn't seen President Meyer take her into the car. On her exit, he took her to one side and told her they could have shot her the moment snipers saw anything that seemed like a gun. But she just smiled beatifically at him, so he tried again, more forcefully. She nodded and claimed she understood.

William, Louise, and Pearl were surprised that Hilda appeared so laid back and relaxed on the return. When they tried to talk of the incident, she merely nodded and agreed she would not repeat it. Then she talked cryptically of higher purposes. She even seemed unfazed by the discovery that her super soaker was missing. There is an apocryphal story that it became a regular source of fun for the secret service team on their breaks. Some say that they even bought a couple more and would often be seen running around in the backyard at The White House. Who can say if such a thing is true? President Meyer did once comment that Chad's suit seemed wet in the afternoon. Had he just spilt a drink on it? Who knows?

Hilda was a good as her word and never mentioned Area 51 to her family or friends, which is just as well. Had she tried to tell them what she knew, they would have referred her to a psychiatrist. After all Area 51 being real and being in Colorado rather than Nevada, aliens visiting Earth as delegates for an intergalactic treaty. If such was what she was told, it would be seen as nonsense. Mind you, it may not be what she was told. Hilda has a very ripe imagination. It would be best to treat her thoughts on aliens and Area 51 very lightly, very lightly indeed. That instruction comes straight from the desk of President Meyer, and he is The President of the United States, so he should know.

A campsite on the outskirts of Washington DC, USA

Next morning, as Hilda sat drinking coffee, Area 51 and the super soaker incident were nowhere in her mind. But she often claimed to have a dreadful memory, so perhaps she had forgotten all about it. Instead, she was looking for some sweets in her bag and found a piece of paper. She gave a squeal of delight and said, 'oh look! My vase list, I forgot about it.'

'What's a vase list?' asked Pearl sharply from the other side of the table. She was still a little aggrieved over the events of the day before. Her memory bore no resemblance to a sieve.

'It's a list of things you want to do,' said Hilda. She spread out the folded sheet of paper on the table.

Pearl read it and said, 'that reads like a bucket list.'

Hilda shook her head and said, 'it isn't a bucket list. That would be a list of things you want to do before you "kick the bucket" wouldn't it?'

'Well, yes,' said Pearl, staring at Hilda and shrugging.

'This is different. I am not planning to die anytime soon. It's my vase list.'

Pearl shook her head, 'alright Hilda, what makes it a vase list rather than a bucket list?'

'It is a list of special things that I want to do while we are in America,' said Hilda.

Pearl seemed like she wanted to speak. But did not.

'Let's see what I have already done?' Hilda checked the list and started ticking things off, 'see The White House, tick, dance with The President, tick.'

Pearl stared open-mouthed at Hilda and then found her voice, saying, 'they were on your list?'

'Of course, dear, now where was I? Meet an alien tick.'

Pearl just shook her head at the astonishing list, then said, 'that was an actor, at least I hope it was.'

Hilda tapped her finger on her nose and said, 'now what else? Feed the bears, tick.' Pearl crossed her arms over her chest. Hilda continued, 'meet an Indian and a cowboy, tick, tick, eat lots of local food, tick, explore the country. Do you think we have done that?'

'Yes, I think so,' said Pearl.

'Dance on Broadway, tick.'

'I can't believe what's on your list. Your expectations of this trip were very high.'

'Aim for the stars, dear. Now, here's something you have missed,' said Hilda.

Pearl checked the list, then up at Hilda, 'what do you mean, I've missed?'

'You've not taken us to any American sporting events.'

'I didn't know that you wanted to see any, or that it was up to me.' Pearl stared at Hilda.

'Of course, you can't come all this way and miss that. Now let me have a read of my list of sporting events I wanted to see,' said Hilda. She held the list close, then far away, and squinted her eyes. Then she showed Pearl the list and said, 'what's that word?'

Pearl stared at it hard, and said, 'it's your writing. I don't know. It could be loothill? No, hang on, I think it's foot hull.'

'Don't be silly, foot hull indeed. What's foot hull? You must have been right the first time, loothill. I'll go and ask someone where we can watch a game of loothill,' said Hilda. She headed out of the RV and accosted a few passing people to ask them about the game of loothill. Funnily enough, no one had heard of it. On her return to their RV, Pearl was again looking at the list. She looked up at Hilda, a smile on her face and said, 'it's football, or at least American Football.'

'That's it.' Hilda clapped hands, 'although I really can't see why they call it football. They hold the ball in their hands most of the time. Have they never heard of rugby? As for all the protective stuff they wear...'

'What else?' said Pearl, interrupting.

'Right, oh, I can't read this next one.' Hilda again stared at her list. After a few minutes they had discerned that the remaining items were basketball, ice hockey and baseball. Hilda said that she wanted to watch The Harlem Globetrotters play basketball. But was happy with any ice hockey and baseball teams. When Hilda mentioned baseball, Pearl sounded worried and said, 'can I just check? You're not planning to tell them they are just playing the children's game, rounders?'

'What a suggestion.' Hilda feigned shock.

'I think we'll need to see what we can fit in; we only have a few days left before we head home.'

Pearl did her usual brilliant job of organising the schedule with the help of her sister. Between them, they planned it so that in the last five days, they could see three of the sports. The first was going to be basketball, The Harlem Globetrotters, they were playing nearby. The following day was a college football match, then two days later, a baseball match.

Harlem Globetrotters

Ruby was a huge fan of The Harlem Globetrotters and with her White House links already had front row seats to watch them. She added two more for Pearl and Hilda. If you are going to watch any sport with Hilda, the last thing you want to do is sit right next to the pitch or court. So, it was not a clever idea to have chosen three seats right next to the basketball court.

Everyone who loves basketball will no doubt agree that it can be an extremely exciting game full of action; especially when you are watching the Harlem Globetrotters. They play exhibition games, and they really play it for laughs. They choose opposition teams that they can more easily beat.

But as seems to be the case with a lot of American sports, there are a lot of time outs. Whether American sports people need a lot of chats with their team members. Or they like to question their coaches is uncertain. But there is a lot of conferring in these 'time outs.'

As Hilda sat watching the match unfold, she was getting impatient. When it came to the fifth time out, she got up and walked over to the teams as they were conferring and said, 'that's enough, get on with the match. We're getting bored waiting for you.'

Both teams looked up at Hilda in astonishment. They could not believe this little lady, with the bright clothes and red hair, was daring to challenge them. They told her to sit down. But she refused. Not only did she refuse, but she walked over and took the ball from them, saying, 'if you don't carry on this minute I will hold on to the ball.'

That really was the limit for most of the team, and they came chasing after her. Hilda was having none of that, and she ran across the court with the ball. Her little legs were no match for the long legs and athletic build of all the basketball players pursuing her. They soon surrounded her, so she hugged the ball to herself. They were not sure what to do. She was quite an elderly lady, and she put on her best frail and pathetic look. They were not keen to be seen by the TV cameras, manhandling her, or in any way injuring her. This left them in a standoff. Hilda was in the middle, holding their ball, surrounded by very tall athletic basketball players. They all seemed lost. Hilda gained confidence.

The audience wondered what was going on. Some started cheering for Hilda and some cheering for the basketball teams. A young man in the audience had an idea, he shouted to Hilda, 'throw the ball through the hoop.' Others joined him in shouting for her to have a go. Not everyone agreed, when does everyone agree on anything, and there were also shouts for her to return the ball. But Hilda only heard the ones that encouraged her to throw the ball through the hoop. Her netball days came back to her memory, and an unrealistic memory it was of her great skill. She was standing at the three-point line.

The basketball players had moved away from her, realising there was nothing they could do to get the ball from her. This gave her a clearer shot at the hoop. It also gave gaps through which the audience could see her more clearly. She lifted the ball and aimed it. Those in the audience that had been against her switched allegiance. Seeing this little old lady standing on the three-point line with a clear shot at the hoop, everyone cheered. A cry of 'Hey! go, hey! go,' rang out around the basketball court from the audience. People stomped their feet rhythmically.

Pearl and Ruby had been watching Hilda's antics in utter shock. Now that they saw what she was planning, they joined in the cry of support, adding 'Hilda,' to their chant. People near them heard the name and gradually everyone was shouting, 'Hey! go, Hilda!' 'Hey! go, Hilda!' over and over. Seeing the little lady about to attempt what seemed like an impossible shot, even a few of the basketball players joined in and shouted, 'go for it.' The auditorium was filled with chants of, 'hey! go, Hilda!' and 'go for it,' it was deafening. Feet were stamping, people were cheering. No one could see any way in which this little old lady could get the ball through the hoop. It was just an impossible dream. We all love to believe in the impossible.

Pearl had watched Hilda at school playing netball. Or standing on the side-lines ignoring the ball. She could not see any way in which Hilda could get the ball through the hoop. Hilda had one big advantage, she never let the impossible stop her from trying something. She was the sort of person to whom failure was not a dirty word. She would always try. Who cared if you failed or succeeded? The important thing was to give it a go. Everyone in the audience, everyone on the benches, and all the team players, and most people watching on TV, were supporting Hilda as she aimed the ball at the hoop. They had totally forgotten; she had interrupted their game. All that anyone could think about was whether this 5-foot 3-inch, seventy-seven-year-old woman could get that basketball through the hoop from the 3-point line? 'Hey! go, Hilda!' 'Hey! go, Hilda!' 'Hey! go, Hilda!' The chanting, the clapping, and the stamping of feet filled the stadium.

Hilda focused, her mind as razor sharp as it had ever been. Which isn't claiming a lot. No daydreaming, well, maybe just one, her scoring. She aimed, pulled back her arm, and threw the ball. Everything went completely silent. The ball sailed through the air, heading straight at the hoop. It hit the side of the hoop, everyone stopped breathing. Time stood still. The ball appeared to balance on the side of the hoop for ever. Was it going to make it in, or was it going to fall to the side? Then one player leapt up and nudged it in. Hilda had scored – with a little help.

The applause could not have been greater if it had been the winning three points in the NBA championship. People were on their feet shouting, cheering, throwing things in the air. The teams lifted Hilda on their shoulders and paraded her around the court for a victory lap. People at home watching it on TV were leaping around on their sofas, cans of beer sprayed everywhere. Confetti canons were let off. Television presenters were proclaiming Hilda to be incredible, amazing and a force of nature. But there was one little boy, sat on the sofa with his dad. In an ordinary house, in an ordinary street, in an ordinary neighbourhood, in an ordinary town. He turned to his father and asked, 'pops, didn't she just interrupt the whole match?'

Out of the mouths of babes and young children. The lesson can be learnt or should have been learnt from the King's new clothes fairy tale. That kids see things clearly and speak the obvious truth. But fortunately for Hilda that lesson had not been learnt. Indeed, it often isn't. Instead of being seen as a nuisance or an interruption, they saw Hilda as a wonderful example of someone overcoming age. Everyone ignored the fact that one of the team had lent a hand to put the ball through the hoop. But facts are not always the most helpful things with legends. Hilda was fast becoming a legend in America. They should declare a Hilda holiday in America, or they should create a Hilda flag - American's love flags. Maybe a Hilda statue could be commissioned? But legends take time to mature and grow. Gradually fermenting and improving, like an excellent wine. So that in years to come, people look back, not at the reality of a person, but at the created legend. That would be extremely helpful, in Hilda's case. Her reality was more tainted than her legend.

The events at the Basketball game had created a media interest in Hilda. Reporters were trying to track her down. One advantage of being in a mobile vehicle was that it made finding Hilda hard. Pearl had a bit of reticence about going to another big event. Hilda was keen and wasn't easily put off anything. But Pearl convinced Hilda that they couldn't fit in the other sporting events they'd planned. She said there wasn't enough time. In the end she won through.

A motel near Washington DC, USA

Jake sat in a motel room a short distance from the campsite, surrounded by papers. He sketched plans, wrote ideas, then stared at them for a while. Getting up, he paced and then, walking to the sideboard, poured himself a drink. He had a smile on his face. Gathering all the papers together, he burnt them, one by one, the window and door wide open to clear the smoke. At last, he had a plan that would work, an infallible plan.

CHAPTER TWENTY-ONE

September 1997

Penelope Kendal's seafront condo, Los Angeles, USA

Penelope Kendall, AKA, Bonbon, sat on her veranda enjoying a morning cup of coffee and croissant. Her security staff were inconspicuously stationed around the extensive grounds. When the duchess, Jayne Milford, had stayed with her, Bonbon had ensured they were out of sight.

Penelope preferred to be known as B by her criminal empire. She had taken it over from her father Lucian on his death. He had trained her up for an early age. She got up and walked to the edge of her veranda and watched some passing yachts; hers was moored at a distance.

B's lawyer had just left. Useful, because during his visit he took a call from his messaging service. It had been Jake. A confirmation of the handover details for the diamonds in two days. After her lawyer left, B had checked on her own plans for the handover. The diamonds would be hers at no cost, and they would deal with Jake. He had become unreliable and old. She had other jewel thieves lining up to take his place.

A helicopter passed nearby - not too close. It's powerful cameras filming the whole time. B glanced up; it bore the logo of a news station. They were a common sight in this playground of the rich and famous. The FBI had 'borrowed' the helicopter for their covert operation. The seafront condo was difficult to approach without being seen. After an extended aerial reconnaissance, they were ready.

The discovery of Penelope Kendal's part in the diamond theft and smuggling had been incidental. They had caught her lawyer in another crime, and he agreed to turn state's evidence for immunity. He had deliberately arranged the visit that day so that a call from Jake would happen at Penelope's home. He had also worn a wire to record her instructions to him.

The FBI had long been investigating her organisation. They were in partnership with the international criminal investigation divisions, ICID. Her organisation was truly worldwide. They were preparing the swoop on her LA property that day.

***

Even after Penelope Kendall was in prison and charged, her friends did not believe it. Jayne, the Duchess of Somershire, was sitting in Claridge's when a friend told her about Penelope's arrest. Jayne said, 'how could Bonbon be a master criminal? She's been my best friend since school.' We believe what we want to believe.

A campsite on the outskirts of Washington DC, USA

The FBI turned up again to chat to Hilda. The UK Intelligence services had viewed CCTV of Jake's departure from Heathrow Airport in London. Slowing it down, they could see him place something in Hilda's bag. Their colleagues in the US had viewed the CCTV at Portland and seen Jake's failure to regain the package. Realising it must be the diamonds; everything made sense. Hilda still had the diamonds.

At first Hilda thought they were mistaken. But when they described the eyes of Hora diamonds as the stolen items, Hilda had a flash of realisation. She went to Pearl's case and fetched the jar of cream. After washing off the diamonds, she handed them to the FBI agents, explaining how she found them. She still thought they were just crystals rather than diamonds. They were far too big to be diamonds. One agent stood staring at them for five minutes. Until Hilda asked, 'are you all right dear? Have you never seen crystals before?' They tried to explain they were diamonds. But Hilda would have none of such nonsense. As she said to them, 'whoever heard of such enormous diamonds? They would be worth millions.'

The lead agent was nodding and said, 'exactly, they are worth millions.' Hilda just laughed.

The FBI agents knew Jake would not let such a prize go easily. So, they planned to catch him, using Hilda as bate; with her very willing consent. She enjoyed the excitement.

A swarm of FBI officers and other backup agents were brought in to protect Hilda. All agents heavily disguised and on high alert. Hilda and Pearl were due to return to the UK the next day; time was running out.

***

Hilda and Pearl had become increasingly famous. As they spent the last day sorting out and packing, they found that their fellow campers kept coming up to chat. They were constantly watched by disguised FBI agents.

The advantage of RV's is that they fit many of them with portable televisions. Their neighbouring RVs had watched Hilda and Pearl on the news. Hilda was famous for two reasons. First, the impossible basketball shot and second, being at The Whitehouse with The President. What people could not understand was why these VIPs kept returning to such a small campsite.

The campers had also seen Hilda get wrestled to the ground by security when she attempted to fire a water pistol at the President. This item was being run continuously as a joke by many networks. The President's press office had released a statement saying it was planned. All of which lent credence to the image of Hilda and The President as being close personal friends.

Hilda made the most of the fame afforded to her, especially as people saw her as the most famous of the two. She offered to give people autographs and enjoyed embellishing the stories of her adventures. She even offered to sketch people. Those who missed out on her earlier sketching antics. When asked why they were not staying in a five-star hotel, Hilda explained she liked to meet real people, which caused murmurs of assent. She missed out on any reference to the cost. Whilst she had a captive audience, she wowed them with tales of how she had even appeared on Broadway as a star. Then she accepted the various offers to have drinks and snacks in her neighbours' vehicles. Pearl stared on in wonder at her friend, the centre of attention and loving it. They overlooked Pearl in the general rush to talk with Hilda. But that gave her time to sit quietly and think back over all the things she had experienced. She needed to take on board the reality of having a sister and finding out about their mother. Hilda fetched her for some invitations.

***

A group within the campsite suggested honouring their special campers, Hilda, and Pearl. They wanted to throw a party and Hilda loved the idea. The centre of the campsite had a large clearing. It already had several picnic tables and an area where some barbecues could be set up. People added extra tables and chairs and brought out food and drinks. They found a few people who could play musical instruments. A fiddle player, two guitarists, someone with a harmonica, and a lot of singers. They got together and worked out what they could all play and sing. The people who liked to plan had a rare old time organising the event. Those who are good at, and enjoyed cooking, did the food preparation. Leaving those who just enjoyed eating to munch away at the delightful treats.

A few of the campers seemed oddly stilted in their preparations. They wore more layers than the others; dressed more formally. All of them seemed to need a hearing aid of some sort; matching each other. They also had matching bulges under their arms. They were undercover FBI agents.

That evening, the weather was glorious, warm, and dry. The sunset was red over the distant mountains. The muggy heat of the day had gone, and it was a pleasant evening. Everyone gathered in the centre of the campsite. The tables overflowed with a fantastic array of food delights. Folk dressed in a variety of styles, from country and western to posh casual and, of course, FBI semi-casual. Hilda wore a dress, but not just any dress. It seemed like it came from the movie 'Oklahoma.' Hidden inside her dress was a microphone. The principal agent had wanted to cover all eventualities. Hilda kept speaking into it, no matter how often they told her to stop. When she danced, she was copying dances from a Rodgers and Hammerstein Musical. So, the musicians took a cue from her. The musicians had produced a very entertaining programme already, but they added several special tunes, for Hilda. They had also cobbled together a makeshift amplification system.

Hilda was in her element; she danced and sang the night away with a variety of partners. She sang extra loud, knowing she was being recorded. Pearl took her turn at dancing, but often she just talked about their experiences with those who sat watching. William and Louise turned up early on. Pearl had talked to them earlier in the day about the evening's entertainment.

William had been a little reluctant, but Louise insisted that they be present as it marked the end of their USA trip. It surprised them they had to pass through a security cordon disguised as a couple of runners. The agents pulled William and Louise to one side and said, 'FBI.' After the shock of an impromptu search, they could enter.

Sometimes people act completely out of character. That was certainly the case for William that evening. Whether it was being in America, the shock of hearing his mother had been carrying around multi-million-pound diamonds. The presence of so many FBI officers, the hot weather, or just his feeling of success with his job. William was not acting his usual reserved self. Some may just put it down to the alcohol being served. Which could be described as 'moonshine,' but let us not dwell on that, because that would suggest someone on the site had an illegal still. The alcohol was certainly strong. FBI agents were preoccupied with guarding Hilda and noticed nothing amiss with it. The company was bright and fun, the music was loud and easy to dance to, the food was tasty. Whatever the reason, William and Louise danced together, and then William danced with Hilda. This made the holiday for Hilda. All the carefree laughing, singing, and dancing. Plus, the added excitement of being a deputised agent. At least that is what she told everyone she was.

The FBI agents thought nothing was going to happen. One or two gazed hungrily at the food. They had been instructed to stay alert and not eat; no drinking was obvious. That is why they missed the moonshine. Hilda tried to grab one agent for a dance, they called out. Not hearing them, she said, 'I want you to do your duty.' After a quick spin, they broke away. Hilda had plenty of partners queueing up; not something she was used to.

One of Hilda's dancing partners whispered in her ear, 'be quiet and come with me.'

'What's that?' asked Hilda.

'Be quiet and come with me,' repeated a disguised Jake.

'The music is too loud,' said Hilda, 'you'll have to speak up.'

'I have a gun and I will shoot you,' said Jake. He held the gun up so that only Hilda could see it.

'Ooo, that's the gun I wanted to see at the beginning,' said Hilda. She squealed in delight. 'It's James Bond's gun. You are a treasure; how did you know?'

'I'm not a treasure,' said Jake quietly in Hilda's ear. 'I'm threatening you with it.'

'Look everyone,' said Hilda, 'this kind young man has brought me 007's gun.' She was not easily intimidated. Having recognised Jake quite quickly, she was just playing dumb so that the FBI agents could act.

The agent listening in to Hilda's singing and inane chatter from her body mic had switched off from listening. It was not until she was talking about 007's gun that he woke up and sounded the alert. By this point, all the agents had already seen Jake pointing the gun at Hilda.

The FBI agents had all drawn their weapons and were pointing them at Jake. Shouting, 'FBI, put your gun down.'

Jake was not a violent man, but this was too much. This woman had taken him to his limit. The FBI had him surrounded, trapped like a rat. This old woman had led him a merry dance across America. He was now known to law enforcement. Here he was, surrounded by the FBI. Enough was enough. They would not take him alive.

'I will kill her if you don't all put your guns down,' said Jake.

A new FBI recruit lowered his gun. The lead agent stared at him; he lifted it again.

'You're the man who stole my bag at Camp David. Why ever would you want that?' said Hilda to Jake, unphased by his gun.

'To get my diamonds back,' said Jake.

'They're not your diamonds,' said the lead agent. 'You stole them from the Duchess of Somershire.'

'Yes, and where did she get them from, eh?' said Jake.

'She inherited them from her husband,' said the lead agent. He glanced around. As if expecting applause.

'I know the history of those jewels. They were stolen from a small African village,' said Jake. He stared at the agents boldly.

An African American agent called, Hannah Rial, glanced from the lead agent to Jake and asked, 'are they the eyes of Hora diamonds?'

'I don't know what they called them. But they are twin, circular and very large,' said Jake, glancing at the agent who had asked.

Hannah stood mouth open, her gun hung at his side. 'The long-lost eyes of Hora diamonds,' she said under her breath.

'Enough of this, give yourself up Jake,' said the lead agent.

Hilda brought the standoff to an end. She could see that Jake was distracted. She grabbed his gun; he let go. Jake could not believe it; this little woman had disarmed him. He stared at her in absolute shock, defeated by an old woman. They led him away. He was no doubt wondering how such a small old lady had beaten him. Although he had a small smile on his face, no doubt feeling secure in knowing that his wife, children, and fortune were safe. He phoned her earlier to arrange everything.

The only person who was undaunted by the events was Hilda. She wanted the party to continue after the FBI left with Jake. But it took a while for everyone's nerves to settle down. Pearl went to bed after hugging Hilda. William and Louise also gave her a big hug. It had badly shaken them watching events unfurl and, after spending a bit of time chatting; they headed back to their hotel.

***

Once the diamonds were registered as having been recovered by the FBI. Special agent Hannah Jerlepze looked up details of the eyes of Hora diamonds on the FBI computer. She sent information back to relatives in Africa. The long-lost eyes of their god had been found.

Panama City Airport

Jake's wife, Laura, was standing in the arrival lounge at Panama City Airport. She was waiting for his planned flight to arrive. Panama was their escape location; extradition was complex, and they had a false identity and properties already set up there. She had gone ahead the moment the police had turned up at their home in the Caribbean. Once Jake realised the FBI was on to him at Camp David, he had contacted her there.

He had told her the details of his plan. Snatch the diamonds at Hilda and Pearl's party. Finally, get the cash for it from his buyer, B. He had the flight booked using his false passport. Laura was to meet him at the airport, and they would begin another life in Panama with all their stashed away cash.

Laura glanced at her two children. They were getting bored and running around. The plane from Washington Dulles had been delayed. Now at last it arrived, and passengers were coming through. Forty minutes passed and the last few stragglers left the airport. Laura looked around for the phones. She called the children and headed towards the bank of phones on a nearby wall. As she arrived at the phones, a woman approached her and said, 'I have a message from Jake. Come this way.'

Laura took her children by the hand and followed the woman. They headed through some doors; they were waved through security. Laura was too distracted to notice. Exiting the main building, they found themselves on the airport apron, heading for a small private plane.

'Is he on here?' asked Laura.

'Up here,' said the woman.

Laura climbed the steps to the private jet. There were five people on-board, all wearing suits, three men and two women. She was told to take a seat with her children. She did this, and asked, 'where's Jake?'

'I'll explain once we're airborne,' said the woman.

The moment Laura and her children sat and strapped in, the plane taxied and took off. Once they were over the ocean, and the seatbelt sign was off. The woman got up and came over to Laura. She instructed Laura to stand a moment and come forward.

When Laura was a little way from her children. The lady said, 'I'm FBI Special Agent Gloria Tern.' Laura stared at her. 'Laura Vort, you are under arrest for aiding and abetting your husband, Jake Vort, in theft, fraud and the sale of stolen goods.' She continued with all the legal requirements.

RV Adventure Hire Centre, Washington DC, USA

The day after the party, Pearl was feeling more her normal self. Hilda sprung out of bed as she always did. Having her life threatened had no real effect. It was their last night in the RV, time to return it.

After returning the RV, Hilda and Pearl headed to a hotel for one last night before their flight home. They talked about their mixed feelings of relief and sadness. It had been an enjoyable and yet tiring adventure. There is something special about being in your own home.

Pearl told Hilda that it frustrated her they had found nothing about her mother, Victoria Worth. Ruby had a few ideas for avenues to pursue, but they didn't look hopeful. Hilda was not fully listening. She had ideas which had not fully developed, but there was time for that.

***

The First Lady was as good as her word. Her friend had researched Victoria Worth and discovered what we already know. That she married Lucian Kendal, the head of a criminal empire. Pearl and Ruby found it hard to hear about Victoria's third daughter Penelope, AKA Bonbon, AKA, B, their half-sister. Especially when they heard she was behind the theft of the diamonds. A big surprise to them all to hear that she had hired Jake to steal the diamonds from her best friend. When they heard Penelope had been initiated into the family businesses from age ten. They felt some sympathy for her. But not a lot.

They discovered that Victoria had moved back to the USA and married again. What they could not understand was why she left Penelope behind. Victoria was now aged ninety-four, widowed, and had borne no more children. She lived in a nursing home in Florida. They had blanks only she could fill in.

Nursing home, Florida, USA

Larry Campbell lent Pearl, Ruby, and Hilda his private jet to get to Florida fast. Arriving at the nursing home, Pearl and Ruby felt a great sense of trepidation. Hilda strode ahead of them, saying, 'come on you two, what's the holdup?' But it wasn't a lack of compassion on Hilda's part, merely her way.

A staff member took them to Victoria's room. It was empty, her wheelchair missing. 'She'll be in the garden,' said the staff member.

They stood looking around the room. No photos of Penelope, which was strange. But in pride of place by her bed was a copy of the photo of Pearl and Ruby, newly born. It was not in a frame but had obviously been well handled; the edges worn. Ruby and Pearl both turned white, and Pearl had to find a seat. Hilda put an arm around her friends' shoulders. There were tears in all their eyes.

The staff member waited until they had recovered, then took them into the garden. The lawns were extensive and sloped down to a lake, trees were dotted around its edge. They provided areas of shade. Under one of them sat a diminutive figure in a wheelchair. She was staring out at the lake. As they drew closer, she turned and looked up. Her face and body transformed. She had been slumped in the chair; her face drawn and white. The change was like a flower that has been watered, the crumpled and creased petals filling and blossoming. The ivory of her skin bloomed into red, her smile like sunlight. She looked up at her long-lost twins, recognition in her eyes and said, 'it's you. I have waited, hung on, hoped, prayed.'

Hilda stood back and watched as Pearl and Ruby embraced their frail mother. It was as well they were near the lake. Tears flowed so freely. But tears can be of joy and so these were. They sat and talked for hours; Victoria explained much of her past to her long-lost daughters. When she spoke of being forced to give them up, it obviously caused her such pain. Talking about Penelope and the night she had left was another time of anguish. When Pearl, Ruby and Hilda left there was a feeling of peace and finality, as if it had laid ghosts to rest. They said goodbye with a sense of endings; they were releasing her - they were right.

Victoria had hung on for her two girls. A feeling had told her they would find her one day. She died that night, happy, serene, and at peace. The nurse called to her side, reported to her daughters that she had smiled and then let out a long sigh. She could at last let go.

***

None of them knew that in a prison on the far side of the country, her other daughter Penelope said a prayer that night. She prayed out loud, saying, 'God, I don't know if you even exist. If you do, I guess you are not pleased with me. But this isn't about me. If my mom is still alive, be with her. I did her a great wrong and I'm sorry.'

***

Victoria's funeral was a week later. The Shilton family and Pearl stayed on for it, extending their stay in America. There was an odd mix of joy and sorrow. Joy from Pearl and Ruby, that they had finally met their mother. Sorrow to have known her for such a short time. They were also still processing about having a half sister who was a crime boss and now in prison. When Pearl and Ruby said goodbye to each other, it was more of a see you soon. Pearl was certainly not very focussed on England as she set out on her journey home. Ruby said to her sister, 'I have an idea. Give me some time to sort a few things.'

***

Hilda, Pearl, William, and Louise had a smooth flight home. Hilda was on her best behaviour. Just as well, because everyone was exhausted. Although she seemed to be thinking a lot, unusual for her.

Orville's homestead, Marlan, Ohio, USA

Back in the USA, Orville was in prison on remand. His homestead was a place that no one ever visited, even the local kids kept away. It was a desolate place. If kids wanted a haunted house, they went to the Big D Farm. There was no reason to visit anywhere else in Marlan. Yet a man hurried up the drive, leading his dog. Every so often, he gave the poor creature an unnecessary jerk on the lead. It whimpered and then trotted faithfully alongside him. On arriving at the house, the elderly man seemed to hear a noise. He stared through grey dead eyes at the surrounding area. Then headed into the house and closed the door. He acted as if it was his home, but then, maybe it was. Hilda was right to think that all was not yet sorted on this case.

Rose Cottage, Stoke Hind, UK

In Stoke Hind, England, the Duchess of Somershire had been so pleased to hear that her twin diamonds had been recovered, and the thief caught. She wanted to reward Hilda. On Hilda's return home, a quality embossed envelope awaited her. Inside a monogrammed letter thanked Hilda for her help and enclosed was a cheque for £200,000. William had many ideas about how his mother could invest the money. She just smiled; an idea had already been forming.

For many people, the first thing on their mind when they get back from such a long and arduous journey would be feet up and a cup of tea. Hilda is not like many people. She was already making plans for her next adventure. Having seen what, to Hilda's eyes, was the ease of cooking, she dreamt up the idea of running a cafe. It would also give her a great place to solve mysteries from.

Before heading back to her own house, Pearl was spending the night with Hilda. As eager as she was to see Merlin, she needed a night's rest first. That evening, Pearl was sprawled on an armchair. William and Louise had stayed for an evening meal. They were lying back on the sofa, full, content and half asleep. Hilda broke her brilliant idea to the drowsy group, which woke them all up.

***

The front door was open, letting fresh air in as it was a hot evening, and the house was full. So, as Josh arrived, coming to find out all about their adventures, he walked straight into a strange scene, everyone sitting upright staring at Hilda. She was standing in the middle of the room, triumphant and glowing. She glanced up and saw Josh. 'Hello dear,' said Hilda. 'Pearl and I are going to buy a tea shop together with my reward money.'

Josh looked at Pearl, who was shaking her head, then said, 'reward money? Tea shop?' 'Mysteries?' He glanced at his parents; William stared at the ceiling. 'Are you starting a detective agency in a teashop?'

'Of course not dear, the very idea,' said Hilda, with a smile.

***

Hilda will be back.
Book 2 *Teacakes and Murder*

Also By Mike Nevin

Other Books by Mike Nevin
Book 2 *Teacakes and Murder*
Book 3 Millennium Mystery
Coming Soon: Book 4 Double Dealing

Find my Books Here:

Printed in Great Britain
by Amazon